MAGGIE CHRISTENSEN

A Christmas Surprise in Pelican Crossing

Dedication

To all my readers.

Also by Maggie Christensen

Oregon Coast Series
The Sand Dollar
The Dreamcatcher
Madeline House

Sunshine Coast books
A Brahminy Sunrise
Champagne for Breakfast

Sydney Collection
Band of Gold
Broken Threads
Isobel's Promise
A Model Wife

Scottish Collection
The Good Sister
Isobel's Promise
A Single Woman

Granite Springs
The Life She Deserves
The Life She Chooses
The Life She Wants
The Life She Finds
The Life She Imagines
A Granite Springs Christmas
The Life She Creates
The Life She Regrets
The Life She Dreams

A Mother's Story

Bellbird Bay
Summer in Bellbird Bay
Coming Home to Bellbird Bay
Starting Over in Bellbird Bay
Christmas in Bellbird Bay
Finding Refuge in Bellbird Bay
Escape to Bellbird Bay
Second Chances in Bellbird Bay
Celebrations in Bellbird Bay
Happy Ever After in Bellbird Bay

Pelican Crossing
The Restaurant in Pelican Crossing
Secrets in Pelican Crossing
A New Dawn in Pelican Crossing

One

It was a glorious November morning in Pelican Crossing. Rachel Mason gazed out her kitchen window to where, in the distance, she could see tiny figures on the beach and surfers out on the ocean, her mind going to the message which had awakened her in the early hours. It hadn't occurred to Alexander his text would disturb his mother's sleep.

Alexander had left Australia soon after finishing university, reaching out to the opportunities he envisaged overseas. He'd been fortunate to have been picked up by a start-up company specialising in computer games and loved his life in London. The company had continued to grow and he with it, going public with a share option the previous year. While he made it home occasionally, his visits were short, and he was fond of telling Rachel and his sisters how narrow and suburban their lives were in Pelican Crossing.

Typical of Alexander, it was a brief message: *Coming home for Christmas. Bringing a surprise. Will explain when I see you. Much love.*

Rachel had pushed herself up against the pillows and sent a reply asking for more information, but the phone had remained frustratingly silent, and she'd forced herself back into a fitful sleep.

Now she was awake, Rachel couldn't wait to talk with Jess to discover if he had been any more forthcoming with his sister, but she doubted it. While they had been close growing up, once he'd left, Alexander seemed to have put everything in Pelican Crossing behind him, his irregular communications focussing on his life in England

and the seemingly endless string of women he became involved with. Rachel had given up hope of him ever settling down.

The large family home where Rachel lived was located on the top of the bluff on the outskirts of town. She and Kirk had bought it when she was pregnant with Jess, and it had been wonderful when Jess, Steph and Alexander were growing up. But after they left, Jess to get married, Steph to live independently and Alexander to seek employment in England, she and Kirk had rattled around in it. Then when Kirk died after a long illness, Rachel couldn't bear the thought of leaving the house that had been her home for so many years. It held too many memories for her to contemplate selling.

Turning it into a bed and breakfast had been the result of a flash of inspiration based on the memory of staying in a series of bed and breakfasts on a visit to England with Kirk many years earlier. Now, five years later, the business had taken off. It suited her well, providing both company and income, and allowing her time to look after her three grandchildren – one-year-old Emily and four-year-old twins Gemma and Indie, who she called the two terrors.

Rachel's West Highland Terrier, Molly, came padding over from her food bowl. Rachel leant down to ruffle her ears. 'What do you think, Molly?' she asked. 'What is Alexander's surprise? Do you think he's found a woman at last, one he wants to spend the rest of his life with?' It was her dearest hope her son would settle down and start a family, though she dreaded the thought that any children he might have would grow up on the other side of the world and speak with a different accent.

Breakfast over, Rachel made herself a cup of lemon and ginger tea and went out to sit in the courtyard on one of the Adirondack chairs she'd recently purchased, Molly joining her and dropping down at her feet. She had two couples staying with her at the moment, but one of the advantages of running a B&B was that her guests were out all day, leaving her time to herself to do as she pleased. Jess often took advantage of this to ask her mother to mind the twins, and Rachel loved spending time with the little girls. She'd be sorry when they started school next year. Emily was lovely too, but too small to be much company, and Jess rarely left her with Rachel.

She had barely taken one sip of tea, when her phone rang. Seeing

Jess's number, Rachel's first thought was that she wanted her mother to mind the girls for the day. She was wrong.

'Have you heard from Alexander, Mum?' Jess asked, before Rachel had time to say hello.

'I have. You did too?'

'A strange email about coming home and bringing a surprise. Do you think he's finally found someone and is going to get married?'

Rachel felt a flutter of excitement. 'Do you think so? I did wonder, but you know your brother. He does like to tease.' 'Well, if he has, it must be pretty recent. He didn't mention anyone last time he was here, did he?'

'No.' Alexander's last visit had been so fleeting there had no time for chatting about anything personal. He'd been gone before Rachel had time to enjoy seeing him again. But that had been over six months ago, plenty of time for him to form a relationship.

'Well, I guess we'll have to wait to find out. It's so typical of him to leave us wondering like this. I bet he's only done it to annoy us. Remember how he used to be?'

Rachel laughed, remembering the countless occasions when Alexander had managed to get the better of his older sister, graduating from frogs in her bed to spreading rumours about her interest in the older boys at school. The latter backfired, when one of his targets actually liked Jess, and invited her on a date. Being younger, Steph had often escaped his teasing.

Rachel finished her tea and went back inside, Molly following her as usual. She rarely let Rachel out of her sight. 'You'll be glad to see Alexander again, Molly, won't you?' she said to the little dog. Alexander aways made a fuss of her when he was home, and Molly defected from her mistress to fawn on him.

Rachel sighed. It was over six weeks till Christmas. It seemed like it was for ever.

Two

Luke Findlay re-read the email, leant back, tipping his chair up on its back legs, and pulled on his beard. It was only six months since he'd left his vet practice, deciding that at sixty-two, it was time to retire and spend time doing all the things he'd promised himself he'd do... one day. Since then, he'd barely scratched the surface and the prospect of returning to the town he'd left to attend university held little appeal.

He'd enjoyed growing up in Pelican Crossing, the small coastal town on the Queensland Coast, but when his parents moved to the city soon after he'd started university, he'd never gone back. He'd met his wife at university and the small animal vet practice they'd opened together in a leafy suburb of Sydney had provided him with everything he wanted in life. It had been a shock when Ness had died in car accident, but he'd kept the practice, delighted when their son decided to join him, after spending two years overseas. Now Josh ran the practice himself with the help of a couple of assistants – Guy and Rose, and Luke tried his best not to interfere, spending his time with Nelson, his faithful pet, the boxer he'd rescued when his owner wanted him put down. Now, he couldn't imagine life without him.

'What do you think, Nelson?' he asked. 'Fancy a few months by the beach?'

The dog favoured him with one of his superior glances, seeming to indicate he was no more in favour of it than Luke.

Luke pulled on his beard again and sighed.

The email had come out of the blue, from a guy Luke had met at a conference the previous year. He recalled how, over a beer one evening, he and this guy – Bob Reed – had been reminiscing, and when Luke revealed where he'd grown up, Bob had slapped him on the shoulder. 'That's where I have my practice,' he'd said. 'Great town. Why did you leave?'

The conversation had brought back memories of growing up with the sun, sea and surf, far removed from his current lifestyle, and the recollection of girls with tanned skin and legs that seemed to go on for ever.

Now Bob had been accepted into a three-month programme at Colorado State University and had asked Luke if he'd be willing to look after his practice while he was away.

Deciding he needed a good cup of coffee to help him decide, and knowing he was fresh out of coffee beans, Luke picked up Nelson's leash and, the dog padding eagerly after him, headed out of the house. It was the house he and Ness had bought and renovated when they were first married, before Josh was born, and he couldn't imagine living anywhere else, despite Josh's suggestions it might be time for him to downsize. Luke hated the term and the thought of leaving his comfortable existence.

Once outside, Luke breathed in the fresh air, only partly spoiled by car fumes, as Nelson wandered along at his side, sniffing at the pavement. He loved his home, and the leafy suburb with several coffee shops only a short walk away. He'd miss all this if he took up Bob's suggestion. He couldn't imagine he'd find the same delights in Pelican Crossing. From what he remembered, there had been one café, a fish restaurant and not much else. He supposed it might have changed in the meantime – it had been over forty years ago – but he had no desire to find out.

Luke was enjoying his coffee, along with an almond croissant he'd been unable to resist, and was flicking through the latest edition of the local paper, Nelson lying happily at his feet with a bowl of water, when his phone rang. Seeing Josh's number, he pressed to accept the call.

'Hey, Josh, what's up?'

'Dad, I need a favour. Can Abby and I come over tonight?'

Luke's immediate thought was to wonder if his son needed money. He knew Josh's girlfriend had recently moved in with him, into the tiny one-bedroom unit in North Sydney which was all the young man could afford as he was determined to pay off his HECS (higher education contribution scheme) fee as soon as possible. But Josh had already refused Luke's offer to pay off the debt for him. 'No problem,' he said. 'Would you like to come for dinner?' Since Ness passed away, Luke had worked on his cooking skills, determined not to become one of those men who lived on takeaways.

'Thanks, Dad. That would be great. See you around six-thirty?'

'See you then, son.'

'Well,' Luke said to Nelson, 'I wonder what that's all about? We'd better do some shopping. I think barbecue steak with a nice salad.'

'Woof,' said Nelson, recognising the word steak and clearly hoping a piece of it might come his way.

*

By six o'clock, everything was ready. Nelson had been fed, the barbecue was lit, the salad prepared and in the fridge, and the steak was marinating in a mixture of Worcester sauce, French mustard and rosemary, a recipe Luke had found on Jamie Oliver's website and which had become a favourite of his. He took a beer out to the courtyard while he waited for Josh and Abby to arrive, wondering what sort of favour his son wanted from him.

As was usual with Josh, his arrival set off a flurry of barking from Nelson, and everything was chaotic for a few minutes while they all hugged and the young couple fussed over Nelson who revelled in the attention.

'For you, Dad.' Josh held out a bottle of cabernet sauvignon from Luke's favourite Margaret River winery. *This must be some favour, if he had shelled out on what was an expensive drop of red.*

'Thanks, son. This will go well with the steak.'

'Barbecued steak? Yum.' Josh headed outside to where the barbecue was ready for the meat.

'Can I do anything to help?' Abby asked, flicking back her hair. Luke liked Abby. She was a step up from the girls his son had brought home before her, and this time, it looked as if Josh was serious about their relationship. Perhaps it wouldn't be too long before there were grandchildren running around. *Ness would have loved to have been a grandmother.*

'No, it's all good,' Luke said, grateful for the offer, nevertheless. 'I'm betting you'd like a glass of wine.'

'I'll get it, Dad,' Josh said reappearing, Nelson at his heels. The dog had abandoned Luke as soon as the young couple arrived.

Their meal was over, and Abby had disappeared into the kitchen to make coffee – Luke had replenished the coffee supply earlier in the day – when Josh cleared his throat.

Recognising the signs, Luke said, 'Okay, Josh, so what's this favour you want to ask? If it's a case of money...'

'No, Dad. It's not money.'

Abby reappeared carrying three mugs of coffee which she placed on the table before taking her seat next to Josh and placing a hand on his arm.

Under the table, Nelson snored gently, happy to have been the recipient of several pieces of steak.

'It's like this, Dad.' Josh squeezed Abby's hand. 'My landlord has decided to sell the unit. His mortgage has skyrocketed and so have prices. He wants to cash in. Problem is…' he scratched his chin, '… it's not so easy to find a place to rent at the moment, low vacancy rates, rents have gone sky-high… and Abby and I…' he sent an affectionate glance in her direction, '… we want to save up a deposit. In the current market, it makes sense to buy, not rent.'

Luke had an inkling of what was coming. He was right.

Josh continued, 'We thought… if we could move in here for a bit… just until we get a deposit together… You don't need all of this house, and…' his voice trailed off.

'Well!' When Josh said he wanted to ask a favour, Luke hadn't expected this. He tried to think how Ness would react. He could almost hear her voice. '*We were young too, Luke. He's our son. It's up to us to help him. It was easier in our day. And he's right, you're living in two rooms in this big house.*'

'Dad?' Josh sounded anxious. 'Are you okay?'

'I was just thinking about your mum. If she was here…'

'I don't understand.'

'I was imagining what she'd say, and I know she wouldn't hesitate.' Ness could never deny Josh anything. 'Of course you can both move in. When did you have in mind?'

The young couple shared a relieved glance. 'Would next weekend be too soon?'

Luke swallowed hard. But what did it matter when the move took place, now he'd agreed to it? 'Sure. Need any help?'

'No, we should be right. We can hire a truck.' Josh glanced at Abby again. 'We thought we could store a few of our things in the garage.'

Luke swallowed hard again at the realisation he wasn't only about to share his house with the two young people but was going to have to provide house – or garage – room to all their belongings.

'Thanks, Dad.' Josh gave Luke a warm hug when he and Abby left later that evening, after they'd celebrated the decision with glasses of the vintage port Luke kept for special occasions. He wasn't sure this one called for it, but it pleased Josh.

Once he was alone again with Nelson, Luke poured himself another glass of the port and took it outside, the dog at his heels. As he sipped on the tawny liquid, Luke thought about what the next few months would bring, what it would be like to share his home with the young couple whose lifestyle was so very different from his. Maybe it was time to enjoy some of those things he'd been putting off, to hike the Larapinta Trail, go scuba diving on the Barrier Reef, ride a camel on the beach at Broome, follow the dinosaur trail and dig for fossils at Winton, rent a caravan and travel around Australia, or…

Three

It had been over a week since Alexander's text and there had been no more word from him, despite Rachel's texts and the messages she'd left on his voicemail. To her annoyance, no matter how she tried to arrange her calls at times when she assumed he'd be home, he never answered.

Today was the monthly lunch with her three friends and she'd be able to share her frustration with them. The four women had met as young mothers, and their friendship had continued over the years, now having evolved into lunch once a month with them taking turns to host, although Rachel often met a couple of them individually in between times.

Today they were meeting at Gill's, and Rachel was looking forward to seeing her again and to hearing her news. Rumour had it that Gill had finally decided to form a relationship with their local mayor, and Rachel was eager to discover if it was true. She'd seen Gill's embarrassment the previous month when Liz tried to quiz her about it and had no intention of distressing her. But the town rumour mill was working overtime – Joe was a popular mayor – so Rachel wanted to hear it from Gill herself.

It was strange, Rachel thought, as she walked Molly on the beach, her feet sinking into the wet sand at the water's edge, Molly running back and forth in and out of the waves, how only a year ago, all four of the women were single. Now Poppy and Cam were a couple, Liz had recently paired up with Finn, the editor of the local newspaper, and it looked as if Gill was finally going to settle down with their local mayor, Joe Harris. Only Rachel was still single and likely to remain so. She had no desire – or room – for a man in her life. Her memories of Kirk were still so strong, and her life was full with her B&B guests and her grandchildren.

Back home, Rachel wiped the sand off her feet and dried Molly off. There was just time to shower and change before she set off for Gill's.

After a welcome shower, she pulled on a pair of elastic-waisted pants and one of the loose shirts she'd bought as her weight ballooned after Kirk's death. They said grief made you lose weight. It had the opposite effect on her, though the extra kilos might also be the result of the snacks she shared with her granddaughters who loved Grandma's cookies, and the large breakfasts she cooked for her guests – and ate herself. As she examined herself in the mirror, she made a vow to lose weight.

Telling Molly to behave while she was gone, Rachel checked her phone to see a text from Steph. *Alexander???* She closed the phone, deciding to reply later. Steph and her partner had been visiting Tasmania for the past week, so she'd no doubt only read Alexander's message when they returned.

It always came as a shock to Rachel to walk into Gill's home. The sparsely furnished apartment, with its white walls and minimalist decor was so different from her own cluttered house, it was almost like visiting another planet. But it suited Gill who was the most private member of the group and who'd lived there alone since her husband left, until her daughter returned home a few months earlier.

Poppy and Liz were already there when Rachel arrived, seated on Gill's balcony with glasses of white wine.

'We didn't wait for you, so you'll need to catch up,' Liz said, holding up her glass, even though it was obvious she'd barely touched the wine.

'Hush, Liz,' Gill said, but she quickly poured a glass for Rachel, who took a seat by the others. 'Busy morning, Rach?' she asked.

'One elderly couple and a family of three for breakfast, then I took Molly for a walk,' she said, before taking a welcome sip of wine.

'I don't know how you do it,' Gill said, 'having strangers in your home.' She shivered as if the thought scared her.

'It's company. The house felt so empty after Kirk… And the money helps, of course. We don't all have a lucrative law practice, Gill.'

Gill had the grace to look embarrassed, making Rachel wish she had been more tactful. It was rare for anyone in the group to mention money.

'Anyway,' Poppy said, 'what news of you and the mayor, Gill? Rumour has it that…'

Gill didn't allow her to finish. 'I don't know what you've heard,' she said, two red spots appearing on her cheeks, 'but, yes, we have become… more than friends. And that's all I'm prepared to say at the moment. As you may also have heard, we had a pretty hairy time with Joe's brother-in-law appearing in town then dying suddenly. His sister has gone back to Perth to be with her son and his wife and await the birth of her granddaughter. Now, can we talk about something else?'

'Freya?' Rachel asked, aware Gill's daughter had applied for a position at Sydney University after spending the past few years teaching in a university in California.

Gill smiled, more relaxed now the focus was off her and Joe. 'It's good news. She's been offered the position in Sydney. She starts there in January.'

'Oh, congratulations. You must be so pleased,' Rachel said.

'I'm relieved she's staying in Australia,' Gill said, accepting the congratulations of the others too. 'My worst fear was she'd decide to return to the States.'

Rachel nodded. She knew what it was like to have a child living overseas.

As if reading her mind, Poppy asked, 'Any news from Alexander, Rachel? I know you were disappointed he didn't stay long last time.'

Rachel took a deep breath. 'I heard from him last week. He's coming home for Christmas and bringing a surprise.'

'Ooh!' Liz said. 'Has he met someone?'

'Your guess is as good as mine,' Rachel replied, 'but it's a distinct possibility.'

'What else could it be?' Poppy said. 'I'd lay bets on him having finally found someone. I'm so pleased for you, Rach. I know how good it feels to have all your chicks settled down.'

'I agree with Poppy, Rach,' Gill said. 'It sounds as if he's bringing someone home to introduce her to you.'

'I hope you're right.'

Once Gill served lunch which was a variety of salads with slices of rare roast beef, the conversation became more general. They all found it difficult to believe their next lunch would be their December one. It hardly seemed to have been any time since the previous Christmas, but so much had happened since then. They parted, with Liz reminding them it was her turn to host their December lunch and suggesting they have Secret Santa again. They all groaned, but Rachel knew they'd go along with it. It had been fun last time, and it was always difficult to dampen Liz's enthusiasm.

Rachel was already in bed when she heard her guests return that evening. It was like when the children were teenagers, she thought. She could never settle till she knew they were home. Now she turned over and closed her eyes, thoughts of who Alexander might be bringing home swirling through her head till she finally fell asleep.

Four

It was only a week since Josh and Abby moved in, but already Luke was beginning to feel the house didn't belong to him any longer. It was strange how two people could manage to take over and turn his home into… He didn't have a word for it. All he knew was that he could never find anything in the kitchen, the music which blasted out whenever the young couple were home threatened to burst his eardrums, and there were strange scents in the bathroom. Even Nelson seemed different, choosing to spend more time curled up in his bed than before.

He wondered what Ness would have thought but knew she'd only have been delighted to have their son back home, and would have regarded the inconvenience as a small price to pay. Maybe Luke was becoming grumpy in his old age, but sixty-two wasn't really old, was it? He didn't feel old, but somehow, seeing Josh and Abby leave the house dressed in their gym gear made him feel as if life was passing him by.

Today, he'd waited till they left before opening his laptop and googling Pelican Crossing. He still hadn't given Bob Reed an answer, and it didn't do any harm to check out what the town was like these days.

What he found was a surprise. The sleepy little fishing village he remembered had become a mecca for yachties from all over the world and was now on the tourist route for many international travellers, while still managing to retain its unique ambiance. From what he could see, some of the original buildings were still standing, while many had been renovated. The old fish and chip shop he remembered was now a classy restaurant called *Crossings*, was touted as one of the best restaurants on the coast, and had been featured on the popular television programme, *Weekender*. There also appeared to be several cafés with good reviews on TripAdvisor. Maybe it wasn't such a backwater after all. Luke stared at the screen, undecided, then looked down at Nelson whose expression seemed to be one of encouragement. Acting as locum for the Pelican Crossings vet wasn't on Luke's bucket list, but it would provide some relief from Josh and Abby, and maybe by the time he returned either they'd have managed to save a deposit, or he'd be more willing to accommodate them.

Before he could change his mind, he typed a reply to Bob, offering to help and asking him when he planned to leave.

That done, Luke fetched Nelson's leash and the pair set off for their morning walk to the park. As they followed their usual path, Luke tried to imagine what it would be like to walk on the beach instead of the concrete pathways they were used to. Nelson had never seen the sea, never felt the sand beneath his paws. He wondered how the dog would react to the different environment. It would be a big change for both of them, but one he was beginning to look forward to. He decided not to get too excited, however. Given the time he'd taken to respond to Bob's email, it was quite possible the other man might have already found someone else to fill in while he was gone.

It was a relief when his phone rang, and he heard Bob's voice. 'Got your email, Luke. I was about to give up on you, but I held off contacting anyone else. I'm delighted you've agreed to look after my practice for me. You won't regret it.'

'I hope not, Bob. Sorry it took me so long to reply. I wasn't sure about going back there, but a few things have happened…' No need to say how he felt like a stranger in his own home. 'What sort of timeframe are we looking at?'

'Well…' Bob paused, '… the programme doesn't start till January, but if you could get yourself free, I'd really like to travel around in the States a bit before then. How soon could you get up here?'

For a moment, Luke didn't speak. It wouldn't take him long to pack what he'd need for a few months. With Josh and Abby there, he had no need to worry about the house while he was gone. He took a deep breath. 'I could be there next week if it suits you.'

'Couldn't be better. I can spend a few days with you to do a bit of a handover, then it's all yours till the end of March. Call me when you're on your way.'

When the call ended, Luke looked down at Nelson who had remained standing at his side, his head cocked as if trying to figure out what was happening. 'Well, mate, looks as if we're going to Pelican Crossing,' he said. 'You're going to find things a bit different there – the scent of the ocean, the sand underfoot and the pelicans.' Suddenly the image of those magical creatures filled Luke's mind. How could he have forgotten the birds from which the town got its name, though that wasn't quite right. Didn't the name come from the nearby Boodalang River, boodalang being the Aboriginal word for pelican?

Nelson nodded his approval. Now, all Luke had to do was to break the news to Josh and Abby.

*

Luke waited till after dinner, which they'd eaten in the courtyard – a pasta dish Abby had cooked for them and which proved to be very tasty, though not a patch on Luke's mother's cooking, which she'd learned from her own Italian mother.

'I had an interesting email from this guy I met at a conference last year,' Luke began.

'The one in Canberra?' Josh asked, nodding.

Abby fussed with Nelson, displaying no interest in the conversation. The dog enjoyed her attention but kept his eye on Luke clearly sensing something was up.

'That's the one. He has a practice in Pelican Crossing where I grew up.'

'I think I've read about it or seen it advertised. Isn't it in Queensland?' Abby asked, showing she was still following the conversation.

'It is.'

'What did he want, Dad?'

'He's been accepted into a programme at Colorado State Uni and asked me if I'd take care of his practice while he was gone. Now you two are here to take care of the house, I've said I will.'

'Will what? Go to this Pelican Crossing place? What's it like? You never talk about it.'

It suddenly occurred to Luke that he had never mentioned it to Josh, or if he had, the young man had forgotten. 'It used to be pretty quiet and laid back, but I checked it out on the internet, and it seems to have changed since I lived there. It's no surprise. It was over forty years ago.'

'Wow!' Abby said, as if she couldn't imagine anything that long ago. She probably couldn't.

'How long are you talking about?'

'The programme lasts for three months, January till March, but Bob's keen to get off. I said I'd be up there sometime next week.'

Josh's eyes widened. 'I hope we're not chasing you out of your own home, Dad. It's a bit odd you deciding to do this just after we've moved in. Abby and I… we've tried to fit in, not to disrupt your life here. I know it must feel different, when you've been on your own since Mum passed, but you did agree…'

'No,' Luke lied, 'it's nothing to do with you and Abby.' He smiled at the girl who now had a worried expression. 'I'd been thinking about it for a few weeks. It's time I got out of my comfort zone, and this might just be the first step.'

'To take care of another vet practice?' Josh sounded doubtful.

'To move away from the city for a bit, to…' Luke waved his hands in the air, not knowing exactly what he meant, if he meant anything at all.

'Well, if you're sure. We'll take care of the place for you.' Josh shot a glance at Abby who nodded enthusiastically, giving Luke the impression they'd be glad to see the back of him and have the house to themselves. He'd probably have felt the same at their age.

'I'm sure. I think this calls for a drink.' Luke rose to fetch three glasses and the port from the sideboard. 'To the next four months,' he said, raising his glass.

The other two followed suit, then, 'Hey, we could join you for Christmas. It's always a quiet time. The practice will be closed for a few days and Guy and Rose could carry it for the rest of the week. What do you say, babe?' Josh said to Abby. 'How do you fancy a beach Christmas in this place Dad grew up?'

'Sounds good to me.'

'Sounds like a plan,' Luke said, glad the matter seemed settled. It would be good to see the pair of them in Pelican Crossing for the holiday. By that time, he'd have found his way around, met some locals. In a tiny corner of his mind, he wondered if there was anyone he knew still living there.

Five

Rachel had spent the last hour in her garden making up for lost time. It was difficult to do any work there when she was minding the twins and, while she loved her granddaughters to bits, the plants needed regular trimming and the weeds seemed to appear from nowhere. She straightened up and put one hand to her back, the ache a reminder she was getting older. Molly, frolicking at her feet, seemed to have no such challenge, and was ready for a walk.

'Okay,' she said to the little dog, 'but I need to have a seat first, and maybe a cup of tea with a slice of the carrot cake I made yesterday.' That was the problem, she thought, too many slices of carrot cake, banana bread and blueberry muffins, but Gemma and Indie loved her baking so much, and the cakes and slices went so well with a cup of her favourite lemon and ginger tea. Just one slice, she promised herself, opening the tin, cutting a generous serving, and vowing to start a diet tomorrow, as she always did. But tomorrow never came. Rachel sighed. What did it matter? At her last checkup, her doctor told her she was healthy, and there was no man in her life for her to please. Though, when Kirk was alive, he didn't mind her adding a few kilos – he called them her love handles. She tried to forget that these days the love handles had expanded to form a definite muffin top.

Drinking her tea, Rachel thought again about Alexander. While she was delighted he'd be home for Christmas, she couldn't help wondering about the surprise he was bringing with him. It had to be a woman, but why couldn't he just say so, rather than keep them all in suspense? Steph had received the same brief text as she and Jess and was equally puzzled. A nurse, Steph had been on night duty since returning from Tasmania but tonight she and Chloe were coming to dinner, and Rachel was sure Alexander would be one of the main topics of conversation. It wasn't like him to be so mysterious. He was normally an open book, unlike his sisters had been with their relationships.

Her tea finished, Rachel rose, much to the delight of Molly who had been waiting impatiently at her feet.

Taking Molly's leash from its hook, and popping on a wide-brimmed hat, Rachel and the dog climbed down the steps to the beach. This stretch of beach was more secluded than the main Pelican Crossing beaches, protected as it was by the headland. This morning it was practically deserted, only a few surfers sitting out waiting for a wave to bring them in to shore. Rachel loved it when it was like this, when she could almost believe she and Molly were the only two living creatures on the planet. She raised her face to the sun and breathed in the salty air.

Her peace was disturbed by her phone ringing. It was Jess wanting to know if Rachel could take care of the twins that afternoon. Of course she agreed, but it would mean she'd need to take time to shop this morning. She sighed but knew how much it meant to her to have both her daughters here in Pelican Crossing and to be able to help out when necessary. Without them and her B&B guests, her life would be very empty. She might even envy her friends who had found love a second time around.

An hour later, Rachel had completed her shopping and was ready for lunch. She'd left Molly at home, but knew the little dog would be happy in the yard for a bit longer, so decided to treat herself and made her way to her favourite café. Lou, the owner of *Books and Coffee* was a good friend of Rachel's. She had been one of her sister's best friends at school and, when Becky married and moved away, she and Rachel had become friends, drawn together by their mutual love of books.

'Good morning, Lou,' Rachel said to her friend, stopping for a moment as she passed through the bookshop section of the shop which, as its name suggested, was a combination of bookshop and café. Lou managed the bookshop section, while the café was run by

Ron and Denny, a couple of guys who cooked the most delicious food and whose witty repartee was legendary in Pelican Crossing.

'Rachel, how lovely to see you. Here for lunch?'

'I am. I don't suppose you have time to join me?' Rachel glanced around the bookshop which, given it was Monday, wasn't busy. She saw Lou's assistant – a young woman called Zoe – busy tidying and dusting the shelves.

Lou's eyes followed hers. 'Why not?' she said. 'I have to eat sometime. Can you take over here, Zoe?' she called to her assistant, before joining Rachel.

Rachel was pleased Lou was able to join her. They didn't often get the opportunity to have lunch together and it was several weeks since they'd last spoken.

'What news of Becky?' Lou asked, when they were comfortably seated at a corner table and had both ordered panini – Rachel's with grilled chicken and avocado, and Lou's with turkey, pear, bacon and cheese. Both women also ordered coffee.

Rachel's lips turned down. It had been three years ago when she'd received an email from her sister to say she was having memory problems, two since the shock news Becky had been diagnosed with Alzheimer's. 'It's not good, Lou,' she said, a tear coming to her eye. 'She hasn't been able to talk to me on the phone or use the computer for ages. She seems to have gone downhill so quickly. I can hardly believe it. I have no way of contacting her. It's as if she's died.'

The two sat in silence for a few moments, remembering the bright young woman who had always been so full of life, the first in her group to try something new.

'Oh, Rach!' Lou put a hand on Rachel's arm. 'I'm so sorry. It doesn't seem possible.'

'I know.' Rachel wiped her eyes and sniffed. 'Sorry. It just gets to me sometimes. Andy's good at keeping me in the loop, but there's nothing I can do. Last time I visited we were able to chat and go out for afternoon tea. I'd like to go down again before Christmas, but Adelaide's such a long way away and…'

'I know… your guests and the grandchildren. They're well, Jess's three littlies?'

'Very well, thanks. I don't know what I'd do without them.'

'And it'll soon be Christmas, a lovely family time.'

The mention of Christmas reminded Rachel. 'Alexander's coming home for Christmas,' she said, 'with a surprise.'

Lou's eyes widened. 'He's found someone at last?'

'It's the obvious explanation but being Alexander, he's keeping all of us in the dark. What about you?'

'Christmas? Oh, you know. I'll have a few days off from here, spoil myself, then come back and do it all over again.' She grinned, but Rachel knew her grin hid a hurt Lou would never talk about.

'Here you are, ladies.' Denny placed their coffee and paninis on the table with a smile and a wink. 'Taking it easy for a change, Lou?'

'Less of your cheek, young man,' Lou said but her tone was affectionate. 'He and Ron are like family to me,' she said when he'd left. '*I* don't know what I'd do without *them*. But there's something up.' She followed Denny with her eyes. 'The pair of them have been very mysterious for the past few days. They're keeping something to themselves, and I'm determined to find out what it is.'

Rachel laughed, her earlier mood broken, 'You're like my Molly with a bone when you get something into your head. I pity those two if you've got them in your sights. You must let me know if you discover their secret.'

'Mmm.'

Rachel didn't really think the two young men had a secret, sure it was all in Lou's imagination, but she was happy to humour her. She often felt sorry for her friend who didn't have any children or grandchildren to keep her mind occupied. The two guys who manned the café were a poor substitute for children of her own.

Rachel was still counting her blessings when she returned home to Molly's enthusiastic welcome, the welcome she received from the little dog whether she'd been gone for five minutes or an hour. She picked her up and gave her a cuddle. 'I have you too, Molly,' she said rubbing her nose in the dog's wiry coat, 'and we have Gemma and Indie arriving soon and Steph and Chloe coming to see us tonight.' She pictured Lou going home to her empty home and shivered at the thought it could have been her life if she hadn't had Kirk, if they hadn't had children, if…

Six

It had taken two days of driving, and Luke was exhausted when he finally saw the sign for Pelican Crossing. For a moment, he wondered if he'd made a mistake, if it was wrong to go back, to try to recapture his youth. But that wasn't why he was here, and it was too late to change his mind now. Bob had changed his plans. He intended to leave next morning and there were animals who needed a vet's care. The grateful email he'd received with details of the practice had listed three animals in the hospital section of the clinic, and a full schedule of appointments.

As he drove into town along the main street, Luke recognised several of the buildings, but many had obviously had a facelift since he was last here. He passed a café and gelato shop, and the marina located at the end of the street had grown in size and now boasted a lowset building named *Pelican Marine*. Similarly, the harbour now housed a variety of craft and there was a large sign advertising a dive school. Things had changed, and with Christmas approaching, many of the shops were sporting Christmas displays, the poinciana trees were in bloom and tinsel garlands had been strung from the lamp posts. Everything looked very festive.

From his vantage point in the back seat, Nelson peered eagerly out the window as Luke followed Bob's instructions to a bluff on the outskirts of town, to stop in front of a modern building with the sign which indicated it was *Pelican Crossing Vet Clinic*. Next to the clinic was an equally modern house with large glass windows looking out to the ocean. So, this was where he was to spend the next few months. As if reading his mind, Nelson gave a loud bark. Luke killed the engine and got out of the car before leaning into the back to release Nelson who immediately put his mark on the low wall outside the clinic.

'Hey! Glad you made it.' Bob appeared in the doorway of the house, his hand outstretched. 'Come on in. You too,' he said to the dog who was sniffing at his feet as Luke and he shook hands. 'I didn't open the clinic today. I've had another change of plans and have to leave later today. Thought we could have a quick handover before I go. You have my number, but you shouldn't have any problems. It's all pretty basic, and it's a good community. Well, you know that, you grew up here. My receptionist, Wendy, has been with me for years. She'll be able to steer you right.'

Luke might have grown up here, but from what he'd seen already, the Pelican Crossing of today was very different to the one he'd left. But perhaps the people hadn't changed much. He guessed he'd find out. It would certainly be different to his city practice and to living in Sydney.

He and Nelson followed Bob into the clinic where the vet took him through to where two cats and a dog were in cages, each in different stages of recuperation from surgery, then into the clinic itself which impressed Luke with the display of modern instruments and the state-of-the-art equipment. The vet's own office was both comfortable and practical. It would be a pleasure to work here.

'Guess you feel like a beer and a bite to eat after your long drive,' Bob said.

'Sounds good, but what about Nelson?' he gestured to where his dog was standing, tongue hanging out.

'We can go to *The Grand*. They have tables outside and they'll provide a bowl of water for your dog.'

'It's still there?' Luke asked in surprise. *The Grand Hotel* had been where he and his mates enjoyed their first beers, where he'd spent many a Saturday night till they were ejected at closing time, where he'd taken his first girlfriend and tried to impress her by ordering white wine when they were both underage.

'It sure is. It's undergone a few changes of owner and renovations, now serves craft beer from a local brewery, but the place hasn't really changed much. It'll always be *The Grand*.'

Sure enough, when they reached the hotel, Luke easily recognised it. The façade hadn't changed in the past forty years, though it had clearly been repainted a few times.

Bob chose a table on the outside and brushed off Luke's offer to pay. 'Pie and chips do for you?' he asked.

Luke nodded and took a seat, Nelson choosing to lie at his feet and stare around at the new setting, his nose in the air sniffing up the different scents.

Before long, Bob reappeared carrying two beers, a waiter accompanying him with a bowl of water for Nelson which the dog lapped up eagerly.

'Thanks,' Luke said. 'Cheers.' He raised his glass and took a long draught, the icy liquid going down a treat.

'Cheers,' Bob responded. 'Here's to a successful few months.'

'I'll drink to that,' Luke said, already beginning to feel at home.

When they returned to the clinic, Bob gave Luke a quick tour of the house, before heading off and leaving Luke and Nelson to settle in. Once he'd carried their gear into the house, Luke took a more leisurely look around, Nelson padding at his heels. The house was bigger than he'd expected, knowing Bob lived there alone. It comprised four bedrooms, the master with a magnificent view of the ocean, as did the open-plan living/dining/kitchen area. The entire place was tiled, making it cool underfoot in summer and easy to clean, and it opened out onto a courtyard shaded by a tall poinciana tree.

Seeing Nelson was restless, and knowing the dog would be in need of a walk after the long trip, Luke popped on his hat and led the dog to where he could see steps leading down to what appeared to be a secluded stretch of beach. Once there, Nelson immediately rushed off to investigate this strange new world, undeterred by the unfamiliar feel of the sand underfoot, while Luke followed at a more leisurely pace. The smell of the sea and the roar of the waves brought back memories of a time Luke had almost forgotten, and he began to relax, already confident he'd made the right decision in coming here. According to Bob, the vet practice was rarely busy. He'd have time to relax and enjoy life away from the buzz of the city, maybe time to catch up on his reading, even to start the research on his family history he'd been meaning to do for ages, but never seemed to find time for.

Gazing up at the bluff above the beach, he could only see one other house besides Bob's. There was a set of steps leading down to the beach from it too, then further along, yet another set of steps and what appeared to be a car park with a couple of vehicles. He supposed they belonged to the surfers he could see riding in on a wave. It had been years since he surfed, not since he left Pelican Crossing. He could still remember the feeling when you caught that wave and glided in to shore. *Was it too late to have another go? Was he too old?* Being back here, where he'd grown up, where he'd learned to swim, to surf, where he'd had his first beer, his first kiss… it was like going back in time. But he had to remember, he wasn't eighteen anymore, and at sixty-two he was no longer in the first flush of youth.

Seven

Rachel had just popped the chicken casserole into the oven when Steph and Chloe arrived. It had been a surprise to her when her younger daughter told her she was in love with the girl who had been her best friend through school, but Rachel had immediately realised how well suited they were. Now the pair were happily settled into married life.

After the usual round of hugs, and when the two women had made a fuss of Molly, Steph handed Rachel a bottle of prosecco. 'What are we celebrating?' Rachel asked.

'Later,' Steph said, giving Chloe a secret smile which made Rachel wonder what it was about. They'd only recently returned from Tasmania. She hoped they hadn't decided to move there.

Putting the prosecco into the fridge on Steph's instructions, Rachel poured three glasses of chardonnay and they went out to sit in the courtyard, Molly following and choosing to plop herself down at Steph's feet.

'So,' Steph said, 'what do you think about Alexander? I spoke to Jess, and it seems he sent the same message to all of us… no details, just a surprise.'

'He's met someone,' Chloe said. 'What else can it be?'

'I think you're right,' Rachel said, but it irked her she'd been unable to contact him for more information.

'Your brother's always been a bit of a dark horse,' Chloe said. 'It's just like him to want to keep everyone in the dark. I wonder what she'll be like.'

'Well, we'll soon find out,' Steph said. 'It's not long till Christmas, and I expect he'll arrive at least a few days before the big day. You *are* going to do your usual Christmas, Mum, I hope?'

'Of course.' Christmas wouldn't be Christmas without the big tree in the living room, Rachel's special Christmas Eve dinner, and Christmas Day breakfast and lunch. It was a tradition she and Kirk had started when the children were little, and she'd continued. It brought back so many good memories. 'It's so much fun with Gemma and Indie, and Emily is old enough to enjoy it too this year. Christmas is for children, and I love to see my granddaughters' faces when they open their presents. It's part of the joy of Christmas.'

Steph and Chloe laughed, and Rachel saw them glance at each other and share that secret smile again. There was definitely something up.

The oven pinged and they went inside to where Rachel had set the table in the dining room. Steph and Chloe helped her carry in the chicken along with a salad she'd prepared earlier and the remainder of the wine, Molly following in the hope of some titbits.

It wasn't till they had finished eating and Rachel had heard all about the Tasmanian trip, that, after a glance at Chloe, Steph rose and went to the kitchen to return with the now chilled prosecco. Rachel gave a sigh of relief. She was finally going to discover what the secret smiles and glances were all about. She crossed her fingers they weren't going to tell her they planned to leave Pelican Crossing. She loved having both her girls living so close to her and being able to see them regularly. It almost made up for Alexander's absence.

Steph filled their glasses with the sparkling wine, then took Chloe's hand in hers. Both women smiled at Rachel. 'Chloe and I have decided to have a baby,' she said. 'We wanted you to be the first to know.'

Rachel was speechless. When Steph and Chloe got together, she'd resigned herself to the fact Steph wouldn't provide her with any grandchildren. While she knew many same-sex couples did have children, it had never occurred to her Steph and Chloe would be one of them.

'Oh, I'm thrilled,' she said, trembling with excitement. This was the best news they could have given her. 'How? When?'

Steph laughed. 'We're still in the early stages, but we've been speaking to the two guys who work in *Books and Coffee*. They're more than willing to go along with us, for one of them to donate his sperm and for them to be honorary uncles to the baby. They say it'll be the next best thing to having one of their own.'

Rachel was glad she was sitting down. This was a lot to digest. Another baby, another grandchild and a link to those delightful young men who worked with Lou. 'Who?' she asked, looking from Steph to Chloe and back.

'I'm going to have this one,' Steph said. 'We drew straws.'

Rachel gasped. *They drew straws for who would become pregnant?*

'It's not as crazy as it sounds,' Steph said, clearly understanding Rachel's surprise. 'We don't want this one to be an only child. We want him or her to have a brother or sister, so I'll have this one and Chloe will have the next. I loved growing up with a brother and sister, but Chloe was an only child, and we don't want that for our child.'

'I… see.' Rachel did, but it wasn't always that simple. She thought of her friend Poppy's oldest daughter who had such difficulty in becoming pregnant, but as a nurse, surely Steph would be aware of the possible pitfalls.

'And your folks, Chloe?' Rachel looked at Steph's partner. She was aware Chloe's parents hadn't been happy about the two women getting together and had only attended their wedding under protest.

Chloe reddened. 'That's one of the reasons Steph will have our first child. Mum and Dad… We want them to get used to the idea before it's my turn.'

Rachel didn't say anything. She knew Chloe's parents and doubted anything would change their minds. She could only hope the arrival of a grandchild would soften their attitude to their daughter and her partner. She suddenly realised they'd been so busy talking their glasses were still full. She raised hers. 'To the new addition to our family, my next grandchild, and its two very special mothers,' she said.

Steph and Chloe raised their glasses too. 'To our first child,' they said together as they clinked their glasses and took a sip.

The rest of the evening was spent in a discussion about names for the baby, and with Rachel wanting to know when they intended to set this in motion. She was unable to receive a definite answer, but Steph assured her she'd be the first to know when she became pregnant. 'After

Chloe,' she said, laughing. There had been a lot of laughter, proving to Rachel the two women had given their decision a lot of thought and would be good parents. Rachel couldn't wait for her new grandchild, a cousin for Gemma, Indie and Emily, and to wonder if this one would be a boy or another granddaughter. It suddenly occurred to her that this must be the secret Lou had imagined the two young men were keeping from her.

When Steph and Chloe had left and Rachel was alone again with Molly, she sighed with happiness. While unexpected, Steph's news had filled her with delight, but it made her wish Kirk was here to share it with her. As she prepared for bed, she picked up his photo from the bedside table as she always did. It was one taken just before he had become so sick. In it, he looked the picture of health. He was standing on the beach with a fishing rod, wearing his old straw hat, a silly grin on his face. She kissed the image of the man she'd never stopped loving, before replacing it carefully. 'You'd be so proud of Steph,' she told him. 'She's made a good life for herself and is going to become a wonderful mother.'

Eight

It was a week since Luke had arrived in Pelican Crossing, and he felt as if he'd never left. He'd slipped seamlessly into Bob's practice, and into life here in Pelican Crossing. Bob had been correct when he said it wasn't a busy practice. Now, the three animals in the vet hospital had returned to their owners, he'd only had a few routine appointments to deal with, plus a cat who'd managed to get into a fight and lost a patch of fur.

He was enjoying the slower pace of life, and Nelson seemed to be enjoying the change too. Each morning, Luke rose early, and he and Nelson climbed down to the beach where he had an early morning swim and Nelson joined him. So far, they'd had the beach to themselves. Some days, he even braved the waves on a surfboard he'd found in Bob's garage. On these occasions, Nelson chose to remain on the beach and watch him with a jaundiced eye, while Luke relived his youth, albeit with less energy than when he was in his teens. It felt as if life was one long holiday.

Returning home from the beach, Luke washed the sand from Nelson, then took a shower himself, before pulling on a pair of shorts and a tee-shirt, reflecting as he did so, how different this was from his life in Sydney. In his call the previous evening, Josh had assured him all was well with both the house and the practice and said how much he and Abby were looking forward to seeing Luke at Christmas. Luke was looking forward to it too but was surprised how little he missed Sydney and his son's company. It was as if he'd had a new lease of life since arriving here.

Today being Sunday, the vet clinic was closed, so Luke had the day to himself. He planned to investigate the café he'd seen opposite the marina. *The Blue Dolphin Café* advertised breakfast and, since there were outside tables, Nelson could accompany him. Then he intended to spend more time wandering around Pelican Crossing to reacquaint himself with the town and note the changes which had taken place. He'd already made another visit to *The Grand* and was interested in visiting the brewery which produced the craft beer he'd enjoyed there.

When he and Nelson approached the café, Luke could see one of the outside tables was already occupied by a couple who looked a few years younger than him, a chocolate labrador lying at their feet. The dog raised its head as they walked past, but Nelson chose to ignore it. Luke didn't recognise the couple, but why would he? It had been a long time since he lived here. A lot had happened in the meantime and there was no reason to believe the community in Pelican Crossing had remained the same.

After studying the menu, Luke ordered the Big Breakfast with an espresso. His mother's Italian background had made him appreciate this rather than the milky drink Ness and many of his friends preferred. When his meal was served, along with a bowl of water for Nelson, the friendly waitress said, 'I haven't seen you here before. Are you on holiday?'

'Not exactly, though it feels that way. I'm the locum at Pelican Crossing Vet Clinic while the usual vet's away.'

'Oh, I'd heard Bob was off overseas. Welcome to Pelican Crossing. I'm Janice.'

'Luke Findlay, and this is Nelson.' At the sound of his name, the dog raised his head.

'Hello, Nelson,' she said, bending down to pat him. 'I hope we see both of you here again. Bob often came in on the weekend.' She disappeared inside the café.

'Well,' Luke said to his pet, 'seems we've made one friend here.' Nelson grunted his agreement.

He had finished his meal, which proved delicious, and was on his second cup of coffee, when the man from the couple he'd noticed earlier came over to his table, hand outstretched.

'Hi there. I couldn't help overhearing what you said to the waitress earlier. I knew Bob was heading off for a few months. I'm Joe Harris, the local mayor. Always glad to welcome new blood to the town but…' he scratched his chin, 'why does your name sound familiar?'

Luke laughed as he shook the other man's hand. 'It's been a while – over forty years – but I grew up here. Left to attend university and haven't been back till now.'

'Of course.' Joe snapped his fingers. 'That's how I know the name. You must have been a few years above me at school. Didn't you play on the rugby team?'

'Wow, you have a good memory.' Luke felt embarrassed. He didn't remember Joe at all, but that tended to be the way of it. You could always remember those older than you, not those younger.

'I'll never forget that amazing try of yours which won the regional trophy,' Joe continued, adding to Luke's embarrassment. It had been his one success in what had been a pretty mediocre sporting career. He'd given up the sport soon afterwards, preferring to focus on his studies and his surfing.

'Anyway, welcome back,' Joe said. 'Bob didn't tell me who was taking his place. You can always find me in the council chambers, and you must come to dinner some time with Gill and me.' He nodded to where his companion was watching them with interest. 'This is a nice fellow,' he said leaning over to ruffle Nelson's ears. The dog made an appreciative sound of approval.

'Thanks,' Luke said. It was kind of Joe, but he doubted he'd take advantage of the offer. When Joe and his companion – and the labrador – had left, Luke finished his coffee, paid for breakfast, then began his exploration of the town. First, he headed to the nearby marina, where he leant on the wall to study the large number of vessels berthed there. It had certainly expanded since the few rows of boats he remembered, but the pelicans hadn't changed. He chuckled to see a couple perched on the wooden bollards which Nelson was regarding with puzzlement. 'Haven't seen any birds like those before, have you, Nelson?' he asked, only to see the dog shake his head.

Luke's next port of call was the building where he'd seen the sign for the dive school. He'd done a bit of diving on a trip in his early twenties and gained his certification. He wasn't sure if it was something he wanted to pick up again, but the water here would be very different to that he'd experienced all those years ago in the water around Sydney, and it would be useful to have the information.

After a friendly chat with a young man called Gary who ran the school, he left with a handful of pamphlets covering not only the dive school, but also kitesurfing the young man also managed, a fishing charter service operated by Gary's father, and hot air balloon rides conducted by another local. Luke certainly had lots of options for outdoor activities here if he wanted to take up the opportunity.

As he wandered down Main Street, Luke came to the building he remembered as the fish and chip shop he and his mates had often dropped into after an evening out. It was almost unrecognisable. The door and windows of the hundred-year-old, two-storey building had been painted a deep shade of ocean-blue and gleamed in the sunlight. Gorgeous twists of bougainvillea adorned the wrought iron balconies on the upper level, and the name *Crossings* was tastefully printed on a sign above the entrance. This was the place he'd seen on the internet. It was impressive. Luke made a mental note to have a meal there while he was in town, perhaps when Josh and Abby came to visit.

The beach in this part of Pelican Crossing was busier than the one where he was staying. Today it was filled with families enjoying the sunshine, and surfers taking advantage of the waves. Luke wasn't tempted to join them. He preferred what he had come to consider his own more secluded stretch of sand.

Seeing Nelson gaze up at him longingly, Luke realised more time had passed than he realised. It was time for lunch. He debated visiting the brewery as he'd planned, but unsure how welcome Nelson would be, he decided to leave it for another day, and headed back to where he'd parked his SUV.

Before long, he was back at the house which was his home for the next few months and after making a sandwich for himself and ensuring Nelson was fed and watered, he settled down in the courtyard with a beer and a book he'd discovered on Bob's bookshelf. It was a history of Italian migration to Australia in the 1950s, and he was keen to discover if it made any mention of his mother's family, of whose background he knew very little.

Nine

When Rachel awoke on Monday morning, Molly was nowhere to be seen. Initially, she didn't worry – the little animal often went out the doggy door. She'd no doubt reappear when she became hungry.

After showering and dressing in a loose sundress, Rachel settled into her morning routine of preparing breakfast for her guests. This week, she had a young couple who she suspected were on their honeymoon, as they were very affectionate towards each other, breaking apart with embarrassment in her company. The other guests were a family of four – Mum, Dad, and two teenagers – Rachel wasn't sure why they weren't in school – and the youngsters were proving to be a challenge with their continual whinging. She was glad they were only booked in for a week.

Breakfast over, there was still no sign of Molly, and Rachel began to worry. She stepped outside, calling, 'Molly!' which usually brought the little dog running. Not this morning. Her heart dropped. Where was she? Rachel started to search around the garden, calling out the dog's name as she went, becoming more and more anxious. Then, as she rounded the sundial, she heard a faint whimper, then saw what looked like a white bundle lying under a bush.

'Molly!' Rachel rushed to the dog who tried to get up when she saw Rachel, but she seemed unable to move her back legs. Recognising the signs of a tick, she knelt down and examined her pet, frustrated when she was unable to find the culprit. She had no idea how long Molly had been lying there. She only knew she needed to get her pet to the vet right away.

Rachel bundled the little dog into the car and set off for the vet clinic, driving carefully so as not to disturb her, and glad she didn't have far to go. The clinic was located along the bluff from her home. She'd heard Bob Reed, the usual vet who'd taken care of Molly since she was a tiny puppy, was away and hoped the locum would be as caring as Bob always was. But surely anyone who chose to work with animals must be kind and caring?

Entering the clinic, Wendy, the receptionist who'd been there for ever, welcomed her with a smile. 'Morning, Rachel. Molly poorly? You do know Bob's away at the moment? His replacement's a lovely man.' Wendy's endorsement meant nothing. She saw the good in everyone, but it was some sort of a comfort. Rachel and Molly were the only ones there so she shouldn't have long to wait. 'You're going to be fine, Molly,' she reassured her pet, stroking the dog's head gently.

In only a few minutes, Wendy told her to go in.

Inside the consulting room, the vet had his back to Rachel. All she could see were a pair of long legs encased in blue jeans which had seen better days and a white tee-shirt stretched across a set of broad shoulders. The body was topped by a thatch of white hair. 'Take a seat. Be with you in a minute.' The voice sounded vaguely familiar.

When he turned to face her, Rachel gasped as she recognised Luke Findlay, the boy – now a man – who had been her sister's first boyfriend.

Luke stared at her for a moment, a puzzled expression on his face then, 'Red?'

'Rachel,' she said automatically. What was he doing here? When she was fourteen, she'd had a huge crush on her sister's boyfriend and instead of ignoring her, he'd been happy for her to tag along on some of their dates, calling her *Red*, because of her red hair, the hair which was now faded to more of a strawberry blonde. He'd left for university around the same time his family had moved away too. It was all over forty years ago. But she could easily recognise the younger version of him. Although his once black hair was now silver and the matching beard neatly trimmed, his eyes hadn't changed, eyes of such a dark navy blue, the young Rachel had felt she could drown in them. His features hadn't changed either, the high cheekbones and sallow complexion. Wasn't there an Italian connection somewhere in the mix? All of this went through her mind in a flash, so it was a shock when he spoke.

'Rachel, of course.' His lips turned up in the smile Rachel remembered, the one which had made her senses reel when she was fourteen, and she felt her heart lurch at the memory. 'And who have we here?' he asked, taking Molly into his arms and setting her down on the examination table.

'Molly. She's very lethargic this morning, I think she's picked up a tick, but I can't locate it,' Rachel said, trying to control the butterflies in her stomach. It was nerves about Molly, she assured herself, nothing to do with the man who was now carefully examining the little dog. She wasn't fourteen any longer, and Luke must be… she did a quick calculation… sixty-two. At fifty-eight, Rachel was older than the other three in her group of friends. It was possibly the reason they often confided in her and asked her advice. And she was much too old to have a resurgence of her teenage emotions for a man from her past… from her sister's past, she corrected herself. To him, she'd always been Becky's little sister.

'Let's have a look,' Luke was saying, his long, tanned fingers feeling around Molly's tiny frame, while Rachel watched on anxiously. 'I believe you're right,' he said. 'Good thing you brought her in when you did.'

'What…?'

'I'll just administer a sedative to ensure I can find the tick and don't miss any others. I'll give her an anti-serum to help neutralise the toxin. Then I'd like Molly to stay in the vet hospital for a few days so I can monitor her and provide any additional treatments which prove necessary.'

Rachel felt the colour drain from her face. 'How long will it take? She will recover?'

'I'm sure she'll be fine. It looks as if you found her before the toxin got a hold. But she should stay here for a few days. It can sometimes be a slow process, take up to nine days. You can call in two days' time, and we'll let you know how Molly is doing.'

'And that's it?' Rachel realised she was sounding foolish. But this was Molly who had been with her since she was a tiny pup. What would she do without her, and how would Molly take to being in a cage at the vet clinic?

'I can assure you I'll take good care of her,' Luke said smiling. He was clearly accustomed to dealing with anxious pet owners. 'And, once she goes home again, you'll still need to take care – keep her comfortable with a cool environment and minimal stress or exercise, feed her smaller, more frequent meals and ensure she has plenty of water. It could be up to three weeks before she's fully recovered.'

'Three weeks? That takes us up to Christmas!'

'Is that a problem?' Luke raised an eyebrow.

'No, of course not.' But Rachel was already trying to work out how to incorporate Molly's care with her Christmas preparations, and how she was going to manage to ensure her lively pet got enough rest. Normally, this was a time when Molly liked to be in the thick of everything, excited when the tree went up, and on Christmas morning when the two terrors were unwrapping their presents – and this year there was Emily too.

'Well, then.' Luke stood looking at her, and Rachel realised he was waiting for her to leave.

'Right, thanks. I'll call in two days, then?'

Luke nodded.

Molly looked so sad lying there on the long examination table. Rachel hated to leave her there, but she had to trust Luke. 'Bye, little one,' she said, bending over to place a kiss on Molly's nose, which was warmer and drier than usual. 'Be good.' Then, feeling even more foolish, she turned and left, tears coming to her eyes as the door of the surgery closed behind her.

Rachel drove home in a haze, unsure what had upset her most, having to leave Molly with the vet, or the fact the vet was Luke Findlay, the first boy she'd ever had a crush on – and who she'd never forgotten.

Ten

The house felt very empty when Rachel arrived home. There were none of the usual snuffling noises Molly made, and which Rachel wasn't normally aware of… but their absence made the house seem like an empty shell. She was glad Jess had asked her to take care of the twins in the afternoon. Their company would go some way to fill the gap Molly's absence made.

Rachel fixed herself a salad for lunch and carried it out to the courtyard, but only picked at it. Everything was so still and quiet. She gave herself a shake. Molly was going to be all right. It was only for a few days. It would pass in a flash. Then, she thought, she would meet Luke again. Her mind went back to her shock at the sight of him, of her surprise he'd recognised her after all these years. Back then, she'd been a shy teenager impressed her older sister was dating one of the stars of the rugby team, thrilled when he invited her along to the beach with them a couple of times, and once to the movies to see *Grease*. She'd love the movie, picturing herself as Sandy, and Luke as Danny. It was every teenage girl's dream. But she was only fourteen, and Luke was her sister's boyfriend.

Nothing had changed, she told herself. It might be over forty years later, but Luke Findlay was still way out of her league. What was she doing even thinking of him? The thought of another man had never crossed her mind since she met Kirk… till now. She remembered how, only a few weeks ago, she'd told herself there was no room for another man in her life. But she also remembered once telling Liz that grandchildren were no substitute for a man in your bed. She stopped herself and stared into space. *Where had that memory come from? And why think of it now?* She picked up her plate and carried it inside, determined to dismiss all thoughts of Luke Findlay. The man was Bob's locum. He was taking care of Molly. And that was all. There was no need for her to behave like a starstruck schoolgirl.

*

By the time Jess arrived with the twins, Rachel was in a calmer frame of mind.

'Where's Molly, Mum?' Jess asked, as the twins raced into the house shouting the dog's name – she was usually at the door to greet them.

'I had to take her to the vet this morning, a tick. She'll be there for a few days.' Rachel's bottom lip trembled as she relived her distress about Molly.

'Poor Molly. I heard Bob's off on a trip. What's the new vet like?'

Rachel swallowed. There was no need for Jess to know about her and Becky's history with Luke. 'He seems nice, competent, older than Bob, closer to my age, I think.'

'Oh!' But Jess wasn't really interested. 'Well, I need to go. I have to get Emily to this party. I should be back around four. That okay with you?'

'Sure, we'll have fun, won't we girls?' she said to the two little girls who had appeared again, bewailing the fact they couldn't find Molly.

'Molly's sick,' she told them, when they had waved Jess off. 'She's had to go to hospital. You know, like you did, Gemma, when you hurt your arm.'

Both girls nodded, clearly recalling the incident the previous year when Gemma had fallen out of a tree and broken her arm.

'Will she have a plaster too?' Indie asked – she had been very envious of her sister's plaster.

'No, but she needs to stay in the vet hospital for a few days, then we'll need to be very quiet when she comes home. No running around or rowdy games. Promise?'

'We promise,' they said together. Then Indie asked, 'Can we go swimming? Mum brought our togs.' She pointed to the brightly coloured bag sitting in the hall.

'I think that's a great idea. Why don't you two go out into the garden while I get changed. You can check if any of the strawberries are ripe.'

The girls ran off, and Rachel headed into the bedroom to change. A few minutes, later all three made their way down the steps to the beach.

As Rachel had predicted, the twins kept her busy, so busy she didn't have time to think about what was happening with Molly... or to brood over the reappearance of Luke Findlay in her life. When the image of him did intrude into her consciousness, she quickly dismissed it. After spending a couple of hours on the beach, the girls clamoured to do some baking and in the chaos they always managed to create in the kitchen, there was even less time for Rachel to give in to her thoughts.

When Jess arrived with Emily to take the twins home, all three were sitting outside enjoying the results of their labours, the girls' mouths rimmed with chocolate from the chocolate chip Nutella cookies.

As always, Jess was in a rush. She quickly rounded up the twins, accepted the box of cookies Rachel had prepared for them to take home, and was off, almost before Rachel had time to blink.

Now the twins had gone, Rachel felt Molly's absence more than ever. The little dog was her constant companion and, although she knew her absence was temporary, she couldn't help wondering how she was. It was a shock when the sound of her phone ringing broke the silence of the empty house.

Rachel recognised the number of the vet clinic, and her heart dropped. Had something happened to Molly? Luke had said she'd be fine, but what if... 'Hello,' she said, her heart in her mouth.

'Red?' Luke said. 'I don't want you to worry. Molly's just fine. I could tell from your expression this morning you were anxious about her, and I wanted to put your mind at rest. She's awake. I've given her the anti-toxin and I don't expect any adverse effects. I'm pretty sure when you call on Wednesday, you'll be able to pick her up.'

Rachel breathed more easily. It was as if a weight had been lifted from her shoulders. Her eyes misted. 'Oh, thank you, Luke,' she said. 'And thank you for calling. I was worried about her.'

'No problem. It was good to see you again.' He ended the call.

Relieved her pet was recovering, and somewhat bemused Luke had called her *Red* again, Rachel poured herself a glass of wine, the words, *It was good to see you again*, going round and round in her head. It didn't mean anything. He was only being polite to a client. He probably had a wife tucked away in Bob's house, the house which was only a stone's throw away on the other side of the bluff and which shared the same stretch of beach.

*

Now why had he done that, Luke wondered as he put down the phone. It wasn't his habit to call the owners of animals in the vet hospital to report on their condition. Then to say it was good to see her again… He shook his head. But it *had* been good to see her again. He remembered Becky's little sister – Red. Back then, her hair had been a fiery red, the curls making a halo around her face. It had been a pretty face, he recalled. It still was. She'd aged well… and she'd obviously stayed in Pelican Crossing. He wondered briefly what had happened to Becky, if she was still in town. But he'd known from the start that relationship wouldn't last. Ness had been Becky's complete opposite… actually more like Red… Rachel. He must try to remember to call her Rachel. He expected she was married now, no doubt with a brood of children and grandchildren, whereas he only had Josh who had hurtled from one relationship to another. But he had hopes for this one with Abby. It was the first time he'd mentioned buying a house. Abby was a lot younger than his son – mid-twenties to his mid-thirties, but she was a lovely girl, mature for her years with a caring personality. He'd keep his fingers crossed about her. He was aware he hadn't been much of a father to Josh since Ness's death. At first he'd been too caught up in his own grief, then keeping his distance had become a habit.

Feeling restless, and aware he'd forgotten to do the shopping he'd intended, Luke fed Nelson and told him to stay, before heading out.

As he drove into town, he tried to remember the restaurants he'd noticed on the day he arrived, but the only one that came to mind was *Crossings*. It seemed too upmarket for a casual meal, so he kept driving, past *The Grand Hotel*, which was a possibility, though he didn't feel like the forced camaraderie he'd most likely find there. Then, overlooking the marina, he spotted it. When he was growing up in Pelican Crossing, the yacht club had been the place for celebrating birthdays, anniversaries and any other event. It had been a good spot for a casual meal or a special occasion. Like many of the other buildings in town, it had had a facelift sometime in the past forty years – perhaps more than one – but it still looked as welcoming as he remembered from the night their coach had taken the rugby team there to celebrate their victory. He parked his car and made his way to the entrance.

The restaurant was surprisingly busy for a Monday evening. Luke suspected many of the diners were tourists enjoying an early holiday before the Christmas rush. If what he'd read was true, Pelican Crossing had become a tourist mecca for both interstate and international visitors, eager to spend the holiday season in warmer climes. Luke was shown to a table by a window overlooking the marina by a cheerful waiter and handed a leather-bound menu much fancier than the one he remembered. Gazing out over the lines of vessels in the marina, he marvelled yet again how much the town had changed. The myriad lights glinting in the ocean could have been on the French or Italian riviera instead of his home town.

After a brief glance at the menu, Luke ordered fish and chips with the craft beer he'd enjoyed with Bob in *The Grand* to wash it down and leant back in his seat to observe the other diners. As his eyes flitted over the couples and families, several of whom appeared to be on holiday, his eyes were drawn back to three people seated at the far side of the restaurant. There was something about the set of one of the men's heads, the way he tilted it to one side as he spoke, that was familiar. It took Luke a few moments, then it came to him. He'd seen that head many times before, but back then the hair had been long and blond, prompting the school principal to demand he have a haircut. But Troy Piper had never been one to stick by the rules. He'd managed to get Luke into trouble more times than he cared to remember. So, he was still here?

While Luke was debating whether or not to announce his presence to his old friend, the man turned round and caught sight of Luke. For a moment he looked puzzled then his eyes widened, and his face broke into a grin. He said something to his companions before heading over to where Luke was sitting.

'What the hell are you doing here, Luke?' he asked. 'Thought you were well set up down in Sydney and had forgotten Pelican Crossing and all your old mates.'

'Not so.' Luke rose to give Troy a hug, noticing how the once well-muscled man was turning to fat. 'Stayed there after uni, but I'm retired now.'

'And what are you doing in Pelican Crossing?' he repeated. 'On holiday?' He glanced around as if expecting to see a wife and family.

'I'm on my own. I'm taking care of Bob Reed's vet practice while he's overseas.'

'Right. I heard he had some expert from down south coming to fill in. So that's you?'

'Not really.' Luke wondered what rumours were circulating about him. He remembered what Pelican Crossing could be like regarding a stranger in town. 'Bob and I met at a conference last year. I gave a paper. That's probably what he was referring to. You're still here?'

'As you see.' Troy spread his arms. 'Never left. Took over Dad's landscaping business, married Carrie from school – you'll remember her – three kids, grown now.' His eyes clouded. 'She passed away two years ago, so now it's just me and the dog, but my daughters look after me, make sure I eat regularly and don't burn the house down. You must drop round for a beer while you're here, have a yarn about old times. Those were the days, weren't they? We had good times. Not like the teenagers are today. My grandchildren! You don't want to know.'

'Sure, give me a call. You know where I am.'

'Will do.' Troy glanced over to where his companions were staring at him. 'Have to go. Good to see you again, mate.'

Luke stared after his old friend. Life back here in Pelican Crossing certainly wasn't going to be boring. It might be more interesting than he'd anticipated. There was his meeting with the mayor, now his old schoolmate… and there was *Red*…

Eleven

It had been a difficult two days for Rachel, the house unusually quiet without Molly, despite the presence of her B&B guests each morning for breakfast. But finally, Wednesday was here, and she could call the vet clinic to find out if she was able to pick up her little dog and bring her home. She suppressed the thought that she would also have the opportunity to see Luke again, and the butterflies in her stomach that accompanied it. She was too old to allow such thoughts to take root.

Once her guests had gone out for the day, the teenagers seeming to take for ever to get themselves organised, Rachel washed up then took her own breakfast out to the courtyard along with her phone. She forced herself to eat a slice of toast spread with avocado and cottage cheese, and to drink half her cup of lemon and ginger tea, before deciding it wasn't too early to call the vet.

To Rachel's disappointment, it was Wendy who answered – she didn't know why she'd expected it to be Luke. But, after the usual pleasantries about the weather, the other woman said, 'You need to speak to Luke. He won't be a moment.'

It seemed like a lot more than a moment, as Rachel listened to the recorded message giving the clinic hours and advice on the importance of worming your pet, but eventually, Luke's warm voice said, 'Hello, Red.'

Rachel's heart lurched, drawn back to her fourteen-year-old self at the sound of her old nickname. 'Molly, how is she?'

'Molly's doing very well. I'd like to keep her here this morning, but if you can drop in around four, you can take her home.'

'Oh, thank you!' Rachel could have kissed Luke. It was just as well he was on the other end of the phone. But it wasn't such an unusual response. Bob had once told her that many of his clients hugged him when their pets recovered, so grateful for his assistance though he protested he was just doing his job. She suspected the same happened to Luke.

Picking Molly up at four would work out perfectly for Rachel. Today was her lunch meeting again, their Christmas lunch at Liz's, and the evening before, she had wrapped her gift for the Secret Santa. It was a beautiful Koh tealight candle holder in an Aboriginal design which she'd discovered on a trip to the Ginger Factory with the twins earlier in the year and purchased for just such an occasion. She had fond memories of that trip, of their ride on the ginger train, joining the gingerbread man on his adventure on the boat trip as he evaded the hungry chefs, having fun on the bee jumping castle and the kids' playground, the day finishing with ice cream for the twins, and tea with a ginger scone for her. It had been exhausting, but lovely to see Gemma and Indie enjoying themselves so much.

*

Rachel was first to arrive at her friend's and, after greeting her with a hug, Liz poured her a glass of wine. Before Rachel could open her mouth, Liz began to speak. 'You wouldn't believe the week I've had,' she said. 'We've been short-staffed at the medical centre. I've had to stand in for one of the receptionists and it looked as if I might have had to work today.'

'I'm glad you didn't,' Rachel said, hoping to calm Liz down. 'Did something else happen?' she asked, seeing her friend still appeared distraught.

'Yes…' But before she could continue, there was a knock at the door. 'Later,' she said, heading off to answer it.

When she returned, she was accompanied by Poppy and Gill who had arrived together. For the next few minutes, she was busy pouring wine for them, then ushering all three women out on to the balcony which, as usual, was filled with a collection of plants. Liz loved to tell people how she was inspired by Indira Naidoo's book, *The Edible Balcony*, to create a garden on her balcony containing a variety of vegetables and herbs, plus a few pots of flowering plants. Rachel was going to have to wait till later to discover what Liz had been going to tell her.

At first, the conversation centred around their Christmas plans. This year, all four were going to have a family Christmas, and they had fun sharing how they intended to spend the day. For Gill, this would be the first year for some time that she'd have her daughter with her, along with Joe. She beamed as she described how they were going to have breakfast on the beach followed by lunch at *Crossings*.

Poppy smiled at the news. Her family Christmas was an evening event, after the busy Christmas lunch in *Crossings*, the restaurant she owned and managed. 'But at least I don't have to cook,' she said with a grin. 'We get all the leftovers from the restaurant. And this year, there will be four grandchildren to cater for. I can scarcely believe it. It's been so much fun choosing presents.'

'I totally know what you mean,' Rachel said. She still had to finish her Christmas shopping for the twins and Emily, though she'd already bought gifts for the grownups, plus a baby gift for Steph and Chloe in anticipation of the news Steph was pregnant. As always, Alexander had been the most difficult to buy for. What did you buy your twenty-eight-year-old son who lived overseas and would have to take it home on a plane? She'd settled for a voucher for Iconic, one of his favourite stores, even though she always felt this sort of gift was a copout.

Liz smiled. This Christmas was going to be special for her too, the first with the daughter and granddaughter she'd only recently been reunited with. 'I can't wait,' she said. 'And Mandy's baby's due soon too. That's what I was about to tell you, Rach. Now I can tell you all. We had a scare on Monday evening when Mandy thought she was in labour. We all rushed to the hospital, but it was a false alarm. Good preparation for the real thing, I suppose.'

They all smiled, and Rachel said, 'Looks like you might be getting a very special Christmas present, Liz.'

'I'll drink to that.' Liz raised her glass. 'I can't survive any more false alarms. Now, I hope you're all hungry.'

They all nodded, and Rachel realised she couldn't smell roast turkey, and this was their Christmas celebration. There had been no mention of the Secret Santa either, and she wondered if Liz had forgotten. She should have known better.

After a delicious meal of prawns and lobster, accompanied by salads and followed by a chocolate cheesecake, Liz said, 'Time for Secret Santa.'

They all dropped their gifts into a bag Liz provided, and, eyes closed, took turns in picking one out. To her delight, Rachel picked out a long, beaded necklace, while Poppy got the candle holder, Liz a pair of earrings, and Gill a book which she said she'd been longing to read.

They were enjoying coffee with a final glass of champagne when Liz said, 'I hear there's a new vet in town while Bob's overseas. Have any of you met him yet?' She stared around at her three friends.

Rachel felt herself redden, sure her meeting with Luke was obvious from her expression. 'I have,' she said. 'Molly picked up a tick on Monday. She's been in the vet hospital for the past two days.'

'Oh, no!' Poppy said, her expression mirroring her concern. 'How is she?'

'She's fine now, coming home later today. But it was a worry at the time.'

'It must have been. I must keep an eye on Angus,' she said, referring to her own West Highland Terrier.

'So, what's he like?' Liz asked, refusing to be deterred.

'He seems nice, competent, a bit older than Bob.'

'Nice, competent… That doesn't tell us much. You're the only one of us still single.' Liz pointed at Rachel. 'Is he hot?'

'Liz!' It was Poppy who spoke first, while Rachel was trying to figure out how to respond. Liz did have a habit of making outrageous remarks – she'd only given up briefly when she was herself at the start of a relationship with their local newspaper editor – but this was too much, even for Liz.

'I'm quite happy as I am, thank you,' Rachel said, finally finding her voice. 'Not everyone needs a man to fill her life.' But even as she spoke Rachel knew it to be a lie. Hadn't she spent the past two days thinking about Luke… and wishing…?

Twelve

Luke had had a busy morning. He'd been wakened at the crack of dawn by a call from Josh to ask how to reset the gas water heater as Abby had complained the water was cold in the shower. He'd sighed at the realisation he'd forgotten to leave instructions for this possibility and at how spoiled the younger generation were. He remembered having lots of cold showers when he was younger – his dad said they were bracing.

The phone wakened Nelson too, and unable to go back to sleep, Luke had taken the dog down to the beach for an early morning walk, surprising himself by how much he enjoyed seeing the sunrise over the ocean. But even with a walk along the beach, followed by a swim, it was still barely six when he got back home.

Since Luke was now wide-awake, he fixed breakfast for himself and Nelson before showering and dressing. Then, over a welcome mug of coffee, he sat down to study the book on Italian immigration he'd scarcely had time to look at earlier.

An hour later, he'd reluctantly closed it. So far, he'd discovered that while many Italian immigrants came to work on the Snowy Mountains project, there was also a large group who headed for the cane fields of Northern Queensland. He wasn't sure which group his own ancestors belonged to. He knew nothing about his mother's family and was keen to find out more.

Luke walked across to the clinic with Nelson. One of the advantages of this job was the proximity of the clinic to Bob's house... not to mention the nearby beach. It would be difficult to leave and go back to the city when Bob returned. But that wasn't for another three months. He might have tired of Pelican Crossing by then.

Wendy arrived soon after he did, and the morning routine began. Rachel's Molly had only been the first of many animals to be attacked by ticks, and the cages in the hospital section of the clinic were filling up with a variety of breeds who'd been similarly affected. Luke had just finished treating one such creature when Wendy called through. 'I have Rachel Mason on the phone about Molly. Can you speak with her now?'

'Give me a minute,' Luke replied, surprised how his mood lifted at the prospect of speaking to Rachel and seeing her again. Molly had responded well to treatment and would be able to go home later in the day, freeing up a space for another poor animal.

At the sound of Rachel's voice on the phone, and the relief in her voice, Luke immediately pictured her as she'd been two days earlier. He told her she could pick Molly up in the late afternoon, already beginning to look forward to seeing her again, and berating himself for his foolishness. He was only here for a few months. It would be madness to become involved with a local woman… especially this one, whose sister he had once dated. And… she was probably happily married. But he couldn't stop himself thinking what if…

*

By the time four o'clock came around, the clinic had emptied of patients and their owners. It was closing time, and Wendy was packing up ready to leave.

'Is that everything?' she asked, before she closed off the computer for the day.

'Only Molly's mum to pick her up. I can fix up the payment.'

'Are you sure? I can stay for a bit longer.'

'No, it's fine. Off you go. It shouldn't take long.'

'Right.' Wendy headed off, leaving Luke alone in the clinic with Nelson, the silence only broken by the barking coming from the hospital section.

In preparation for Rachel's arrival, Luke fetched the little Westie from her cage, and carried her through into the reception area, Nelson padding at his heels and glancing up from time to time as if wondering what Luke was doing. He didn't normally bring an animal in like this.

It was quarter past four, and both Nelson and Molly were becoming restive, when Rachel rushed into the clinic. 'I'm sorry I'm late,' she said. 'I was held up. Early Christmas lunch. You know how it is.' Her face was red from rushing – or perhaps from celebratory wine – but she looked good to Luke, dressed in a loosely-fitted red and gold caftan, her curls, reminiscent of the red ones he remembered, though now faded, falling around her face.

'No worries,' Luke said, picking up Molly from where she had been lying on a soft cushion. 'Here's your little lady.'

'Oh, Molly!' Rachel took the now squirming dog from his arms, sending a frisson through him as their hands touched. She appeared unaffected. She raised her eyes to meet Luke's and, for the first time, he noticed how blue they were, a pale blue, the shade of the ocean on a cool day. 'Thank you,' she said. 'She's fine now?'

'She's recovered sufficiently to go home, but you still need to take care.' Luke repeated the instructions he'd given her earlier regarding a cool environment, plenty of rest, lots of water and small amounts of food frequently.

'Thanks,' she said again. 'I remember and I've told my granddaughters. They love Molly too and will hopefully obey my instructions.'

Granddaughters, he knew she'd have grandchildren. Luke's heart sank. 'How old are they?' he asked.

'Four, going on five. They start school next year.'

From her tone of voice, it wasn't something she was looking forward to. Luke wondered what it would be like to have grandchildren that age, if he'd ever know. Josh certainly wasn't in any hurry to make him a grandfather. He cleared his throat to… but he couldn't ask about her husband. He said nothing.

Nelson nudged him. It was as if the dog knew something he didn't.

'Your dog?' Rachel asked.

'Nelson.' He sounded like a fool.

'How does he like it here? You've come from Sydney, haven't you?'

Of course, she'd have known he went there, or perhaps Bob had said something about his replacement. 'Yes. He's loving the sand and the sea, the freedom.' *As I am.*

'Who wouldn't? Pelican Crossing is a beautiful spot, always has been.'

Did Luke sense a note of bitterness? 'My parents left. There was nothing to come back to.' *Why did he feel he had to justify himself to her?*

Rachel seemed to collect herself. 'Of course. How much do I owe you for this little one?' She peered down at her pet who was cuddling into her, clearly pleased to be back in her mistress's arms.

Juggling the little dog in her arms, Rachel took out her credit card and paid the vet bill. Then she turned to go.

Luke wanted to stop her, to say something, anything, that would delay her departure. But there was nothing he could think to say that would make any sense, that wouldn't paint him as a fool, an old fool who was trying to recapture a youth that was long gone. He wondered what had happened to her sister, to the first girl he'd kissed. No doubt that's all he was to Rachel – her big sister's boyfriend. He wondered if she'd tell Becky he was back, back in Pelican Crossing where it had all begun, where he'd started to learn about the ways of the fairer sex, who he'd never fully understood, not even after all those years of marriage to Ness. 'What do you think, Nelson?' he asked his dog. 'Do I have a chance there?' The dog looked back at him pityingly.

Thirteen

Rachel hurried out to the car with Molly in her arms before she could embarrass herself by saying something inappropriate. She'd meant to be on time, but lunch had gone on longer than usual… and there had been that last glass of champagne… followed by more coffee as all of the group, apart from Liz, were driving. Had Luke known she was a bit tipsy? At least she hadn't disgraced herself by asking the question which was foremost in her mind. *Was he married? Was his wife with him in Pelican Crossing?* Two questions, she realised. But what difference would it make? She wasn't in the market for a man, and Luke Findlay wasn't for her, never had been. But a girl could dream.

Back home, Rachel examined the little dog, noticing a shaved area behind one ear. It must be where the tick had been located. She settled her pet, who had lost her normal liveliness, onto the dog bed and placed a bowl of water close by. Then she made herself a cup of tea and chose a seat where she could keep an eye on Molly. She was pleased to have her home, though worried about how listless she was. But she had to trust Luke knew what he was doing, and she was well enough to be here. Three weeks, he'd said. How was she going to cope with Molly being out of action for three weeks? And tomorrow the Christmas tree would be delivered, and Gemma and Indie would be arriving to decorate it, filled with excitement. Maybe, she thought, she could make a spot for Molly in her study. The two terrors rarely went in there. It had actually been Kirk's study, and Rachel had taken it over when he passed, and when she started her B&B business. Once her current guests left at the end of the week, she was free of visitors until mid-January, allowing family time over Christmas – and space for Alexander… and his surprise.

It was a month since she'd heard from him, and he hadn't answered her repeated texts and calls. It would be typical of him to just turn up one day, although he did know about his mother's guests, so would surely give her advance warning of his arrival. It was as if he'd read her mind. Rachel was just thinking about her son when her phone pinged with a text.

Flat out here. Arriving 23rd. Looking forward to seeing everyone. Much love.

It must be early morning in London. Perhaps she could catch him. This lack of information was irritating. Rachel pressed his number on her speed dial, only for it to go to voicemail as usual. Then she tried WhatsApp, but again there was no reply. Damn the boy! He knew how much she wanted to hear from him. This must be some surprise if he was refusing to communicate with his mother and sisters. Although she wished he was arriving earlier, she was pleased he was arriving on the twenty-third. He'd be here for their traditional Christmas Eve dinner… and Christmas Day. Rachel hoped he didn't plan to leave again as abruptly as he had on his last visit.

*

Next morning, Rachel was awake long before her guests and, after checking on Molly, decided to take a short walk on the beach before making breakfast. She'd done most of the preparation the night before and only needed to cook the eggs, bacon and toast that her visitors preferred.

It felt strange on the beach without Molly running beside her, stopping every now and then to sniff at something the waves had brought in, or to leap into the waves after a stick she'd begged Rachel to throw for her. It took Rachel some time to realise that, this morning, she wasn't alone on the beach. At the far end of the beach, a tall figure was running down towards the ocean, a large dog at his side. As she watched, both man and dog leapt into the water and began to swim swiftly out to sea.

Rachel stood for a moment watching their movements before it dawned on her. The only other house facing this stretch of beach was Bob Reed's. The man and dog must be Luke and… what did he call his boxer? Nelson, that was it, a noble name.

Rachel wasn't sure how she felt about seeing them there, on what she considered to be *her* beach. It was as if it had been invaded. Bob rarely came here, preferring the more populated surf beach off Main Street. Rachel glanced around, but there was no sign of Luke's wife. Perhaps she wasn't into an early morning swim. Rachel pictured an elegant woman preparing breakfast for her husband's return. Thinking of preparing breakfast made her realise it was time for her to do the same. She hurried back home.

To Rachel's annoyance, this morning everything seemed to go wrong. First, Molly didn't want to move from her usual spot in the kitchen to the study, only persuaded by a special beef treat. Then, one of the teenagers decided she didn't want the breakfast Rachel had provided, and would prefer poached, rather than scrambled eggs and hash browns instead of bacon. Fortunately, Rachel had a packet of frozen hash browns in the freezer and it was easy to poach a couple of eggs, but it delayed her morning routine. Thank goodness she only had two more mornings of this group, she thought, as she forced a smile to her face and served the alternative meal to the sullen teenager.

The Christmas tree was due to be delivered between nine and ten, and Rachel had barely finished her own breakfast of the leftover scrambled eggs and bacon when she heard the truck drive up at quarter to nine. Molly heard it too, and managed a small bark, no doubt eager to know what was happening. Rachel popped her head into the study on her way to the door. 'It's okay, Molly. Only the Christmas tree, nothing to worry about,' she said, chuckling at herself for giving this explanation to a dog. But Molly was more than a dog. She was Rachel's companion, a member of the family.

It didn't take long for the two men from the Christmas tree farm, from which she had been buying her trees for more years than she could remember, to unload and set the tree up by the window in Rachel's living room. It was an excellent service, not only did they deliver and place the tree where she wanted it, but they collected it again after Christmas. When they had gone, she made herself the tea she hadn't had time for earlier and took it into the study to be company for Molly. The little dog showed her delight to see her by nuzzling close when Rachel settled at the desk. She fired up the computer to check for any bookings which had come in since she last looked, pleased to see her January and February dates were now filling up.

'Sorry, Molly, I need to leave you for a little while,' she said, but when she looked down, she saw the little dog was asleep.

Rachel spent the rest of the morning pulling out the boxes of Christmas decorations and placing them by the tree. Then she checked that all the lights were working. By the time she'd finished, it was time for lunch which she ate out in the courtyard, taking a newly awake Molly out with her, but ensuring she didn't stray far from where she was sitting. Luckily, the little dog showed no desire to make her customary rounds of the garden, content to lie at Rachel's feet. Then, after a small snack, she happily went back to her bed in the study, much to Rachel's relief.

It was such a pleasure to see Gemma and Indie's excitement when they walked in to see the tall tree sitting by the window. Rachel was sure their whoops of delight could be heard as far away as the vet clinic on the other side of the bluff, though she stifled that thought as soon as it surfaced.

'Where's Molly?' the twins asked in unison. 'Is she still in the vet hospital?' Indie asked.

'No, she's back home. But remember how I told you she needed to be kept quiet?' Both girls nodded solemnly. 'She's in the study.'

'Can we see her?' Gemma asked, jumping up and down in excitement.

'Maybe, but only for a few moments, and you need to be very calm and still.'

'You need to do what Grandma tells you,' Jess said. 'Be good for her, or you won't be allowed to decorate the tree.'

The girls became very subdued. 'We promise,' Gemma said for both of them.

'I'll be off now, Mum,' Jess said, giving Rachel a hug. 'See you later. We're going now, girls,' she said, as both Gemma and Indie ran over to hug her. 'I'll take this one out of your way.' She picked up Emily, who had been sitting quietly on the floor, and left.

When she'd gone, Rachel took the twins in to see Molly. They tiptoed in very quietly and hugged the little dog, before tiptoeing back out again. 'She will be all right?' Gemma asked anxiously, when Rachel closed the study door behind them.

'Of course. She just needs peace and quiet while she's getting better.'

The girls seemed to accept this and were soon happily engaged in decorating the lower branches of the tree. Rachel would do the upper branches later, once they had gone home. But before they left, she added the lights and turned them on to a chorus of oohs and aahs from the twins.

By the time Jess picked up the twins, Rachel was exhausted. She checked in on Molly and made sure she had enough to eat and drink then despite her tiredness, she went back to finish the tree decorations. She never liked to leave a job half done, and it would be lovely for her guests to see the finished tree when they returned that evening. Once she had finished, she collapsed into one of her comfortable armchairs with a glass of wine.

When her phone rang as she was preparing to go to bed, Rachel thought it would be Steph, and was surprised to see Liz's number. It was unlike her friend to call her this late, and they'd only seen each other the previous day.

'Liz, is everything okay?' she asked, immediately fearing the worst, though she had no idea what that might be.

'Very okay. How are you?'

'I'm fine.' Rachel was puzzled by the note of excitement in Liz's voice. 'Molly came home yesterday, and Gemma and Indie helped me decorate the tree today. I'm just about to go to bed.'

'Glad I caught you. I wanted you to know what I discovered today.'

Rachel waited. Liz was renowned for her ability to discover gossip. What was it this time that couldn't wait till their next lunch… or even till next day?

'It's about the new vet. He grew up here, then went to Sydney… and he's widowed.' Liz announced the last fact with what amounted to glee.

'So?' Rachel didn't reveal that she'd known the first two, and that he'd been Becky's first boyfriend and her first crush.

'So? So, he's available!'

'Liz!' Despite the tiny flutter in her stomach at the news there was no elegant wife with Luke, Rachel couldn't help feeling annoyed with her friend. 'You called at this time of night to tell me that? I don't know how often I need to tell you I'm quite happy with my life the way it is. I know you, Poppy and Gill claim to have found your happy ever after a second time around, but…'

Liz didn't wait for her to finish. 'I know you always say that, but I also remember something you once said to me… when *I* said I was happy with my grandchildren.'

Rachel flinched. She knew what was coming.

'You said grandchildren were no substitute for the companionship of a good man, and they wouldn't keep me warm in bed at night.' Liz chuckled.

'I may have said that, but I didn't mean it to refer to myself.' But Rachel knew it was a weak response. Liz was right. *She'd* been right. *She did often miss having someone to cuddle up to at night*, she thought, trying to dismiss the image of Luke Findlay which appeared behind her eyes.

Fourteen

Troy hadn't wasted any time in contacting Luke and inviting him over for a beer and the promise of a steak. On the Friday after bumping into him in the yacht club, Luke found himself leaving Nelson in charge of the house and driving into town to the address Troy had given him.

When he got there, he discovered his old friend lived in what had once been an old fisherman's cottage but appeared to have been renovated over the years. It was in a part of Pelican Crossing Luke wasn't familiar with, on the far side of the harbour from the beach where they used to go surfing.

As soon as he walked through the gate, Luke was greeted by a volley of barking, and when the front door opened, a large black dog bounded out to meet him. 'Hello there,' he said, patting the labrador, who lapped up the attention. 'Aren't you a good fellow?'

'He's harmless,' Troy said, following the dog out. 'Makes a lot of noise but wouldn't hurt a fly.'

'He's a fine specimen. Had him long?'

'Six years. You have a dog too, don't you? You should have brought him along.'

'I knew you had one and wasn't sure if they'd mix well. I have a boxer. He can be unpredictable with other dogs.'

'Right. Well, come on in and have a beer.'

Half an hour later, the men were enjoying their second beer, and Troy had fired up the barbecue. He had proved a mine of information about current happenings in Pelican Crossing and what had happened to many of their old schoolfriends.

'I try to keep up with everyone with a regular newsletter,' he said, 'but you fell off my radar when you left town. It's good to catch up again. What's been happening with you?'

Luke filled him in on his life at university, his marriage, establishment of his vet clinic and now, his retirement. 'You're still working?' he asked.

'For my sins, but I enjoy it, and I have cut back a bit since Dan joined me. It's good to keep the business in the family, but you know all about that.' He nodded to Luke. 'You said your son runs your practice now.'

'Josh, yeah.' Luke thought about Josh's call the previous morning and hoped everything at the clinic was running smoothly. It had been different when he was close by to offer advice and fix any problems, but now he was interstate, anything could happen, and he wouldn't know.

'Our dads probably worried about us too,' Troy said, clearly seeing Luke frown. 'But yours wasn't in the same business, was he?'

'No, Dad was in the construction business. That's what took my parents to Sydney. There was more building going on there, more opportunities. It happened just as I left for university. Haven't been back since.'

'Till now.'

'Till now,' Luke agreed.

'And how are you finding the old place?'

'Some changes, but a lot is still how I remember it.' Troy clearly kept a finger on everything and everyone in Pelican Crossing, as well as their old schoolmates. Luke was wondering how to get around to finding out more about Becky's sister but wasn't willing to ask him outright.

He waited till they were standing by the barbecue cooking a couple of T-bone steaks, before casually saying, 'So, what's happening with all the old crowd. Many still around?'

Troy turned the steaks and took a drink of beer before replying, 'Not many. Some stayed around a few years then left, a couple are no longer with us. Remember Lou Chalmers? She owns a business here – *Books and Coffee* – manages the bookshop section. Has a couple of young guys run the café. Never married. She was a friend of that girl you dated for a bit, wasn't she? Becky…?'

'Becky Carr? Yes.' Luke took a deep breath. 'I treated her younger sister's dog this week. A tick.'

'Rachel? She's had a hard life. Her husband died a few years ago after a long illness, but she managed to come good, turned their house into a Bed and Breakfast. Does pretty well from all accounts. Lives on the bluff on the other side of town. She'd be your closest neighbour.'

'Sounds tough.'

'Yeah. I think there are three children. Did some work for the oldest a year back. She has twins, as like as two peas. Sad about Becky.'

'Why? What happened?'

'Heard she had Alzheimer's. Sad case. Not the only one of the old crowd to be afflicted. Gus Swanson too, and…'

But Luke had stopped listening. He had the information he wanted. Rachel was widowed like he was. And he couldn't deny the strange buzz it gave him.

The rest of the evening passed pleasantly, ending with Luke promising to invite Troy back for a meal to repay his hospitality, and agreeing to go along to a fundraiser which the local branch of rotary was co-hosting the following week at *Crossings* restaurant. It would be a good opportunity for him to check out the restaurant before Josh and Abby came to visit.

*

When Luke arrived home, Nelson greeted him as if he'd been gone for weeks. It was a clear night, the stars shining brightly, and Luke was still wide awake, so once he had checked on the animals in the hospital section of the clinic, he decided to take Nelson for a walk. It was too dangerous to go down the steps to the beach at this time of night, so he attached Nelson's leash and set off across the rough grass on the top of the bluff, the moon and stars providing sufficient light to see their way. Although he was loath to admit it, Luke was curious to see where Rachel lived if, as Troy said, she was his nearest neighbour.

There wasn't a proper path here, and it was clear that the official route between the two houses was along the main road some distance away. Rachel must have driven that way when she came to the clinic.

It was pleasant walking along the top of the cliff, the stars shining down and shimmering in the ocean below, the lights of a ship far out at sea just visible in the distance. It was almost a shock when the house came into view. It was large, like an old farmhouse with a lot of windows, many of them lit, and the coloured lights of a Christmas tree twinkling in one of them. Luke remembered Troy saying Rachel had a Bed and Breakfast. He supposed some of the lights belonged to her guests. Luke stopped some distance from the house. What was he doing? He was acting like a stalker. If he wanted to meet Red again – he couldn't think of her as Rachel – there must be a better way of doing it than sneaking up on her home in the middle of the night. He pulled on Nelson's leash and turned to return the way he had come, telling himself he was behaving like… what was he behaving like? A lovestruck fool? A kid with a crush? He gave himself a shake, but still, all he could think of as he headed home was how good she'd looked in that red and gold caftan, her faded red curls falling around her smiling face, cheeks rosy from rushing – or wine – or both. How he had wanted to hold her, to hug her shapely form.

'Down boy,' he said, more to himself than Nelson as the dog pulled on his leash, sniffing at a clump of grass. 'We don't want to be going there, do we?'

Fifteen

Rachel sighed as she dressed for the fundraiser on Friday evening. After the week she'd had, she'd have preferred a quiet evening at home with a good book. She'd recently started a series by an author who was new to her and was eager to continue it. But Gill was organising the event through Zonta in combination with a local Rotary group, and it was in aid of the *Bellbird Bay Women's Centre*. Also, it was to be held at *Crossings*. So, two of her good friends were involved in organising the event. It wasn't one she could wriggle out of.

At least there would be a good meal, she thought, as she checked herself out in her full-length wardrobe mirror, wondering if the black and white dress Jess had encouraged her to buy was really as slimming as her daughter had claimed. Rachel was so accustomed to the loose garments she wore every day, designed to hide her figure, she felt exposed in this more fitted garment which seemed to reveal all her curves.

Deciding she'd do, and it was too late to change anyway, she popped her head into the study where Molly now seemed quite at home. Each day she appeared a little better though as Luke had warned her, it was a slow process. She hadn't seen any sign of Luke since that morning on the beach earlier in the week, perhaps just as well. But Liz's report he was a widower had sent a flood of warmth through her at the realisation he was on his own and lived only a short distance away.

Rachel could hear the noise of chatter even before she pushed open the door to the restaurant, and once she was actually inside it was as if she was being battered by a clamour of voices. Seeing Poppy and Gill in the distance, she pushed through the throng to finally reach them, collecting a glass of champagne on the way. 'Wow, what a crowd,' she said.

'Isn't it wonderful?' Gill said. 'With the entry tickets and the raffles, we should reach our target. Ali will be delighted,' she said, referring to Ali Wells, the director of the women's centre. 'It was a stroke of genius to link up with Rotary. All Joe's idea.' She smiled at the local mayor who was her new partner.

While they were chatting, a young girl came up to them selling raffle tickets. Rachel bought several before realising they were for a hot air balloon ride for two. 'Oh, dear,' she said. 'I don't think I want to win.'

'You could always give it to Steph,' Joe said. 'I'm sure she and Chloe would enjoy it.' Chloe was his PA, and he knew she had an adventurous spirit.

'Maybe.' The mention of Steph reminded Rachel of their conversation about her having a baby. She wondered if the women had done anything about it yet. But even if they had, it was too soon to know if Steph was pregnant.

The evening passed pleasantly. As Rachel had predicted, the meal was excellent but, seated at a table with her three friends and their partners, she felt somewhat out of place. It annoyed her to feel like this. She had no desire to emulate them, to find a new partner. But for the first time since Kirk died, she wished she wasn't on her own.

The meal was over, the raffle drawn – to Rachel's relief she didn't win either the hot air balloon ride or the personal training session with Liz's daughter – when, on the other side of the restaurant, Rachel saw a familiar bearded face. It was Luke Findlay, and he was looking straight at her.

*

Luke couldn't believe it. Rachel was sitting across the room. She looked amazing, wearing a more fitted outfit than he'd seen her in earlier, one which showed off her curves to advantage – and what curves. A man could get lost in them. He swallowed to subdue the unexpected rush of desire which engulfed him. It had been years since he'd experienced anything like this… and this was little Rachel. Not so little, he reminded himself as he gazed across and caught her eye. She quickly looked away, but not before he saw her blushing.

He'd been placed at a table with a group of people who, apart from Troy, he didn't know, and most of the conversation had gone over his head. He realised that, now the meal and the formalities were over, people were beginning to move around, to chat with friends from other tables while they helped themselves to coffee.

'You okay, mate?' Troy asked. 'Sorry if you felt left out of the conversation. Been a good night, hasn't it? Glad you came?'

'I'm good, thanks. Yes, thanks for inviting me. Great meal. I've just seen someone I want to catch up with. Is it okay if…' He gestured to the side tables where the coffee was being served.

'Of course. We'll all be moving on soon. A few of us are heading to *The Grand* after this if you want to join us.'

'Thanks, but I may give it a miss. Work tomorrow.'

'Sure thing. Keep in touch.'

'Will do. I promised you a meal, remember?'

'Good man.' Troy slapped Luke on the shoulder before becoming engrossed in a conversation with the man on his other side.

Luke made his way across the room to where the coffee was being served close to the table at which Rachel was sitting. He was unsure how he was going to approach her but was determined to say something. This was too good an opportunity to miss. He might not get another one for some time. He knew he could have called her – he had her details at the clinic – or dropped in – he knew where she lived – but neither of those approaches appealed to him.

He picked up a coffee and turned towards the table where she appeared to be in conversation with one of the other women. She looked up… and smiled. Luke didn't hesitate. He moved across till he was standing behind her. 'How's Molly?' he asked.

*

Rachel's heart leapt when she saw Luke cross the room towards where she was sitting, only to drop again when he stopped to get a coffee. She tried to show interest in what Poppy was saying, something about Amber's twins, then she was conscious of someone behind her. So much so, it made her skin prickle. She glanced around to see Luke standing there. She smiled, inwardly cursing her burning cheeks.

'How's Molly?' he asked.

'Hi. Yes. Good. Getting better every day.' Rachel was finding it difficult to speak. *What was happening to her?* She swallowed. 'I've been shutting her up in the study, you know, to keep her stress free.' *Damn! She must sound like a fool.*

'Sounds good,' Luke said, smiling at her, his deep blue eyes so bright, so…

'Who's your friend?'

Rachel looked round to see Liz staring at Luke. 'Everyone, this is Luke Findlay, the new vet. He's replacing Bob while he's away.'

'We've already met,' Joe said rising to shake Luke's hand. 'Why don't you join us? I promise we don't bite, though Finn has been known to ferret out your darkest secrets and publish them. This is Finn Hunter, our local newspaper editor, Cam Mitchell who manages the marina and owns *Pelican Marine*, and these lovely ladies are Cam's wife, Poppy, who owns this restaurant, Finn's partner, Liz, who's practice manager at the medical centre, and my lovely partner Gill, our local divorce and family law solicitor.'

'Wow, a collection of dignitaries,' Luke said, shaking hands with the men and smiling at the women.

Poppy shifted around to make a space for him beside Rachel, who quivered as their thighs touched under the table. She was pleased Joe had taken the initiative to introduce Luke. It saved her making a bumbling introduction. But, while it was good to see him, and she was pleased he'd come across to speak to her, he'd only come to enquire about Molly. Now he was caught up with all her friends and their partners, and she could already see Liz's antennae up, while even Gill was giving her a speculative look. It didn't help that, this close, she could smell his distinctive musky scent.

To her relief, Joe took charge of the conversation, reminding Cam and Poppy about Luke's achievement on the rugby team that won the championship.

'I remember,' Poppy said. 'You were a lot older than us. I was still in primary school. We all thought you were like a god.' She furrowed her brow. 'Didn't you date Rachel's sister?'

Rachel blushed. She hadn't thought Poppy would remember.

'I did… for a bit. And there was nothing godlike about me. I was just a guy trying to do the best for his team. It was a lucky break that we won that year.'

The men continued to discuss sport, Joe and Cam vying with each other to recount the wins and losses of their school team over the years.

Poppy nudged Rachel, her eyes filled with questions, but she was too polite to ask while everyone was there. Rachel knew the questions would come later.

Meantime, Liz and Gill who were seated farther away from Rachel had to be satisfied with glances which told her they had questions too. Rachel shifted uncomfortably in her seat, wondering how soon she could leave. This wasn't what she'd bargained for when she agreed to come to the dinner… or when she saw Luke head over in this direction. *Why had he?*

Eventually, everyone rose to leave, Poppy popping her head into the kitchen to thank the staff as she always did.

Once outside the restaurant, the three couples peeled away leaving Rachel alone with Luke.

'I hope I didn't embarrass you… coming over like that,' he said with a wry grin.

'Of course not.' What else could she say?

'It was the only way I could think of to speak to you again… and you looked so lovely sitting there.'

Rachel blushed yet again. *He couldn't mean it… he'd wanted to speak to her again… he thought she looked lovely.* She glanced up at him, but he didn't appear to be joking. 'You wanted to speak to me again… not just ask about Molly?' she risked asking.

'I did. You're a difficult woman to pin down. You have a tendency to rush away.'

Rachel was puzzled, then she remembered her two visits to the clinic. Perhaps she *had* rushed away.

'I would like to see you again, preferably without all your friends around.' He chuckled. 'They're great, but talking about my former exploits on the rugby field isn't my idea of fun. It was all such a long time ago. And you've always intrigued me – even when you were fourteen and my girlfriend's little sister.'

Now Rachel knew he was joking.

'No, really,' he said clearly seeing her disbelief. 'Becky was lovely, but she was an open book, whereas you, Red...' Rachel felt a shiver run down her spine at his use of the old nickname again. 'You were always hard to suss out. I'd like to get to know you better, to find out what makes Rachel Carr tick. Hell,' he pulled on his beard, 'I don't know your married name... or anything about you.'

'Mason, it's Rachel Mason,' Rachel said as if in a dream. *Was this really happening?*

'Well, Rachel Mason, would you agree to coming to dinner with me?'

Speechless, Rachel nodded.

'Is tomorrow too soon? I ate at the yacht club last week. Does that suit you?'

Rachel nodded again, still too overcome to speak.

'We appear to be neighbours. Shall I pick you up at seven?'

This time Rachel did find her voice. 'That would be lovely, thanks.'

'I'll see you then.' Luke put one hand on her arm and gave it a squeeze, before heading off.

Rachel stared after him, still dazed by what had happened. While she might tell the world she was satisfied with her life, without a man, might even believe it herself, the prospect of having dinner with Luke Findlay was like a dream come true.

Sixteen

To Rachel's surprise, she slept well, wakening later than usual to the sound of Molly whining from the study. She jumped up to let her out and, as she stood in the doorway waiting for her to return, she remembered the previous evening. Had Luke really said those things, invited her to dinner? Her phone pinged with a message.

Don't forget. 7 tonight. Luke

Her heart raced. It was true. He really had.

Glad this was the last day she'd have guests for breakfast until after Christmas, Rachel prepared her usual meal, managing to snatch a cup of herbal tea in the process. She was pleased to see Molly looked better and planned to take her for a short walk around the garden later.

Breakfast over, Rachel farewelled her guests. The honeymooners were still starry eyed and, when they thanked her, vowed to return as they'd enjoyed their holiday so much. She was surprised to receive a basket of goodies from the family, who thanked her and apologised for the behaviour of their teenagers. Signs of appreciation like this made it all worthwhile. But she'd be glad to take a break. It was always slightly nerve wracking to have strangers in her home, regardless of the money it brought in, and the company she always said she enjoyed.

It was good to relax with her own breakfast – a tortilla wrap of eggs with mushrooms and tomato – and Molly lying in a pool of sun at her feet, knowing it would be Christmas in a few weeks with all that entailed – and Alexander was coming home. She was still none the wiser about the surprise he'd promised, but they were all agreed he must have met someone special and be bringing her home to meet the family. With that in mind, Rachel had already bought a gift for her, along with those for the rest of the family.

And there was dinner with Luke tonight. Rachel felt a rush of excitement at the prospect of seeing him again, of going to the yacht club with him. Then she felt a curl of apprehension. On a Saturday evening, the yacht club would be packed. There would be a lot of people she knew there. For the first time, she realised how her friends – particularly Liz and Gill – must have felt appearing there with Finn and Joe respectively. It would be a little different for her, since Luke was practically a stranger in town. It was over forty years since he'd lived here. Many of those who'd known him back then had left Pelican Crossing or had passed away. But there would be some who'd remember him, one of whom was her friend, Lou.

Thinking of Lou reminded Rachel she hadn't passed on the latest news about Becky. Last time she'd spoken to Andy he'd said he might be forced to put her sister into a nursing home. It sounded so final. And Rachel experienced a twinge of guilt about the fact Becky was facing this, while she was looking forward to dinner with her sister's first boyfriend. She picked up the phone and called *Books and Coffee*, only to discover Lou had taken the weekend off.

The feeling of guilt persisted, so after taking Molly for a short walk and settling her back in the study, Rachel called her friend at home. 'It's not like you to leave the bookshop in Zoe's hands on a weekend,' she said when Lou answered, 'so close to Christmas too.'

'That's why,' Lou said. 'I need to get some paperwork completed before the big Christmas rush and if I didn't do it this weekend, I don't know when I would get round to it. But I've already been at it since the crack of dawn and need a break. Why don't you drop round for coffee? I can promise you one of Ron's blueberry muffins which I brought home yesterday.'

'That's an offer too good to refuse. I'll see you shortly.'

Rachel checked in on Molly, who was sleeping soundly, then headed off, throwing a glance at the vet clinic and Bob's house on the way. But there was no sign of Luke. He was no doubt busy with his animal patients.

Lou lived on the far side of town in what had once been a fisherman's cottage, one of many such buildings which had been renovated over the years. This one had views of the ocean and a pathway leading down to a stretch of beach which was rarely discovered by tourists. Her large ginger cat greeted Rachel at the door, then slunk off into the garden.

'Don't mind Tilly,' Lou said. 'She doesn't like strangers. Come on in.'

Once inside, Rachel was struck, as she always was when she visited Lou, by how comfortable her friend had managed to make this small dwelling. At one end of the open-plan room, a large picture window looked out onto the ocean, with a sofa and two armchairs positioned to take full advantage of the view. At the other, was a neat modern kitchen and dining area, the two sections divided by a low bookcase. The floor was tiled.

Lou had already placed a plate of blueberry muffins on the low coffee table facing the window, so Rachel took a seat on the sofa, knowing Lou preferred her favourite armchair. She sat there admiring the view until Lou brought in two mugs of coffee.

'Now,' Lou said when she had settled down, her mug clutched in both hands, 'you sounded worried on the phone. Is it Becky?'

'Yes and no.' Rachel took a sip of coffee and eyed the muffins, wondering if she dared have one, remembering the number on her scales that morning. 'The news from Andy isn't good, Lou. Becky's deteriorating more rapidly than we anticipated. Andy's finding it difficult to cope. He's considering a nursing home.'

'No!'

'I know. It's what I feel too. But it's easy for us to say, when we're not living with it every day. It's his decision, even if I don't agree with it.'

'I guess. It's just so sad to think of the Becky we knew…' She shook her head.

Rachel nodded. It was doubly sad that her sister had developed a type of Alzheimer's which had a rapid progression.

They sat in silence for a few moments, the only sounds the calls of seagulls outside the window and the distant roar of the waves.

Then Lou said, 'You said yes and no. What's the no?'

Rachel bit her lip. This was the hard part, but Lou was the only person she could share it with. 'I don't know if you've heard, but the new vet – the one who's taking Bob's place – it's Luke Findlay.'

'I had heard. Not much gets past us in *Books and Coffee*. Strange to have him back here after all this time. You'd remember him of course. Have you met him this time around?'

'Yes. Molly had a tick and I met him then.'

'And? Something tells me there's more to it.'

'It's difficult, Lou. Back then, when he and Becky were dating. I was only fourteen, but Luke was kind to me, sometimes including me when he and Becky were together. I had the most enormous crush on him.'

'You and just about every girl in Pelican Crossing. All the girls were swooning over him, but he chose Becky. So, what's so difficult?'

'We met again at the fundraiser at *Crossings* last night and… he's invited me to dinner.'

'Good for you. It's about time you found another special someone. I know how close you and Kirk were, but you can't grieve for ever, Rach.'

'Thanks, Lou.' Trust Lou to put it bluntly. 'The thing is, although I'm thrilled he's noticed me, wants to see me again, I can't help feeling a little guilty. He was Becky's boyfriend first.'

'Listen to yourself, Rach. All that with Becky was over forty years ago. She's moved on since then, you have too, so probably has Luke. He's been married too, hasn't he?'

'Ye…es. He's widowed.'

'There you go. And from what you've told me, sad though it is, Becky's past caring. And, even if she wasn't, she married Andy. Do you really think she'd worry about a little thing like you dating Luke Findlay?'

'When you put it like that…' Rachel began to feel a little better, so much so that she picked up a blueberry muffin and bit into it, savouring the sweet taste. Lou was probably right. She was getting her knickers in a knot for nothing. If she knew, Becky would probably laugh at the thought of Luke dating her little sister.

'So,' Lou took a bite from a muffin, 'when are you seeing him again?'

'Tonight… at the yacht club.'

'Wow! He doesn't mess around, does he?'

Rachel blushed. 'It can't come to anything, Lou. He's only here while Bob's gone… three months, I think.'

'A lot can happen in three months – especially at our age. It doesn't pay to hang around.' She chuckled. 'So, the yacht club. What do you plan to wear?'

'Wear?' Rachel hadn't even thought about what she'd wear. Definitely not the outfit she wore last night, the one which showed all her curves. She sighed, looking at the half-eaten muffin. She knew she shouldn't have…

'Not one of your caftans,' Lou said before Rachel could suggest it. 'How about that outfit you wore to the Melbourne Cup Luncheon last year? You looked great in it.'

'I did?' Rachel pictured the cream wide-legged pants topped with the calf-length tunic. She'd bought it on a trip to Brisbane with Jess, worn it once, then stuck it into the back of her wardrobe and forgotten about it. She seemed to recall it had been flattering to her fuller figure. 'Hmmm. I might see if I can still get into it.'

'Of course you can. I often think you exaggerate your size and try to hide your lovely curves with those loose shirts and caftans.'

Rachel flinched, but she knew Lou was right. Luke had said she looked lovely… and he had made arrangements to see her again. Maybe it *was* time she changed her style, bought some clothes which fitted her, as Jess was always urging her to do.

'Thanks, Lou,' Rachel said when she was leaving. 'Thanks for listening and for your advice… about my outfit too.' She chuckled. 'You should become my stylist. Jess would approve.'

Lou only laughed and, now that Rachel was leaving, Tilly, the cat, reappeared to curl around Lou's ankles.

*

Lou was right, Rachel thought, as she admired herself in the mirror. She did look good in this outfit which skimmed her curves and made her look slimmer. And she'd left it languishing at the back of her wardrobe for more than a year. Maybe she should make a trip to the boutique in Bellbird Bay where she knew both Poppy and Liz shopped. They always looked good.

'What do you think, Molly?' she asked the little dog, who she'd permitted to join her in the bedroom to give her a change of scene. Molly gave a bark of approval.

Rachel heard Luke's car before she was emotionally prepared. She was trembling with a combination of fear and anticipation. Not only was she about to go on a date with Luke, but this was also the first time she'd dined alone with a man since Kirk had passed. She had a brief attack of nerves. *It was too soon. She was making a mistake.* Then there was a knock at the door, and shepherding Molly back into the study, she went to open it.

When she saw Luke standing there, looking incredibly handsome, his pale blue shirt sleeves rolled up to the elbow to reveal his tanned arms, his cream chinos a neat fit, his deep blue eyes twinkling down at her, what felt like an army of butterflies started doing cartwheels in her stomach. 'Hello,' she said, suddenly feeling shy.

'Hi there. How's the patient?'

'Oh!' For a moment Rachel was confused. 'Would you like to see her?'

'Why not?'

Rachel led him inside and opened the study door, whereupon Molly, showing more energy than she had since she came home, padded over to greet him, her tail wagging.

Luke crouched down beside the little dog, talking to her quietly and gently examining her. 'Looking good, Molly. Won't be long before you're back to normal.' He stood up again and met Rachel's eyes. 'She'll be right pretty soon. Ready to go?' He took out a tissue to wipe his hands.

'Yes, of course,' Rachel said, as Molly settled down on her bed again. 'Thanks.' She seemed to be always thanking him for something.

As she'd anticipated, the yacht club was busy, it being Saturday, but they were shown to a table at the far side of the restaurant, overlooking the marina. It was one of Rachel's favourite spots and highly sought after. She wondered how Luke had managed to snag it. 'You booked?' she asked.

Looking embarrassed, Luke nodded. 'It seems the club's now owned by one of the guys I went to school with. Came in handy.'

'Phil Cook, of course.' How could she have forgotten? Another of Becky's old friends… and Lou's.

If Rachel had thought the evening might have been awkward, she'd have been wrong. Starting with a conversation about their dogs, they soon discovered they had a lot in common, sharing a love of books and movies – even the same ones. As a result, Rachel found herself relaxing and enjoying Luke's company even more than she'd anticipated. It was strange, she thought, how she and Luke had more in common than he and Becky ever had. Did it mean she was more compatible with Luke than her sister had been? She decided not to delve too deeply into that idea, but to enjoy her time with him.

As the evening progressed, Rachel found herself sharing amusing anecdotes about her B&B guests and laughing at some of Luke's experiences as a vet. It was almost as good as watching *Bondi Vet*, one of her favourite television series. She'd always been interested in the life of a vet. Perhaps if she and Kirk hadn't met when they did, it would have been a career she'd have pursued. It was almost a surprise when, after sharing a sumptuous seafood platter, followed by a chocolate brownie with vanilla curd ice cream – she'd start that diet tomorrow – Luke said, 'Coffee or are you ready to leave? They appear to be packing up.'

Glancing around, Rachel could see that most of the other tables were empty, and staff were stacking chairs ready for closing. 'Oh, I guess we should leave. We can have coffee at my place.' As soon as the words were out of her mouth, Rachel wished she could take them back. It sounded as if she was in the habit of inviting men back for coffee after a first date, and coffee sometimes meant… more, or it had done when she was younger. She felt the heat rise to her face.

Seventeen

Luke didn't want the evening to end, so when Rachel offered to make coffee for them, he didn't hesitate. 'That sounds like a good idea,' he said. 'They may have turned the coffee machine off here, anyway.' He could see Rachel was embarrassed at having offered coffee but couldn't see what the problem was. Surely the days had gone when coffee was a code word for more than the caffeine drink? And they weren't kids anymore. Neither of them would see fifty again, and some days he felt like Methuselah. Not today, though. Rachel's company was making him feel younger than he had in a long time.

On the drive back to Rachel's, Luke kept up a steady stream of conversation, hoping to ease her embarrassment. It seemed he succeeded as at one point after he'd been describing some of Nelson's antics, she laughed out loud. There was an awkward moment when he stopped the car, then it passed.

Once inside the house, Luke was impressed by how cosy it was. In the living room, the lights from a large Christmas tree twinkled in one corner of the room in front of a tall window. It was dark outside, but he could imagine the ocean view in daylight, not unlike the one from Bob's place. It hadn't occurred to him to do anything about a Christmas tree. Perhaps he should. Josh and Abby would like that. Ness had always insisted they put up the tree in early December, but since her passing, he hadn't had the heart. Maybe this year he should make the effort. 'Looks good,' he said, gesturing to the tree.

'Thanks. I always do it for the kids, and it cheers the room up too. I'll just fetch coffee – or would you rather have tea?'

'Coffee for me, please. And why don't you let Molly join us?'

'Good idea.' Rachel visibly relaxed. Maybe she'd been worried he expected more than coffee and, while it had crossed his mind, he wasn't crass enough to suggest it, to even imagine it was on offer.

Rachel had turned on a floor lamp and the light from it, plus the lights on the tree, gave the large room an intimate atmosphere. They sat together on the sofa drinking coffee, for all the world like an old married couple, Molly lying contentedly at their feet. Luke was surprised how comfortable he felt in Rachel's company. She was different from her sister, different from Ness, but Luke had the strangest feeling he'd come home.

'Tell me about yourself,' he said, 'You mentioned kids, and two granddaughters. How many do you have?'

Rachel leant back, her coffee mug clasped in both hands. 'Three granddaughters, all belonging to my eldest daughter, Jess. Gemma and Indie, who I call the two terrors are four. Twins. I may have mentioned them to you. They turn five in January and start school next year. I'm really going to miss them. I often look after them,' she explained. 'Then there's Emily who's only one.'

'So, one daughter.'

'Two, and a son. Steph is in a same-sex relationship, hoping to become pregnant, and Alexander works in London. They'll all be here for Christmas.' She smiled, clearly looking forward to the festivities. 'What about you?'

'One son. He's taken over my vet practice. Ness and I ran it together until… she was killed in a car accident. No one's fault. One of those things.' The memory of that dreadful day hit him, as it often did out of the blue. He'd been at the clinic. Ness had gone home early to prepare dinner. The police had come to the clinic. He didn't believe them at first. It couldn't be Ness. But it was, and his world had never been the same since. It was only now, since meeting Rachel, that he felt he might be able to develop feelings for a woman again.

'I'm so sorry. And your son?' Rachel's voice came as a shock, and Luke realised he'd been lost in the past.

'Sorry. Josh? He's bounced from one relationship to the next, but I think this one might last. He and Abby are joining me for Christmas.'

'That's good. Christmas is for families.'

'I guess.' Luke hadn't bothered too much about the holiday after Ness passed. She had been the one to make a fuss about it. For him, it had just been another day, one which he tried to make it through without letting his memories pull him down. Josh had often chosen to go overseas for the holiday, so there had been no one to celebrate with. This year it would be different. 'You've given me an idea,' he said. 'I'll put up a tree, try to get into the Christmas spirit.' He should do it for Josh's sake and somehow, he felt it would be for his sake too. It was time to let the past be the past and look towards the future.

Luke realised that, while they'd been talking, he'd finished his coffee, and Molly, clearly tired of their company, was snoring gently at their feet. 'I should go,' he said, putting his mug down on the coffee table and getting to his feet. 'Thanks for the coffee, for your company. I've enjoyed this evening… a lot. In fact, I don't know when I last enjoyed myself as much,' he surprised himself saying. It was true. Rachel had proved to be restful company. An attractive woman who didn't make things all about her. She hadn't had an easy life, but had worked on making it positive, and look at what she had created for herself, for her family, for Christmas.

Stopping in the doorway, Luke gazed up at the clear sky. It was going to be another glorious day tomorrow, a time to rejoice, to be grateful for his blessings, for this woman who had come into his life so unexpectedly. 'I have no idea how to go about selecting a tree,' he said. 'Would you be willing to help me? Maybe tomorrow?'

He saw Rachel hesitate. Perhaps he had been too pushy. After all, they had only met properly the previous evening. But he was only here for three months. He wanted to make the most of it… and he did need help in choosing a tree.

'I suppose so,' she said somewhat reluctantly, 'but it will have to be late morning or afternoon. I'm having breakfast with Steph and Chloe, her partner.'

'No problem. How about I pick you up around two?'

'That should work.' Rachel smiled, her smile tempting him to pull her into his arms and kiss her, but he resisted the temptation… for now.

'Thanks, I appreciate it,' he said, giving her arm a squeeze before walking away.

Eighteen

Rachel closed the door behind Luke with a tinge of regret. It had been a lovely evening. He was so easy to be with. She hadn't wanted the evening to end, had expected the goodnight kiss that didn't happen. Luke seemed to like her company, but perhaps he didn't think of her in that way. She sighed. At least she could help him choose a tree tomorrow. That was one thing she could help him with. And if he didn't feel the spark she did, then so be it. That was life. She'd never expected to feel desire for another man after Kirk died. This feeling for Luke, the way his touch made her quiver with emotion, had taken her by surprise.

She picked up Molly who had wakened and was stretching out on the floor, her little pink tongue peeking out. 'Just you and me again, Molly,' she said. 'You like Luke too, don't you?' Feeling the need for comfort, she took the little dog into the bedroom with her and didn't object when she begged to join her in the bed. Sometimes you just had to bend your rules.

*

To her surprise, Rachel slept soundly, to awaken with a wet nose pressing into her cheek. 'Molly!' she said, remembering how she'd brought her pet in to comfort her. Now the little dog was urging her to get up.

Pulling on a pair of pants and a loose shirt, Rachel fetched

Molly's leash and the pair headed out for the short walk the dog was allowed. When they returned, Rachel ensured Molly had food and water, before heading into the shower. As the water flowed over her, she thought about Luke and the previous evening. There had been nothing in his behaviour to suggest he considered her to be anything other than a friend. He had been kind, but he had been kind to the fourteen-year-old Rachel too. He probably didn't know many people in Pelican Crossing, and she was his neighbour and Becky's sister. She wondered if he knew about Becky. Perhaps she should tell him, but how did you bring up a subject like that? To say, 'Your old girlfriend has Alzheimer's,' sounded too crass, and he hadn't asked about Becky.

She went into the bedroom to pull one of her many caftans out of the wardrobe, and caught sight of herself in the mirror, grimacing at the rolls of fat around her waist and thighs. She sighed, remembering the sweet dessert she'd eaten… and the rest. She pulled in her stomach, remembering Lou's words. Maybe she wasn't as fat as she imagined. Maybe, if she chose carefully, she could look good in garments other than caftans and the other loose garments she favoured. She'd felt good last night, and Luke had appeared to think so too, but… She sighed and slipped on the caftan.

Rachel had arranged to meet Steph and Chloe at *The Blue Dolphin Café* at nine and as she was early, she took the opportunity to wander along Main Street and gaze into the window of one of her favourite shops. *The Mousehole* was a tiny shop which always looked as if it had been squeezed between the two neighbouring buildings as an afterthought. This morning, the backdrop to the window was a magnificent patchwork quilt which Rachel knew had been made by Anna, one of the cooperative of local women who owned and managed the shop. Sitting in front of it, were two pottery and very lifelike giraffes made by Kelly, the potter of the group, and to one side sat a painting of a group of pelicans, so realistic they looked as if they could step out of the painting and take flight.

Having stood admiring the display longer than she intended, Rachel hurried along to the café where Steph and Chloe were already seated at a table just inside the door. Smiling to Poppy and Cam who were just leaving, Rachel joined the two young women.

'Hi, Mum.' Steph rose to hug Rachel, followed by Chloe. 'Mum,' Chloe said too.

Rachel had been thrilled when Chloe started to call her Mum after their marriage. She loved this girl who had made Steph so happy.

'Heard you went on a date last night… with the hot, new vet,' Steph said, once they had ordered breakfasts and been served with coffee.

'How…?' Rachel asked, halting her coffee midway to her mouth and blushing.

Steph chuckled. 'We bumped into Lou at the garden centre yesterday afternoon. To be fair to her, she thought we already knew. She said she'd told you to wear that lovely cream outfit. You did, didn't you?'

'Yes.' Rachel placed her coffee on the table. 'Is nothing secret in this town?' But she knew it wasn't.

'Not when you go to the yacht club on a Saturday evening. Half of Pelican Crossing must have seen you.' Steph chuckled again. 'So, did you have a nice time?'

'Very nice, thank you. I knew Luke years ago, when he was dating your Aunt Becky.' As soon as she spoke, Rachel knew it was too much information.

'Aunt Becky? Wow! You must have been…?'

'Fourteen.'

'Wow!' Steph said again. 'And did you swoon over him?' She rolled her eyes.

Rachel blushed again. This was too close to the truth. 'Of course not. He was my big sister's boyfriend. He was kind to me, that's all. And it's what he's being again. He was concerned about Molly's recovery, and…' She stopped there, knowing she was on weak ground.

'Leave it, Steph,' Chloe said as the waitress appeared with their meals. All three had ordered eggs benedict with smoked salmon and the servings looked delicious.

She should come here more often, Rachel thought, now she was free of guests for a few weeks. It was nice to have someone else cook breakfast rather than to be slaving in the kitchen for guests who didn't always appreciate the effort it took to have everything ready at once.

But Steph hadn't finished. 'Just one more question,' she said, avoiding Chloe's frown. 'If he's being so *kind* to you, are you seeing him again, and is he really as hot as Lou says?'

'That's two questions.' But Rachel was forced to laugh. Steph was just being her usual self. Jess would have been equally curious but would have been more tactful. 'Yes, I am seeing him again. He's asked me to help him choose a Christmas tree, and as for Luke being hot… I'm not sure I'm qualified to answer that.' Rachel bit her lip at the outright lie. Luke Findlay was hot in anyone's opinion, especially hers.

'Choose a Christmas tree?' It was Chloe who spoke next. 'That sounds like he values your opinion, but surely he's done that before now. Sounds like an excuse to see you again. What do you think, Steph?'

'Oh, definitely. He's interested in you, Mum, and he'd be Aunt Becky's age. Perfect.'

'Stop it, girls, or I'm going to leave right now.'

Both Steph and Chloe giggled. 'Sorry, Mum,' Steph said. 'We were just winding you up. We think it's great you've found someone.'

Rachel could hear the *at your age* which she didn't add.

'He's just an old friend who's being kind and has asked for my advice. Now are you finished? Can we enjoy our breakfast?'

'Okay,' Steph said, but Rachel knew she'd be on the phone to Jess as soon as they left the café, then Jess would call and… She sighed at the challenge of having daughters who had been urging her to move on with her life for the past two years. Now she'd provided them with ammunition.

The rest of the meal passed without any cause for concern. They ordered more coffee, then Steph clasped Chloe's hand and said, 'We have some news too. We've done the deed, so now it's only a matter of waiting to see if it worked.' She and Chloe grinned.

'Oh!' Rachel wondered exactly how it had been done but wasn't game to ask. Better she didn't know. 'I wish you every success,' she said, raising her cup as if it was a glass.

'Thanks, Mum,' the two women said in unison. 'If it takes, it'll be a spring baby,' Steph said.

'How lovely.' Rachel couldn't wait to find out. Hopefully, next Christmas she'd have four grandchildren to love and fuss over.

Nineteen

Luke wondered if he'd gone too far in asking Rachel to help him with a Christmas tree. He'd been aware of her hesitation, but she had agreed, and he knew he had to make every effort to spend time with her before Christmas, before they both became embroiled with family. He had no idea for how long Rachel's family celebrations would continue, or how long Josh and Abby intended to stay. And he had the distinct impression that if he allowed matters to slide, it would be more difficult to pick up their friendship again after the holiday season. The clinic would no doubt become busier with the influx of tourists, and Rachel's B&B guests would be demanding her attention. It would be all too easy for one or both of them to find excuses not to meet.

'She's special, Nelson,' he said to the dog who was giving him a puzzled look. 'I don't want to mess things up.' Nelson nodded his head as if to agree.

Luke had spent the morning on the beach, swimming and lying on a towel with a book, while Nelson lay by his side, wandering off from time to time to splash in the waves, before returning to shake seawater over Luke. He didn't complain. It was refreshing.

Now, after a lunch of a fresh roll from the bakery spread with avocado, tomato and topped with bean sprouts, washed down with a can of beer, he was ready to go.

Luke tried to stifle the tingle of excitement he felt as he drove around to Rachel's home. He felt like a teenager on his first date. Only he was sixty-two and far from his first date, and it wasn't even his first with Rachel.

She was waiting for him in the doorway wearing one of those loose things he'd seen her in at the clinic, the sort of garment Ness had sometimes worn around the house. Rachel had looked so good at *Crossings*, and again last night. He wondered why she chose to hide her beautiful, voluptuous figure under an outfit that looked like a tent. Not that she didn't look good in it. She did, but he suspected she'd look good in a sack which, come to think of it wasn't much different from what she was wearing.

'Hey,' he said, getting out of the car to help her into the passenger seat. 'How's Molly today?' Luke remembered how asking about Molly the previous evening had relaxed her. It helped to relax him too.

'She's good. We went for a short walk this morning, but she misses the beach. Do you think maybe… if I carried her down the steps?'

'Maybe, but better to wait a bit. If she's anything like Nelson, she'll go mad in the water.'

'Mmm. Maybe if I kept her on a leash?' Rachel tipped her head to one side. *Did she know how irresistible that made her look?* In any other woman it would be flirting, but he would bet Rachel never flirted.

'Maybe,' he agreed. 'You'll have to give me directions,' he said as he started up the car, 'I have no idea where the Christmas tree farm is.'

Rachel chuckled. 'It didn't exist when we were growing up but does a roaring trade at this time of year. It's outside town, in the hinterland. It should take us over an hour to get there. And, before you ask, they deliver… and pick up.'

'That's a relief. I had envisaged driving back with a large tree tied to the top of the car.'

Rachel chuckled again. It was good to hear her so relaxed. She'd been tense for a large part of the previous evening.

Luke tuned the radio to the local station which was playing Christmas carols, and they sang along like a couple of big kids as he drove, making the trip go quickly. It was a surprise when he saw the sign bearing a painted Christmas tree, and Rachel said, 'We're here.'

Once inside the property, it was easy to see why it was so popular. They joined a group of people selecting trees and before long, Luke was paying for a tall tree and giving the assistant his address.

When they were on their way back, Luke saw a sign at the side of the road which he hadn't noticed earlier. *Crossing Craft Beer* was the brewery Bob had told him about, the one he'd been meaning to visit. Luke slowed the car and pointed to the sign. 'I've heard it's an interesting place to visit and I like their beer. Fancy stopping?' He threw a glance at Rachel, unsure if visiting a brewery was her thing.

'Sounds good. I've heard about it from Steph and Chloe. They went to some beer tasting event there and raved about it… but I thought it was for a younger crowd.'

'I've never been one to let that stop me. What about you?'

'Absolutely not! I'm up for it.'

Luke drove in and parked beside a number of other cars, utes and motorbikes. It was clearly a popular spot on a hot Sunday afternoon. Once inside, the sound of voices echoed in the large open area. There was a bar at one end, the rest of the room being filled with small round tables, most of which were occupied by groups of all ages. At the far end of the room, a man dressed in shorts and a bright flowered shirt sat on a raised section, strumming a guitar and singing Australian ballads, his voice almost drowned out by the noise of chatter.

Making their way to the bar, Luke enquired about the beer tasting. He was directed outside again where he saw the sign he'd failed to notice earlier pointing to another building.

Inside, they were met by a young man who introduced himself as Brett, one of the owners and master brewer, and indicated they should follow him to a large shed where there were huge vats of beer and a strong yeasty aroma permeated the air.

As they made their way through the brewery, Brett explained the process of malting – drying and cracking the grains, extracting sugars and flavour from malt and other substances to make the sweet mash that became beer, followed by the addition of yeast to ferment it, then the bottling and aging.

At the end of the tour, they entered the tasting room where both he and Rachel were provided with wooden paddles, each containing five glasses of different brews. Each was numbered and they were given sheets on which they could comment on various aspects of the beer.

'This is fun,' Rachel said, when she had sipped two of them. 'It's nicer than many of the beers I've had in the past. I'm not really a beer drinker – I prefer wine – but I could become addicted to this one.' She pointed to the glass marked 2 on the board.

'It's a pretty good drop.' Luke had already tasted all four and found number 3 was his preference.

'Shall we go back and find a table, or have you had enough?' he asked, when they had completed their tasting and filled in the charts.

'Probably enough for now,' Rachel chuckled. 'It's not like wine tasting where you only take a small sip then spit it out – or you're supposed to. We've already drunk four small glasses of beer, and we still have to drive home.'

'You're right.' Luke always drank responsibly. 'I just want to buy some to take back with me,' he said, heading for the sales section.

The worst of the heat was over when they left the brewery, and a slight breeze had blown up. Luke stacked the carton of beer he'd purchased into the boot, and they headed for home. On the way they chatted, comparing beer and wine tasting experiences, and talking about their plans for Christmas. Luke was surprised how detailed Rachel's were and vowed again to make more of an effort this year than he had in the past. The purchase of the tree was a good start. He felt guilty he'd let things go after Ness's death and was glad Josh had found Abby. She was such a compassionate person, a lot like Ness had been when they first met.

The road passed Bob's house and the clinic before it reached Rachel's. On an impulse, Luke slowed at his gate. 'It's getting late. I have a couple of steaks in the fridge and the makings of a salad. Want to have dinner?' He held his breath as he waited for her reply.

Twenty

It had been a pleasant afternoon, and Rachel enjoyed Luke's company. She was feeling more relaxed with him now, and the visit to the brewery had been enlightening and fun. It wasn't somewhere she'd ever thought of visiting, but she'd enjoyed it more than she'd expected. Even the beer had tasted good.

When she sensed the car slow down as they approached Bob's house, Rachel felt her stomach lurch, and when Luke suggested dinner, her first impulse was to refuse. But he was right. It was getting late. The trip to the brewery along with the tour and the tastings had taken longer than she anticipated, and her stomach was telling her it had been a long time since lunch. With the option of returning to an empty house where Molly was still a shadow of her former self and the prospect of leftovers for dinner, or a barbecued steak with salad in Luke's company, she knew she couldn't refuse. 'Thanks, it's kind of you to offer,' she said, to see his mouth turn up in a smile which sent a shiver down her spine.

Rachel had never been inside Bob's house so, when she followed Luke in to be greeted enthusiastically by Nelson, she gazed around. The house had the same aspect as hers did, but there the similarity ended. Whereas Rachel's home resembled a cosy farmhouse, this one obviously belonged to a single man with its dark furnishings, tiled floor and leather sofa and armchairs. One wall held a large television screen, and the others were filled with bookcases. In one corner was a bar which, at first glance, held about every type of spirit and liqueur

Rachel could name, plus a few she wasn't familiar with. A large sound system took pride of place beside the television.

'A bit different from your place,' Luke said, pulling on his beard. 'I take it Bob never married?'

'I think there's a story there,' she said with a smile, 'but no one seems to know the details. He's been on his own as long as I can remember.'

'It's comfortable enough. Suits Nelson and me. And there's lots of room for when Josh and Abby come to visit.' He slid open the French windows and stepped out onto a flagged courtyard in the centre of which was a fire pit. Around the pit were several seats fashioned from logs. 'Seems Bob's a bit of a woodworker,' Luke said.

Rachel looked more closely at the seats, noticing they were hand carved, as was a large table sitting closer to the house. It featured a set of regular canvas chairs which looked the worse for wear. On a wall at right angles to the house stood a top-of-the-range barbecue.

'This won't take long,' Luke said, turning on the gas and lighting it.

'Can I help?' Rachel wasn't used to being waited on.

'You'll find the salad makings in the fridge, and if you could bring out the steaks…'

'Sure.' Rachel headed inside, followed by Nelson who, like Molly, knew when food was on offer. She easily found the steaks and salad fixings. The steaks were already marinating, making her wonder if Luke had planned this. But he would have had to eat anyway… though two steaks? She carried them to where Luke still stood at the barbecue, then went back inside. This time, Nelson didn't follow her, the scent of the meat proving more attractive than either her company or the salad.

By the time the steaks were done, it was almost dark, and Luke turned on a wall light attached to the house which provided just enough illumination to eat by and an ambiance not unlike the one at her home the previous evening.

'This is lovely,' Rachel said, accepting a second glass of the red wine which Luke had thoughtfully provided for her, preferring to drink beer himself. The steak was cooked to perfection and Nelson, having gulped down a small piece of steak, seemed satisfied to lie at their feet. She could hear the roar of the ocean in the distance and, looking up, could see the stars twinkling in the sky.

'I agree. Good food, good drink and good company, what more could I ask for?' Luke said.

'Mmm.' Rachel agreed. She wasn't convinced he was being honest about the company but a tiny voice in her head told her not to belittle herself.

Before coming outside, Luke had turned on the sound system to play a medley of tunes from the eighties through an outside speaker. When the music finally died away, he rose to go inside, obviously to change it.

'I should go now,' Rachel said, rising too. 'Thanks for today, Luke. It's been lovely. I've really enjoyed it. But I need to get back. Molly will be wondering where I am. I need to let her out, give her something to eat and check her water. No,' she said, seeing him take his car keys from his pocket, 'I can walk back over the bluff. It's not far.'

'I don't like to think of you walking back alone in the dark. I'll come with you. Nelson needs a walk, and I need to stretch my legs too.'

Rachel didn't refuse, the prospect of spending more time with Luke too good to miss.

It was pleasant walking together in the dark, their way only lit by the light of the moon and the stars. When Rachel stumbled on a clump of grass, Luke steadied her and didn't remove the hand he'd placed on her arm once they moved on. A wave of warmth flooded her. Rachel felt as if she was in a dream.

They stopped when they reached Rachel's gate. The house was in darkness apart from the Christmas tree lights which she'd left on. It made the place look cheerful. 'Thanks again,' she said, turning towards him.

'Thank *you*, Rachel,' he said, his voice suddenly hoarse. Then his lips met hers in the gentlest of kisses.

Rachel felt herself sink into him, returning the kiss which was the last thing she'd expected. Their lips parted then met again, brushing together as gently as before.

'I'll be busy this week, but I'll be in touch,' he said, as Nelson started to whine, tired of standing still.

Rachel put a finger to the lips he'd kissed, her heart racing as she watched him walk away.

Twenty-one

When Rachel wakened next morning, she felt something momentous had happened. Then she remembered. Luke Findlay had kissed her. It was the first time she'd been kissed since Kirk died and, although it had felt strange, unfamiliar, it had been good. But, she reminded herself, he was only here for a few months. There was no point in becoming involved. And, no matter how much Luke seemed to like her, for him she was probably only someone to while away his time in Pelican Crossing with, before he headed back to Sydney.

So, despite how much she was tempted, despite the hints of her friends, there was no way she was going to allow this relationship – if that's what it was – to go any further than friendship. Rachel enjoyed Luke's company and it was a pity they lived so far apart, but her life was here, and his was in Sydney. There was no way they could be together even if… Her imagination started working overtime before she reined it in.

It was only a week till Christmas, and Rachel had a lot to do before then, enough to keep her so busy she had no time to think about the man who lived only a short distance away and who was proving to be such a good companion. Companion… she liked the word. That's how she'd consider him. And no more kisses. It would be too easy for her emotions to become involved and trick her into wanting more. She wasn't used to having feelings. It had been so long, she'd forgotten what it was like. It was dangerous.

Having made her decision, Rachel rose and showered, before

pulling on one of her favourite caftans and going to let Molly out of the study.

The little dog greeted her with more enthusiasm today, ready for the beach walk Rachel had planned. She picked Molly up and collected her leash, before making her way down the steps to the beach. To her relief, there was no sign of Luke and Nelson. One of the challenges of the proximity of Bob's house was the risk of meeting the pair on the beach.

Molly was delighted to be back in one of her favourite spots, straining against the unfamiliar restrictions of the leash, but happy when Rachel allowed her to splash at the edge of the water. For Rachel, it was a relief to get back to some sort of normality with her little dog beside her on the beach. She did seem to be a lot better. Maybe in a couple of days, she could allow her to run free again.

Back home, with Molly fed and watered and once more settled in her usual spot in the kitchen, Rachel made her own breakfast and sat down at the kitchen table to make a list of all the things she needed to do in the week ahead. First, now her guests had gone, she'd do a full clean of the house, then make up the beds for Alexander... and his surprise – two in case they didn't want to share. She remembered when she and Kirk got together, she'd felt embarrassed to sleep with him under his parents' roof before they were married.

Next, was the garden. She wanted to make sure it looked its best for the big day. Maybe a trip to the garden centre was in order. And she still had a few last-minute gifts to buy for the grandchildren. When the twins, then Emily, were born she'd bought special red felt stockings for each of them and took delight in filling them with lollies and small surprise gifts. Then she needed to do the large Christmas food shop before the shops became too busy.

Last, but not least... Rachel looked down at the outfit she was wearing. She remembered Luke's comments, what Lou had said, and wondered if she could fit in a trip to the boutique in Bellbird Bay before Christmas and surprise everyone with her transformation. She knew she'd need help. She couldn't trust herself not to return with one more caftan. It took her only a moment to decide to ask Poppy for help, giving herself the excuse that Liz would be working. But she knew it was more than that. Poppy would be more tactful than Liz, would gently steer her in the right direction, help her choose garments which were flattering and not too extreme.

Satisfied she had covered everything, Rachel picked up the phone. Ten minutes later, she had arranged to spend Wednesday with Poppy in Bellbird Bay. Now, she needed to ensure everything else on her list was completed before Friday when Alexander was due to arrive.

*

The day passed quickly as Rachel set to cleaning the house to the sound of Christmas carols, singing along and smiling a lot, remembering singing the same tunes with Luke in his car. By late afternoon everything was spic and span, the beds ready, and she had even made a start on the garden, accompanied by Molly. When her phone rang, and she saw Luke's number, her heart was suddenly racing. She was tempted to ignore it, but with the word *companion* at the forefront of her mind, she pressed to accept his call.

Despite her vow, Rachel felt her stomach give a slight flutter at the sound of his voice. She managed to subdue it sufficiently to speak normally. 'Hello, Luke.'

'Hello, Red. I've been thinking of you. How was your day, and how's Molly?'

'Busy, and Molly's a lot better. We went to the beach today and she enjoyed getting her paws wet again.'

'And you? What's been keeping you busy?'

'Cleaning.' Rachel chuckled. 'Now all my B&B guests are gone for a while, I need to get ready for my son to arrive, and for Christmas.'

'About Christmas. I need some advice.'

Rachel sighed. Keeping Luke at arm's length wasn't going to be as easy as she'd thought. And it was compounded by the fact she really didn't want to. 'Yes?' she said.

'The tree arrived today, but it looks very bare standing there in the window. Nelson's beginning to get ideas about it.'

Rachel laughed. He sounded so forlorn. 'What would you like me to do about it?'

'We…ell,' he took a breath, 'yours looks so good. I thought you could give me some advice on decoration, lights and so on.' He paused.

Rachel laughed again. He did have a way of getting under her defences, but she said, 'You'll find lots of both in the local store, and I'm sure someone as capable as you can work out how to hang them.'

'Hmm. I don't suppose you'd come with me?'

Rachel hesitated. This wasn't part of her plan for the week, but... 'I suppose I could,' she said. 'When did you have in mind?'

'What about tomorrow? The clinic closes early on Tuesdays. I'll buy you dinner as a thank you.'

Rachel thought quickly. 'Tomorrow won't work. I'm minding my granddaughters all day, then Jess and Paul are going to his work Christmas party. The girls are staying for a sleepover.'

'Oh!'

Rachel hardened herself to the disappointment in Luke's voice. She could have invited him to join them, sure the girls would enjoy shopping for Christmas decorations, and the twins would love having a new person to try out their jokes on. But who knew what it might lead to once the girls were asleep? 'I'm sorry,' she said, in an attempt to soften the blow.

'I am going to see you again before Christmas to celebrate Christmas together?'

Rachel hesitated again. It was a reasonable question, and a reasonable request. After spending so much time together, it would seem odd to suddenly refuse to see him before they were both tied up with family. Tuesday was out, she didn't know when they'd get back from Bellbird Bay on Wednesday, but it would be churlish to refuse... and she knew she wanted to see him again. 'I can be free on Thursday evening,' she said.

'Wonderful. I'll book a table at *Crossing*s. I understand they have a special menu all week.'

*

What was he doing? Luke pulled on his beard when he ended the call. Kissing Rachel last night hadn't been planned, but she'd looked so lovely standing there in the moonlight, her upturned face, lips parted, just waiting to be kissed. He hadn't been able to resist. It had been a sweet kiss with no hint of the strength of his desire for this woman who'd appeared in his life so unexpectedly when he'd thought himself past all that.

But, he reminded himself, while he wanted to see more of her, to take what they'd started further, it wasn't fair to Rachel. He was only in Pelican Crossing for a few months. When Bob returned at the end of March, Luke would be off back to the big smoke, back to Sydney, to his own home, to Josh and Abby. He flinched at the prospect of sharing his home with them again for however long it took for them to save the necessary deposit. But it was what he'd agreed to, what Ness would have wanted.

Ness. Luke had barely thought about Ness since he set foot in Pelican Crossing. It was as if he'd travelled back in time. But his life wasn't here. Luke sighed, and Nelson made a similar sound in sympathy. 'Life's not fair, Nelson,' he said. 'Just as I meet the woman who could make me happy, help me move on with my life, she lives here in Pelican Crossing… and my life's in Sydney.'

It was still light outside and warm after another glorious day. One thing Luke couldn't dislike about Pelican Crossing was the weather… and the beach. Nelson loved the beach too, so, giving in to the pleading expression on the dog's face, Luke headed out and down towards the stretch of white sand. Once there, on discovering the tide was out, he took off to pound along the beach, Nelson at his heels, no doubt surprised by his master's turn of speed.

When he came to the far end of the beach, Luke stopped for breath, leaning over, hands on his knees, the ache in his joints reminding him he wasn't eighteen any longer, not even close. But the run had done what he intended. He felt a lot better about himself and determined to remain friends with Rachel and to make every effort to avoid any situation which tempted him to be anything else. Friends was good, he thought. We all need friends, and as we grow older new friends are more difficult to find. He conveniently ignored the fact that there were others he could call friends right here in Pelican Crossing, men who'd been his friends when he was growing up, men with whom he shared memories – Troy and Phil to name only two. And he was sure he'd meet others before long, especially if Troy had anything to do with it. Thinking of Troy reminded Luke of his offer of a beer and a meal to his old friend.

As soon as he got back to the house and ensured Nelson had food and water, he called Troy. By the time the call ended, he'd arranged for Troy to come round on Wednesday evening. When he bought the tree decorations, he'd stock up the pantry and fridge ready for Josh and Abby's visit and ready to prepare a genuine Italian meal for his old mate.

Then he poured himself a beer and settled down to lose himself in the book about Italian migration, wishing he'd asked more questions when his mother was still alive, and wondering if anyone here in Pelican Crossing would know anything about her parents, his Italian grandparents.

Twenty-two

Rachel was awakened by two small bodies leaping into her bed and a wet tongue licking her face.

'Can we go to the beach?' Gemma asked. 'And have a swim before breakfast?' her twin finished for her. 'Please say we can, Grandma, please.'

Rachel smiled. She could never resist the two terrors when they pleaded with her like this, and it was a beautiful morning, the sun shining through the venetian blinds. It was going to be another glorious day.

'Only six more sleeps till Santa comes,' Indie said, her hand in Rachel's as they made their way down the steps to the beach, 'and Mummy says Uncle Al will be here with a surprise.'

Rachel laughed. The twins had found it too difficult to say Alexander when they were younger, so he'd become Uncle Al.

'What do you think his surprise will be?' Gemma asked. Emily had her grandmother's other hand and Gemma was skipping along beside them. This morning, Rachel had decided to dispense with Molly's leash and hope the dog was okay.

'What do you think?' Rachel asked, and the next few minutes were filled with their suggestions which included a motorbike, a unicorn – both twins were mad on unicorns at the moment, a cat – Indie would love to have a cat but Jess was allergic, and various other toys they'd seen on television. There was no mention of the special someone Rachel was hoping for.

When they reached the edge of the ocean, Rachel opted to stay in the shallows with the girls and Molly rather than have a swim herself. It was still early, but Jess would be picking the three girls up at eight, and Poppy and Rachel were planning to set off for Bellbird Bay at nine and make a day of it. 'It's ages since I had a girls' day out,' Poppy had said, and Rachel had been happy to agree. Once Alexander arrived and the Christmas celebrations began, she'd be flat out preparing food and ensuring everyone was happy. There would be no opportunity for her to have any time to herself.

Back home, Rachel helped Emily dress and popped her into a highchair with a Sippy cup of milk, then whipped up some banana pancakes. It was a recipe she'd got from Liz and which had proved a favourite with the girls. While the pancakes were cooking, Gemma and Indie played with Molly who seemed to have regained her customary level of energy, though Rachel noticed the girls were still being gentler with her than usual.

They had just finished breakfast when Jess arrived, in a rush as usual. With a flurry of hugs and kisses and promises to catch up for an early dinner on Christmas Eve followed by the carol singing by the marina, they all left, giving Rachel time to shower and pull on one of her caftans ready for Poppy to arrive.

Before Rachel had time to check herself in the mirror, she heard Poppy's car and, with a quick, 'Goodbye and be good,' to Molly, she headed out to join her.

'The tree looks good,' Poppy said.

'Thanks.' At the twin's request she'd turned on the lights when they returned from the beach and hadn't taken time to turn them off again. 'I always think it's a special part of Christmas. It wouldn't be the same without a tree.'

Intent on turning the car ready to drive off, Poppy only nodded. As they passed Bob's house, Rachel caught sight of Luke's decorated tree. She was glad she'd helped him choose it, and it appeared he'd done a good job of selecting the decorations by himself. She hoped his son would appreciate the effort he'd made, her stomach giving a little flutter at the sight of his back as he entered the clinic accompanied by Nelson. Fortunately, Poppy made no comment, though Rachel noted her eyes following the tall figure and his dog.

The pair chatted amicably on the drive south, sharing news about what they'd bought their grandchildren, and Poppy laughing at the twins' suggestions for what Alexander's surprise might be. Rachel shared the fact she'd prepared two rooms – just in case – and that she'd already bought a Christmas gift for Alexander's anticipated partner. 'What else could it be?' she asked, when Poppy suggested she might be wrong.

'I can't imagine,' Poppy replied, 'but you know Alexander. He has always liked to play pranks. So, don't get your hopes up, and don't be too disappointed if he arrives on his own.'

Rachel felt her heart drop. But she was sure Poppy was wrong. She was only trying to protect her from disappointment if Alexander didn't produce a partner.

It was after ten when they reached Bellbird Bay, and Rachel was ready for the coffee Poppy suggested. They parked close to the esplanade, and Poppy led the way to a café which she said she'd visited on an earlier trip. *The Bay Café* was situated on the esplanade close to a bookshop and not far from *Birds of a Feather*, the boutique where Rachel hoped to find the garments which would transform her. *Fat chance*, she thought, but it was how Poppy had described their shopping spree.

The café looked promising, not unlike their own *Blue Dolphin Café*, Rachel thought, with its sun-bleached wooden tables and views of the beach. They chose one of the outside tables and ordered coffee and friands, which Poppy said were delicious and were baked by a local woman. She was right, Rachel thought, as she bit into the hazelnut and apple confection.

'Are you sure this is a good idea?' Rachel asked. Now they were about to actually visit the boutique she was getting cold feet. Maybe they should enjoy the coffee and friands, then turn around and go home.

'You're not going to pike out on me, are you?' Poppy said with a frown. 'You're going to love Greta's stock, and I promise you, she won't try to foist you off with anything that makes you look silly.'

'Okay.' Rachel sighed. She could see Poppy wasn't going to let her get away without buying at least one new garment – and she was driving, so Rachel was stuck here till she chose to drive her back to Pelican Crossing.

Rachel stared into the window of the boutique. The two garments on display were brightly patterned with tropical flowers and parakeets. She'd look ridiculous in something like that. 'I don't think…' she said, but Poppy had already pushed open the door, so Rachel had no option but to follow her.

An elegant woman with short blonde hair greeted them. She was wearing one of her own creations and on her it looked good. 'Good to see you again,' she said to Poppy. 'And this is?'

'Rachel,' Rachel said.

'Welcome to *Birds of a Feather*, Rachel. I'm Greta. How can I help you today?'

'Rachel is looking to revamp her wardrobe,' Poppy said, before Rachel could speak.

Greta eyed Rachel speculatively, but somehow it didn't make her feel uncomfortable. 'I see you've fallen into the trap of many of us as we reach middle age, and elected to wear clothes which hide your figure instead of enhancing it.'

Rachel flinched, Greta had seen through her right away, but she would, wouldn't she? She wanted to sell her outfits.

'What I'd suggest,' Greta said, 'is that you invest in a couple of items of shapewear. These days they're nothing like the garments our grandmothers, even our mothers, used to wear. They're comfortable and will help smooth and shape your curves. You can buy them in somewhere like Big W or online. I sometimes wear one myself when my back is bothering me – I'm on my feet too much.'

'Oh!' It was something Rachel had never considered. Her caftans and the loose pants and shirts in her wardrobe were so comfortable, and it didn't require any effort to slip them on. But this was about change, wasn't it? 'You don't stock them?'

'Sorry. But let me see what I have that would suit you. I'm guessing you don't want anything too extreme… or too tight? Though I expect you have a lovely figure under that caftan.'

It was almost exactly what Lou had said. Could they both be wrong? Rachel straightened her shoulders. She could do this. 'Right.' She watched as Greta pulled garments off the racks which were dotted around the walls of the shop. Poppy had taken a seat and was watching with interest.

Finally, Greta came back to join Rachel, her arms filled with different coloured garments. She studied Rachel again. 'Yes, I think we'll go for wide-legged pants with tunics, and perhaps one of these dresses.' Hanging a selection of garments in one of the change rooms, Greta held up several loose dresses. They were not too unlike what Rachel was wearing but appeared to have been cut to flatter a figure much slimmer than hers. The pants and tunics were similar to the cream outfit she'd worn to dinner with Luke.

'Okay,' she said, entering the change room and reminding herself that she didn't have to buy anything. The mirror in the change room wasn't designed to flatter. When Rachel removed her caftan, she averted her eyes. She looked at the clothes hanging there. The pants were of a solid colour, as were the dresses, while the tunics varied between solid-coloured ones which complemented the pants and a couple with more vibrant patterns, though not as wild as those she'd seen in the window. She had to admit that Greta seemed to understand what she was prepared to wear and had avoided presenting her with anything featuring a more exotic print.

First, Rachel tried the pants with one of the tunics. She turned this way and that. Yes, she could wear this. Then she tried another of the tunics, a more vibrant one this time, surprised how different it made her look and feel. She almost didn't recognise herself. She was in her undergarments and taking one of the dresses down from the hook when she heard Greta outside the change room. 'How are you doing in there? Need any help?'

Rachel was about to refuse when, pulling on the dress, it became stuck. 'Maybe,' she said, whereupon Greta opened the door.

'Oh, I see what's happened.' Greta helped Rachel remove the dress, then put it on again. This time it slid on without any effort. 'I was right, you know,' Greta said. 'You do have a lovely figure. Many women would kill to have curves like yours. This dress looks great on you. Why don't you go out and show your friend?'

Rachel looked at herself in the mirror. The deep blue linen sleeveless dress wasn't anything she'd have chosen, but she did look good. The dress skimmed her figure and swirled around her calves making her look slimmer than she had in years. Maybe everyone else was right and she'd been hiding behind her caftans.

'Wow!' Poppy said, when Rachel walked out and twirled around. 'You look wonderful, like a different person. You must buy it.'

By the time they left the boutique, Rachel's credit card was a lot lighter. She was now the owner of two pairs of the wide-legged pants, three tunic tops – one solid-coloured and two of the vibrantly coloured ones with geometric patterns, the bright blue dress, and an orange one which she couldn't resist.

'Thank you so much, I hope to see you again, ladies,' Greta said as she showed them to the door.

'Thank *you*,' Rachel said. It had all been so much less painful than she'd feared, and she was looking forward to wearing her new outfits, already planning to wear the blue dress to dinner with Luke next evening.

'Are you pleased with your purchases?' Poppy asked, once they were back outside.

'Yes, I think I am. I'd never thought I could wear outfits like these, but Greta… She's very good, isn't she?'

'Why do you think I keep coming back?' Poppy laughed. 'She's magic, knows exactly what suits your figure. Now, lunch. My treat.'

'No, you've done enough, driving me here,' Rachel said.

'Nonsense. I love coming here and seeing what Greta has on offer. I'll probably pop down again after Christmas, so if you want to make another trip…'

'Oh, I don't think so.' Not as soon as that, but Rachel knew she would visit *Birds of a Feather* again, with or without Poppy.

Back in the car, Poppy drove through the town, stopping in the car park of *The Leonard Family Resort*. Rachel recognised the name. There had been a big article in the local paper when Leo Carlson had chosen to sell off his chain of international hotels to renovate this one in Bellbird Bay.

'Leo Carlson… Isn't he…' Rachel said, when they were seated in the restaurant.

'Yes, he and Greta are married. Another happy ever after second time around.' Poppy gave Rachel a pointed look.

Rachel flinched. She didn't want to talk about Luke today. She picked up a menu and studied it.

But Poppy wasn't to be sidetracked. 'What's going on with you and the vet?' she asked. 'A little bird tells me you've been seen together at the yacht club.' She waited expectantly.

While Rachel was glad it was Poppy asking, not Liz who wouldn't have hesitated to interrogate her till she got an answer, Rachel was aware of Poppy's interest… and concern.

'You don't have to tell me anything if you don't want to, but sometimes it helps to share.'

Rachel put down the menu and twisted her fingers. Perhaps Poppy would understand. Like her, Poppy had been widowed before she and Cam got together, though *her* husband's death had been sudden – a freak sailing accident – whereas Kirk had died after a long illness had taken its toll on Rachel. It was when she had started to gain weight, unwilling to leave his bedside and snacking on whatever she found in the pantry.

'Oh, Poppy. I'm in a fix. As you know, Luke was Becky's boyfriend.'

Poppy nodded and took a sip of the wine which had already been served.

Rachel took a sip too, before continuing, 'Like every other girl at school, I had a huge crush on him. He was gorgeous and he was kind to me. It wasn't like I was only Becky's little sister. He really seemed to take an interest in me. Oh, of course, I knew I was far too young for him – I was only fourteen. But he sometimes included me when they went to the beach, and once to a movie.' She stopped and closed her eyes, remembering… 'Anyway, he left school, left Pelican Crossing. Becky went to Sydney, married Andy, I married Kirk. I rarely thought of him… Well, perhaps sometimes, as you do.'

Poppy nodded again, and Rachel wondered not for the first time, if she'd fancied Cam back then before she and Jack got together.

'Molly gets a tick. I take her to the vet, and there he is.' She swallowed. 'Then we met again at the fundraiser. You were there. You saw. After that he invited me to dinner… twice. We're neighbours. I helped him choose a Christmas tree. That's about it.'

'And?'

'There's no *and*, Poppy. He's here for three months, then he'll be off again. Back to Sydney.'

'But you like him?'

'Who wouldn't?' The words were out before Rachel could stop them. She bit her lip. But this was Poppy. She'd been there.

'Oh, Rach!'

A waiter appeared and they placed their orders, Rachel choosing the first item she saw on the menu which luckily was a coconut chicken salad, not something fattening. Poppy chose the same.

'If he wasn't leaving, would you feel differently?'

Rachel sighed. It was the question she'd been asking herself. She hadn't come up with an answer, but the prospect was appealing. She'd lain awake thinking about it. 'But he is, Poppy. There's no point in imagining otherwise. So, best I don't even think about it.'

'What about him?'

'What do you mean?'

'How do you think he feels?'

'Poppy, it's been less than a month since he arrived.' She paused. *It seemed much longer.* 'But he says he wants to get to know me.' Rachel blushed, remembering some of the other things he'd said… remembering the gentle touch of his lips on hers…

'Are you seeing him again?'

Rachel sighed again. 'Tomorrow night… but only because it's Christmas. I have all the family events, Alexander's coming home. And Luke's son and partner are coming up from Sydney.'

'And after Christmas?'

'I hope we stay friends. I enjoy his company.'

'Friends? Sounds to me as if you're more than friends already.'

'No, really. He probably still thinks of me as Becky's little sister.' *But there had been that kiss.*

'Widowed or divorced?'

'Widowed.'

'Something else you have in common.'

'Hardly enough to build a relationship on.'

'So you *have* thought about it?'

Their meals arrived, and Rachel tried to avoid any further conversation about her and Luke as she forked up the salad. 'This is very good,' she said.

'I know what you're doing,' Poppy chuckled, 'but I won't say any more. Only, do think about it. I can speak from experience when I say that love can be just as sweet second time around. Don't dismiss a relationship with Luke because he's only here for three months. A lot can happen in three months.'

'Thanks, Poppy.'

Rachel didn't know whether she was thanking Poppy for deciding to stop talking about Luke, or for her suggestion a lot could happen in three months. She didn't want to think about that... not yet... not now.

Twenty-three

Luke gazed at the brightly lit and decorated Christmas tree in the corner of the window, pleased with what he'd achieved. When he'd come home the previous evening, his car filled with a collection of food and decorations, he'd spent over an hour decorating it, hindered by Nelson's efforts to help. It might not look as professional as the one in Rachel's living room but would pass muster, and for him, it was an achievement. 'What do you think, Nelson?' he asked the dog, hoping he wouldn't attempt to lift his leg on it. Nelson looked up at him, seemingly disgusted that he had brought a tree into the house only to smother it with lights and coloured baubles.

Luke chuckled and headed to the kitchen where he poured himself a beer – one of the craft beers from the brewery – and sniffed the aroma of the lasagne he was cooking for dinner. It filled the room, reminding him of his mother. He'd always loved her food and, in his teens, had persuaded her to teach him to make some of his favourites. 'Not for you, Nelson,' he said to his dog who was nosing around the oven, as he filled the dog bowl with food which Nelson ate rapidly before returning to his previous spot. Luke shook his head. The dog had a mind of his own, especially where food was concerned.

He decided they'd eat outside, but at the table rather than by the firepit which would be good when the weather turned cooler. By the time Troy arrived, Luke had everything ready and had even tuned the sound system into a playlist of Christmas carols.

'Looking good, mate,' Troy said, when Luke greeted him at the door. 'See you're getting into the Christmas spirit. Don't bother, myself. My oldest lays it all on and I spend the day with her and the family.'

'My son and his partner are arriving at the end of the week, so I thought I should make an effort.'

'And what do I smell?' Troy sniffed appreciatively as he followed Luke into the kitchen where Nelson was still positioned by the stove.

'Move!' Luke said to the dog who only did so to sniff at the visitor's feet.

'Good looking animal,' Troy said. 'He probably smells my Jacko.' He bent down to ruffle Nelson's ears. 'Smells like your mother's kitchen, you know. Brings back memories.'

'It's one of her recipes. I like to keep my hand in and you're my first visitor.' Luke conveniently forgot the steak he'd cooked for Rachel, preferring to keep that to himself.

'I always loved Mother Findlay's dinners. You didn't invite us round often enough.'

Luke chuckled. When he was growing up, his home was the focal point for the neighbourhood, his mother's cooking legendary. It was a rare week when one or other of his mates didn't share a meal with them, and they were always Italian dishes, usually pasta. 'Beer, mate?' he asked.

'Thanks.' Troy took a seat on one of the high stools at the kitchen bench while Luke took a beer out of the fridge. Then he lined up the supplies from his shopping trip on the benchtop – a romaine and radicchio lettuce, a tub of cherry tomatoes, jar of olives, red onion, chilli peppers, shaved parmesan, and croutons, the ingredients for the Italian salad to accompany the pasta. His mother would be proud of him.

Troy chatted about his day then said, 'Wow!' watching as Luke put together the salad, then mixed the herbs, red wine vinegar and oil to make the Italian dressing. 'You missed your calling, mate. Should have been a chef.'

Luke laughed. 'Wouldn't have the patience to do this every day, but it's worth it from time to time, and I do enjoy it.'

'You mean you don't eat like this all the time? You're a pie and chips man like the rest of us?'

Luke laughed again, knowing he probably had a healthier diet than many his age. His mother had trained him well. These days people raved about what they called the mediterranean diet. It was how he'd eaten all his life.

Luke waited till they'd finished eating, and Troy had praised the meal. They were on their third beers, and he was feeling mellow, mellow enough to ask Troy about what was troubling him. 'As I said, Mum taught me her recipes, the ones she'd got from *her* mother. You know she was Italian, obviously. But…' he pulled on his beard, '… I've been trying to figure out more about her parents, my grandparents. I don't remember much about them, only an old man sitting in an armchair smoking a pipe and a tiny woman dressed completely in black. You were here back then. I wondered… are your parents still alive?' He waited with bated breath.

'Sorry, Luke. Dad's been gone a few years now, and Mum suffers from dementia. If she knew anything about your folks, it would have gone long ago.'

'Oh, I'm sorry about your mum.' Luke's heart sank. After a few moments he asked, 'Would there be anyone else?'

'Not from our crowd.' Troy took a sip of beer and gazed into space. 'Tell you what. Remember old Agnes, lives by the river, hippie type?'

'Vaguely.' Luke tried to picture who Troy was talking about and came up with a shadowy image of a woman with long hair wearing loose, brightly coloured clothes. 'She's still there? She must be…'

'No one knows how old she is. She takes care of sick pelicans these days, has done for years now. She'd be your best bet. She's been around for ever.'

'Not quite.' But Troy was right. Agnes would have known his mother, maybe even his grandparents. 'Thanks, Troy. I'll talk to her, probably have to be after Christmas.'

'You might have to go easy with her. She can be a tad edgy, but it's worth a shot. She has a dog, a spaniel,' he added as if thinking it would make a difference. Maybe it would.

It was late when Troy finally left, and Luke had agreed to going sailing with him after Christmas, something Josh and Abby would probably enjoy too. He had also made tentative arrangements to meet his old friend at the Christmas Eve carol singing and to attend a school reunion in February. It seemed, without any effort on his part,

Luke was being pulled back into life at Pelican Crossing. And there was dinner with Rachel tomorrow to look forward to.

Twenty-four

Rachel had spent the day in the garden, with Molly happily lying in the shade close by. The little dog was clearly glad to be back to normal and able to run around when she felt like it. But today, the heat was proving too much for her. It was almost too much for Rachel too, but she was determined to get everything looking good for Christmas. And the effort of gardening prevented her from thinking too much about dinner with Luke, and what Poppy had said.

It had been different for Poppy, Rachel reasoned to herself, when she finally finished in the garden and went inside for lunch which consisted of an apple and a piece of cheese. Despite what everyone seemed determined to say about her curves, she did want to lose weight and it would be hard to cut back over the festive period. Maybe if she starved herself for a couple of days, it wouldn't matter if she over-indulged on Christmas treats.

By the end of the afternoon, she was pleased with what she had achieved. There was just time for a relaxing bath to soothe her aching limbs before dressing for dinner. But as she lay in the bath, scented with the fragrant lavender and bergamot oil which had been a gift from Steph and Chloe, her mind returned to Luke Findlay and to how she couldn't understand why he was bothering with her. Several of his old school friends still lived in Pelican Crossing. Surely he'd prefer to spend time with them, rather than an overweight woman whose life centred around her grandchildren and the guests who stayed at her B&B?

Whatever the reason, Rachel had butterflies in her stomach at the prospect of seeing him again, at having dinner with him at *Crossings*. She hadn't told Poppy where they were dining. Perhaps she should have. She knew Poppy and Cam often went there themselves. Although Poppy had cut back on her time at the restaurant, she still often ate there, saying she was only making sure everything was going well.

The water was turning cold by the time Rachel stepped out of the bath to dry herself on a fluffy towel. She took the blue dress she'd purchased at *Birds of a Feather* out of the wardrobe and held it up against her. It was unlike anything else in her wardrobe, and she loved it. Slipping it over her head, she felt transformed, no longer the drab grandmother, the B&B landlady. She felt like Cinderella going to the ball. She chuckled at the comparison, at comparing Luke to the prince. It was what he'd been to her all those years ago. Now she was older and wiser, but it still gave her a thrill to know they were meeting again that evening.

*

The restaurant was decorated for Christmas. There was a large Christmas tree in one corner, its lights twinkling merrily, and garlands of red, green and silver festooned the walls. Christmas carols were playing quietly in the background, almost drowned out by the sound of voices. At first glance, it appeared every table was filled, but Rachel and Luke were unerringly led to a vacant spot in the far corner of the restaurant. There was no sign of Poppy.

'This is lovely. Very different to my last visit.'

'The fundraising?' Rachel smiled, remembering how Luke had made an effort to speak to her that night. 'It can be very adaptable,' she said. 'You should see how Poppy decks it out for the Melbourne Cup Lunch.' She bit her lip, remembering Luke wouldn't be here next November to see it.

'I'd like to see that,' he said. 'I remember this place when her parents owned it. It was a fish and chip shop. They made the best fish and chips.'

'I remember that too.'

A waiter approached with menus and handed Luke a wine list. 'How about champagne since it's almost Christmas?' he asked.

'That would be lovely.' The evening was already promising to be memorable. Luke's expression when she opened the door to him had been priceless. It had been a full minute before he said, 'You look lovely, Red.' She hadn't corrected him. There was something appealing about his use of her old nickname.

Besides the regular menu, there were a number of seasonal options. Both Rachel and Luke chose the baked salmon served with crispy potatoes, roasted cauliflower with herb crust, and green beans, followed by creamy eggnog ice cream with raspberries.

'That was delicious. Thank you for inviting me,' Rachel said at the end of their meal. She looked up to see Luke watching her. A shiver ran down her spine. *What was he thinking?*

'It was my pleasure,' he said. 'It's good to meet a woman who enjoys her food.'

'Oh!' Rachel blushed. *Had she seemed too greedy?*

'I mean it. Since Ness, I haven't dated much, but when I did, I discovered women who were afraid to admit they like to eat. After a few experiences like that, I stopped dating. It all seemed too hard.'

'Oh!' Rachel said again, unsure how to respond. 'Tell me about your wife.'

'Ness?' Luke gazed into space. 'She was the love of my life, my soulmate. We met at uni, set up the practice together. She was the driving force behind it. I'd probably have been happy to work for someone else.' He sighed, then glanced across the table at Rachel. 'She wasn't unlike you in some ways. I sense you have that same drive to succeed. But she's been gone a long time now. I've grown used to living alone, to my own company – and Nelson's, become a grumpy old man. I guess that's why I found it so difficult to adapt to Josh and Abby moving in.'

Drive to succeed? Did she really have one, Rachel wondered. She'd only turned her home into a B&B because she couldn't bear to leave it, but she supposed it said something about her determination. 'How are you finding being back in Pelican Crossing?' she asked to cover her confusion.

'Different to what I expected.'

'Different how?'

'Pelican Crossing is different. Many of the people I knew back then have left and those who've stayed have changed. I guess I've changed too.'

'We all have. We're older for a start.'

'Yeah, but it's not only that. I don't know what I expected exactly. Take you, for instance. When I left, you were a young teenager full of the usual teenage longings. And now…'

Rachel held her breath.

'… now you've grown up into this desirable woman who frankly scares me.'

Rachel gasped. *What did he mean?*

'Sorry, that came out wrong. What I meant was…' he pulled on his beard, '… hell, I'm out of practice at this sort of thing. I like you, Red. I like you a lot, but I'm well aware I'm only filling in till Bob gets back. It wouldn't be fair to start something that can't go anywhere.'

Rachel knew he was right. It was what she'd been thinking too, what she'd said to Poppy. So why did his words make her feel discouraged?

'That said, I have something for you.' Luke fished in his pocket and took out a small packet wrapped in Christmas paper. 'Merry Christmas!'

'Oh! Thank you!' Rachel was overcome. She hadn't expected a gift. 'I'm sorry. I don't have anything for you. I didn't think…'

'No worries. I didn't expect anything. Open it.'

Rachel fumbled with the wrapping, to reveal a small box which, when opened, contained a pair of drop earrings in gold and blue, the blue almost the exact colour of her dress. 'Oh, thank you,' she said again, holding them up to let them swing in the light. They were different from what she normally wore, but in keeping with the new image she wanted to project.

'I thought of you when I saw them,' Luke said with a smile.

Rachel's heart skipped a beat. She took out the small pearl studs she was wearing and replaced them with the new earrings. She moved her head from side to side, loving the way they swung against her neck. 'I love them,' she said, beaming.

'They look good on you… with that dress. You're a lovely woman, Red.'

Rachel blushed. How she wished Luke was here to stay. He was such a lovely man, and he seemed to like her too. Life could be so unkind.

'Coffee?' he asked.

'Yes please.' So, there was to be no coffee at her place or his tonight? One part of her was glad, while another was filled with disappointment. Despite what Luke had said about not wanting to be unfair to her, was three months of happiness better than nothing?

Driving home, they chatted about their dogs, discovering that both liked to wrap up some treats or toys for their furry friends to open on Christmas Day. Rachel sighed to herself as he stopped the car outside her house. He was such a nice man. If only…Then they turned to face each other.

'Red…' Luke said, that one word sending a flood of warmth through her. Then he pulled her into his arms and kissed her. This was no gently brush of the lips, but a kiss that seemed to go on for ever, a kiss that sent Rachel's senses reeling and made her forget everything but the man holding her.

Twenty-five

For the past two days, Rachel had been walking on air, the memory of the kiss in Luke's car and the promise it contained, sending her stomach into freefall. She was unaware of smiling all the time, till Jess asked her the reason. Rachel brushed it off by saying she was looking forward to Alexander's arrival, but she knew it was more than that.

Alexander was arriving today, and she banished all thoughts of Luke to concentrate on the joy of seeing her son again. It had been too long since Alexander visited Pelican Crossing. It seemed he was happy to make his life on the other side of the world, away from her and his sisters.

Rachel intended to make sure this Christmas was the best ever. She'd welcome Alexander's partner as one of the family, just as she had done with Paul when Jess first brought him home, and Chloe, even before Steph revealed they were partners. Maybe, she thought, his new lady would like Queensland so much, she'd persuade him to return home. Surely he could develop his computer games just as well here as in London? But she knew he loved the life there. Moving back home wasn't an option.

The day seemed to drag. Rachel had everything prepared. The brightly wrapped gifts were sitting under the tree and, so far, she had managed to prevent Molly from destroying them. The fridge was filled to the brim with food for the holiday, and the pantry groaned with more food than they could possibly eat. Kirk used to tell her that she overdid it, but Rachel hated to think she might run out of something so continued to shop madly at this time of year.

She'd taken Greta's advice and bought herself several pieces of shapewear, astonished at the difference they made. She had even managed to fit into two pairs of three-quarter pants which had been relegated to the back of the wardrobe. She was wearing a pair now, with a loose shirt, and decided to take Molly for a walk on the beach.

As they made their way down the steps, Rachel could see several people were already there and a game of beach cricket was in progress. She knew if she went close to the game, Molly would want to run after the ball, so headed in the opposite direction. She was wandering along in the shallow water, Molly bounding along beside her, when she saw a tall figure and a dog coming towards her. Her heart leapt. She hadn't expected to see Luke again till the festivities were over.

The two dogs met first, sniffing each other before their tails wagged and they ran into the sea together.

'Well, that's one problem solved,' Luke said, joining Rachel. 'Nelson can be tricky where other dogs are concerned. He's fine in the clinic, but elsewhere…' He pulled on his beard. 'How have you been? I've been thinking about you.'

'I've been good. I've been thinking about you too.' Rachel's stomach was churning. She hoped her expression didn't reveal what she had been thinking, some of which had been X-rated. She was glad she was wearing the pants over the shapewear which made her look slimmer. Luke was as attractive as ever, wearing a pair of khaki shorts and a white tee-shirt with the logo of a brand she didn't recognise. Like her, he was barefoot and carrying his sandals.

'Molly seems to be fully recovered,' Luke said, his eyes following the two dogs gambolling in the ocean.

'Yes.' Rachel felt tongue-tied. This was ridiculous. But meeting Luke like this was so unexpected – though she didn't know why. They shared this beach. It shouldn't have been a surprise to see him here. 'Not working today?' she asked.

'Taking a short break. The clinic has been pretty quiet today. I think everyone's getting ready for Christmas – and they haven't started feeding their animals chocolate and other sugary treats yet.'

Rachel nodded. She could remember Bob complaining about the influx of sick animals after Christmas when their owners had allowed them to indulge in the wrong sort of treats. As soon as they were old enough to understand, she'd warned the twins about sharing their own treats with Molly who would eat anything she was given.

'Your son not here yet?'

Rachel shook her head. Alexander was due to arrive late afternoon. Since next day and on Christmas Day they would be having a big meal, she was planning to serve something lighter tonight. They'd probably be tired after the long flight and wouldn't feel like a heavy meal. Yesterday, she'd cooked her special honey glazed ham. It would form part of the Christmas meal, but she'd cut a few slices for tonight's dinner and serve it with a potato and green salad. 'He'll be here around four,' she said. '*Your* son?'

'Tomorrow. I need to finish food shopping. Maybe you could advise me. Ness always cooked a turkey on Christmas Day, but I'm not sure… I seem to remember it took all day to cook.'

Rachel chuckled. It wasn't like Luke to sound helpless. 'Why don't you buy one of those rolled turkey breasts from the supermarket? It should be enough for the three of you and will only take an hour to cook. You can serve it with salads.'

'Good idea. I'm okay with steak, salads, and can turn my hand to a few pasta dishes, but I've never had to master a roast.'

Rachel chuckled again, then the mention of pasta dishes reminded her. 'Your mother had an Italian background, didn't she?'

'That's right. I've actually been trying to find out more about that side of the family while I'm here. I've discovered some Italian immigrants came to Queensland to work on the cane fields but don't know if my grandfather was one of those. Troy suggested I talk to old Agnes.'

'Of course. She'd be one of the oldest people around, apart from some of the residents of *The Haven*. It's a retirement village and has an aged care home which some residents graduate to when they require more care.'

'Thanks. I'll keep that in mind.'

'I hope you find what you're looking for.' Rachel wondered what it would be like to have no real knowledge of your background. Her family – both her mother's and her father's – had all been born and spent their lives right here in Pelican Crossing. Both grandfathers had been fishermen in the days when Pelican Crossing had been a fishing village. She'd grown up with a strong sense of identity, imagining everyone else did the same.

'Thanks.' He dragged a hand through his hair. 'Guess I should be getting back. Nelson!' he called to his dog, who came running along with a very wet Molly.

'I should too,' Rachel said, suddenly realising how the time had flown while they were talking.

'I…' Luke seemed loath to leave. He moved closer, till Rachel could see the crow's feet beside his eyes. 'I wish…'

He didn't need to say any more. 'I do too,' she said.

He put his hands on her shoulders, and she glanced around. The cricket group had gone the beach was deserted. When Luke pulled her into his arms, she didn't resist, revelling in his closeness, in the now familiar musky scent of him – and became lost in his embrace.

Luke pulled away. 'Now, I really have to go. I'll try to call you…'

'If you're at the carol singing tomorrow evening, we might see each other there.'

'Good idea.' He grinned.

But it wouldn't be the same, surrounded by family and most of the other residents of Pelican Crossing.

Then he was gone, loping off, his dog at his heels.

'Let's go home, Molly,' Rachel said. 'Alexander will be here soon. You'll like that, won't you?' Molly gave a short bark. She loved Alexander who always spoiled her.

Back home, Rachel fed Molly and filled her water bowl. She just had time to shower and change before Alexander arrived with his *surprise*. Rachel wondered what she would be like. She hadn't met any of his more recent girlfriends, but as a teenager he'd always chosen slim blonde girls. She tried to picture the one who would arrive with him, probably a sophisticated blonde, tall, slim, elegant, and hoped she'd fit in with everyone else.

Rachel had decided to wear a pair of her new pants and one of the brightly coloured tunics tonight, keeping one of the new dresses for Christmas Day. It was almost four o'clock when she walked into the living room. She turned on the Christmas tree lights and the sound system – not such a sophisticated one as Bob's – to the Christmas carols she'd been listening to. She had butterflies in her stomach at the thought of meeting whoever Alexander was bringing home to meet his family. They must be serious about each other if she was coming all this way, leaving her own family at Christmas. Rachel wondered if the wedding would be here or in London. It was customary to marry from the bride's home. Would she be travelling across the world sometime in the next year to see her son marry?

Four o'clock passed, four-fifteen, four-thirty. Her stomach churning, Rachel checked her phone, but there were no missed calls or messages. Then, at almost five o'clock, Molly, who had been lying by the tree, got up and ran to the door barking loudly. At the same time, there was the sound of a car stopping, then a car door opening and closing.

Her heart in her mouth, Rachel opened the door.

Alexander was standing there holding the hand of a small child who was clinging to his leg, a little girl with fiery red curls, exactly like Rachel's used to be. 'Hi, Mum' he said. 'This is Verity.'

Twenty-six

When Rachel awoke next morning, it took her a few minutes to remember. Then it came back to her – Alexander, and his surprise, not a partner, but a little girl, Verity. They'd eaten with very little conversation. Her normally laid-back son seeming distraught, the poor little girl overwhelmed, as well she might be, arriving in a strange house, in a foreign country, after a long plane trip, merely saying 'yes' and 'no' and hiding her face in Alexander's chest. Even Molly's attempts to make friends went unheeded. Then Alexander put Verity to bed, disappearing himself soon after, claiming he was too tired and would explain everything in the morning. Too wired to sleep, Rachel had sat up with a glass of wine trying to figure out what it was all about. Alexander was clearly Verity's father. The little girl was the image of photos of Rachel at that age – she'd always regretted neither her daughters nor her granddaughters had inherited her red hair. But who was Verity's mother, and where was she?

Sighing, Rachel rose and dressed, before heading to the kitchen where Molly was awake and ready for her walk. Since there was no sign of Alexander or Verity – she'd agreed to Alexander's request they share a room – Rachel decided to take Molly to the beach.

The heat of the day was already making itself felt and she was glad it was still early enough to make it pleasant to walk along the sand. This morning, to her disappointment, there was no sign of Luke and Nelson.

It was peaceful, strolling along at the edge of the water, the only sounds in the still morning the cries of the seagulls and the whoosh of the waves. It gave Rachel time to think, time to digest Alexander's surprise. Verity was indeed a surprise, one she had never anticipated. And, typical of Alexander, he'd gone off to bed leaving her without any explanation. The little girl was three, a little younger than the twins, one of the few pieces of information she'd managed to elicit at dinner. The twins… how would they react to meeting her? It suddenly dawned on Rachel that she'd been prepared for the arrival of the woman in her son's life, not a child, and it was Christmas tomorrow. She'd need to find time to shop for presents for the little girl. How could Alexander have been so insensitive as to just turn up with a daughter in tow at this time of year? She sighed. Verity was a lovely little thing. But to drag her all the way here, then back to England was pretty unfair. Why hadn't he prepared Rachel for this, why had he kept her existence secret for so long? And where was her mother?

Without coming to any conclusion and having walked to the end of the beach and back, Rachel called to Molly and they went back up the steps to the house.

Alexander was in the kitchen making coffee. 'Hey, Mum,' he said, bending down to ruffle Molly's ears, the little dog having immediately abandoned Rachel and gone to rub herself against his ankles.

'Sleep well?' Rachel asked, as she filled Molly's bowls.

'Not really.' The bags under his eyes which she'd noticed the previous evening seemed to indicate he hadn't slept well for some time. 'Verity's still out for the count.'

'About Verity…'

'Yeah. Coffee?'

'I prefer tea in the morning. I can make it.' Rachel could see it was going to take Alexander some time to explain his daughter to her. She fixed herself a cup of lemon and ginger tea and joined him at the table in the courtyard where he'd taken his coffee. Molly had joined him, having gobbled down her breakfast.

'Well? I think I need an explanation.'

'Yeah,' he said again, sounding distressed. 'She's mine… obviously.'

'Obviously. She's the image of me at her age. You said she's three?'

'She'll be four in March.'

'Why did you never tell me about her? Why keep her a secret?

Regardless of the circumstances, you know I'd have welcomed the news.'

'I didn't find out myself till recently.' Alexander took a drink of coffee and dragged a hand through his hair.

He looked so like his father, it took Rachel's breath away. She felt a niggle of guilt which she quickly suppressed. Kirk would approve of her friendship with Luke, even if it became something more.

'Anthea… we worked together, we were mates, then one night, after a party… It was a one-night stand. Neither of us wanted anything more. Then she left, said she'd decided to go freelance, didn't tell anyone she was pregnant… It was only the once, Mum.' He gave Rachel a pleading look, the one he'd always used to get out of trouble.

She waited.

'Anyway, a few months ago, she got in touch with me. She had breast cancer, stage four. She hadn't long left. And there was this little girl who was my daughter. Can you imagine? I freaked out. Me, with a daughter? She wanted me to meet her.'

'Her family?'

'There's no one. Her parents died in a car crash when she was nineteen. No siblings. No aunts, uncles, cousins.'

Rachel's heart went out to this unknown woman.

'So, I did meet her, get to know her,' Alexander continued. 'She's a bright kid, not usually as quiet as she was last night. It was a long trip and…'

'The poor child was exhausted, then to bring her into a strange house, meet a strange person. She'd just lost her mother. No wonder she was quiet. Everyone will be here for dinner tonight. I hope it won't be too much for her. You never guessed…?'

'How could I?' Alexander dragged a hand through his hair. Rachel thought he was going to cry. 'Anthea… she… She never thought of me that way, even though…' he swallowed, '… if I'd known about Verity, I'd have… I missed out on three years of her life. And now Anthea's gone…'

Rachel could see he was trying hard not to break down. She drew him into a hug. He might be a grown man, a father, but he was still her little boy.

'Thanks, Mum.' He pulled away as if embarrassed to have her see him like this. 'I've told her about everyone – you, Jess. Steph, the twins, Emily. She was looking forward to meeting the twins, but since Anthea died, she's retreated into her shell. It's as if she can't understand what happened.'

'No wonder. The poor little mite.' Rachel's eyes moistened. To lose her mother at such a young age, to be thrust into the care of a father she didn't know, brought across the world to meet a strange family…

A thought occurred to Rachel. 'You had no trouble getting custody, bringing her to Australia?'

'Anthea is – was – Australian, so Verity is an Australian citizen. And I'm named as the father on her birth certificate. It was really quite simple. It's almost as if Anthea knew.' Alexander gazed into space, a tear in the corner of his eye, and Molly, sensing his distress, got up on her hind legs and put one paw on his knee.

'Sounds as if she cared for you… and you her?'

'We worked together, were good mates, often had a drink together, a few laughs, talked about home. She was a great girl.'

At that moment, there was the patter of tiny feet, and Verity ran out of the door and flung herself against Alexander, turning to stare at Rachel.

Molly immediately began to lick Verity's bare feet, triggering a tiny laugh.

'I'm hungry, Daddy,' Verity said into Alexander's chest, her voice muffled.

'Good morning, Verity,' Rachel said gently. 'I'm your grandma. Do you remember meeting me last night? And this is Molly,' she added as Molly made her presence felt.

Verity nodded.

'Would you like me to make you some breakfast?'

The little girl nodded again.

'I have two other granddaughters close to your age. They like my banana pancakes when they have a sleepover. Would you like me to make some for you?'

Verity nodded again.

'Good.'

'I'll have some too, Mum,' Alexander said, as Rachel rose to go into the kitchen, Molly following in the hope of food.

Once in the kitchen, Rachel couldn't stop thinking of Verity and what she'd been through. It was difficult enough to lose your mother at any age, but at three, when she was all you'd ever known. Then to be thrust into the care of a father you barely knew, to meet a grandmother you didn't know existed, in a foreign country, at Christmas… She found herself beating the pancake mix more thoroughly than necessary as her eyes filled with tears.

She was proud of Alexander for stepping up. Some men would have run a mile. But it was the way she and Kirk had brought him up. He'd never been one to shirk his responsibilities, though no one could have predicted this situation. Rachel wondered how he'd cope when they returned to London. Perhaps he'd go freelance, as he said Verity's mother had. Surely game design lent itself to that? A lot of technology workers seemed to work from home these days, or so she'd read.

By the time the pancakes were ready, Alexander and Verity were already seated at the table. Molly had taken up position below the little girl's chair, and Alexander had poured Verity a glass of milk and himself another mug of coffee.

When Rachel joined them, Verity observed her warily over the top of the glass of milk. When Rachel placed a pancake on her plate, and Alexander topped it with strawberries and maple syrup, she picked up her fork and began to eat, gazing at Rachel from time to time.

When Verity finished eating, she slipped down from her chair and out of the kitchen, Molly following her like her shadow.

'She's sweet,' Rachel said, 'but I worry she doesn't speak.'

'She will. It's all very strange to her.'

'Of course.' Rachel remembered about the gifts she needed to buy. 'What do you plan to do today? Since I wasn't expecting Verity, I don't have any presents for her, so I need to go shopping. I hate to leave you both when you've only just arrived, but she's lost her mother. She needs to experience a proper Christmas.'

'Sure, Mum. Do what you have to. I should have thought.' He paused and shrugged. 'We can maybe go to the beach or catch up with Jess.'

'Right. Better forewarn your sister if you plan to drop in.'

'Will do.'

Rachel stared at her son. He appeared very laid back about his situation, but he could no longer only think about himself as he had done for years. As the only boy in the family, he'd got away with a lot all of his life. Now, there was a little girl to consider. And she did wonder if he'd cared more for Anthea than he was willing to admit.

*

It was almost a relief to Rachel to get out of the house. She'd forgotten how busy the stores would be on Christmas Eve – she had always made sure she shopped well in advance so as to be able to relax as the big day drew near. Luckily, she was able to find toys similar to those she'd already bought for Gemma and Indie, plus a few extra for all three. Then, not quite ready to return home and feeling the need for a pick me up, she popped into *Books and Coffee.*

'I'm surprised to see you here today,' Lou said, when Rachel made her way through the bookshop which was teeming with customers seeking last-minute gifts. 'Alexander arrive with his surprise?' She grinned.

'Quite a surprise,' Rachel said, then added, 'Tell you later,' as another customer appeared to demand Lou's attention. Why had Rachel thought her friend would have time to listen to her on this, her busiest day of the year?

She purchased a few more books for the girls, then passed through to the coffee shop. It was busy too, but to her delight, Rachel spotted Poppy sitting at a table almost hidden behind the door. She ordered coffee and a strawberry and white chocolate muffin from Ron, who, despite the crowd, kept up his normal bright repartee, then joined her friend.

'I didn't expect to see you here today,' she said, almost repeating Lou's comment to her. 'Thought you'd be too busy at the restaurant.' She knew Poppy liked to be at the restaurant for special occasions.

'I had a few last-minute gifts to buy,' Poppy said, 'but what about you? I thought you'd be busy with Alexander and his new lady.'

'About that… Thanks, Denny,' she said, as her coffee and muffin arrived. 'Alexander's surprise is a three-year-old daughter called Verity.' She was glad to be able to share the news with someone, and Poppy would understand her shock.

Poppy's eyes widened. 'Wow! And her mother?'

Rachel took a much-needed sip of coffee before repeating much of what Alexander had told her. 'She'd a dear little thing,' she said, 'red hair, just like mine was. I had to come out to buy gifts for her.'

'Of course you did. How thoughtless of Alexander not to warn you.'

'Yes. But it is what it is. The poor mite hasn't said a word since they arrived. I think she's in shock.'

'It must seem very strange to her, but she couldn't be with a better person. Out of all of us, you have the most experience at being a grandmother.'

'Maybe,' Rachel sighed, 'but nothing prepared me for this.'

'How long does he intend to stay?'

'I haven't asked him. It was enough to have to digest the news about Verity. I guess it was a shock to him too, but you know Alexander – he has always been able to come out smelling of roses.'

'Maybe not this time. A child is quite a responsibility.'

'I've already thought of that. I'm pleased he's taken it on, but I do wonder what sort of father he'll make. Having Verity will certainly curtail his social life.'

'You don't think…? No, forget it. Will we see you all at the carols tonight?'

'I hope so. I'm hoping Verity will come out of herself once she's become used to being here, and when she's met the twins. I don't think anyone could remain shy in their presence.' She chuckled at the thought of the two terrors, wondering if Alexander had dropped in to see Jess, and how it had gone if he had. She hoped Gemma and Indie's exuberance would evoke some reaction from Verity and wouldn't send her further into her shell.

'You're probably right. I hope so, for your sake, and hers… and Alexander's. What an interesting Christmas you're going to have. I'm sorry, Rach. I need to go now. See you tonight.'

'Sure. And, Poppy, I'm so glad I bumped into you. I needed to tell someone, to get it off my chest. Sharing with you has helped.'

'No problem.' Poppy hugged Rachel before leaving.

Apart from Liz, Poppy was the friend most likely to understand how it felt to suddenly have another grandchild – the shock and delight – though each of hers had been expected and eagerly awaited, as had Rachel's other three granddaughters. She finished her coffee, had the last bite of muffin and picked up her bag. Despite Alexander's arrival, and the surprise of Verity, she still had a lot to do to prepare for tonight's dinner and for lunch tomorrow.

Twenty-seven

Before going to the clinic that morning, Luke had checked everything twice to ensure all was ready for Josh and Abby's arrival. He planned to close at lunchtime, assuming any prospective clients would be tied up preparing for the next day. As it was, he had only a few appointments.

He was surprised how much he was enjoying working with animals again. Maybe he'd retired too soon, but Josh had been eager to take over, and Luke remembered the thrill of setting up his own practice with Ness. He wanted Josh to experience the same, and he was a good vet. Luke knew the practice was in good hands. Also, he had his bucket list, though the list of adventures he'd carefully researched and put together no longer seemed as attractive as they had when he handed over the keys of the clinic to Josh.

He looked up as Wendy ushered in his first client, an elderly woman with long untamed white hair. She was wearing the sort of outfit Ness would have described as hippie and was carrying a golden cocker spaniel.

'I'm Agnes,' the woman said, before Luke could speak. 'I remember you. You're Sonja Findlay's boy. I heard you were back.' Her eyes raked him up and down. 'You take after her side of the family.'

For a moment, Luke forgot where he was, forgot there was a dog needing his attention. This was the woman Troy had told him about, the one who might have known his grandparents. Then his professional manner took over. 'Who have we here?' he asked, taking the dog from Agnes and placing her on the examination table.

'This is Lady. She's not well this morning. She seems to be bleeding from her mouth and her poo is tarry.'

Luke frowned. This didn't sound good. 'Let's have a look at Lady,' he said. 'How old is she?' he asked, while examining the dog who was lying very still. Her owner was watching closely.

'She's not a young dog. I've had her for twelve years. She was just a pup. She's normally very lively. What do you think is wrong?'

'Are you aware of her having eaten anything out of the usual?' Luke asked, noticing some bruising spots on Lady's gums and abdomen, a sign of rat poison. The symptoms Agnes described would fit with that diagnosis too.

'No, I'm always very careful, though she does tend to be attracted to whatever she finds on the beach. Do you think she's been poisoned?'

'It's likely. Do you have any chemicals lying around, or rat poison?'

Agnes drew herself up to her full height. 'I'll let you know, young man, that I'm well aware of the dangers of those things and, no, I do not have them anywhere Lady could access them.'

Luke had to stifle his amusement at being called a young man. He supposed to Agnes, he was. He believed her, remembering what Troy had told him – she cared for injured pelicans. She would know the dangers of having toxic substances around. 'I'll take a blood sample so I can check if it's what I think.' Luke was glad Bob had installed a diagnostic machine which would enable him to analyse for blood clotting. 'Why don't I have Wendy get you a cup of tea or coffee while I do that?'

It was clear Agnes didn't want to leave her dog, but she allowed Luke to ask Wendy to make tea, and followed her to the waiting room while Luke took care of Lady. It was as he'd thought. The time taken for the blood to clot was a sign of rat poison. He frowned, hoping the dog had picked it up somewhere accidentally.

'What happens now?' Agnes asked, when Luke told her his diagnosis.

'I've given her a shot of vitamin K and here are some tablets to take home with you. I'll need to see her again in forty-eight hours to check if the clotting has improved and again when the tablets are finished in three weeks' time.'

'Will she be all right?' Agnes asked, when Luke had completed his treatment of the dog.

'She should be. Just keep her comfortable. Make sure she has plenty of water and only give her small amounts of food. I'd like you to bring Lady back the day after Christmas so I can check her again.' He stroked the dog's head.

'That's Boxing Day,' she said. 'Won't the clinic be closed?'

'Lady's health is more important than the holiday. Arrange a time with Wendy before you leave.' Luke lifted the dog down. She immediately moved to lean against Agnes's legs.

'If that's all,' she said.

Luke wanted to ask her about his grandparents, but now wasn't the time.

'Okay. Have a good Christmas,' Agnes said, before she and Lady left.

'You, too.' Luke gave a sigh of relief. He hoped this was a one-off. The last thing he needed at his time of year was a spate of dog poisonings.

Fortunately, the rest of the morning passed without incident. There were no more cases of poisoning. Whatever Agnes's spaniel had ingested must have been an unfortunate occurrence. Lady should recover well, and perhaps he'd have an opportunity to talk with Agnes when she returned on Boxing Day.

After farewelling his final client for the day, Luke wished Wendy a Merry Christmas and handed her the box of chocolates he'd bought for her, then went through to his office where Nelson was lying, waiting for him.

'Good boy,' he said, still somewhat worried about Lady's poisoning and wondering how it had occurred. He knew he'd probably never find out. 'You're okay, aren't you?' he said to the dog who was prancing around ready for a walk after being stuck in Luke's office all morning. 'Okay, mate, let's go.'

Luke was ready for some exercise too, so headed down to the beach, Nelson running beside him. Today, Luke kept an eye out for any unusual objects or foreign matter on the sand. Agnes had mentioned the beach, but he'd never seen her on this one. He suspected she was referring to the more popular dog beach which was on the other side of the headland. As usual, this beach was deserted, the sand pristine, the only signs of life a group of surfers some distance from the shore.

It was relaxing to stroll along at the edge of the water, playing fetch with Nelson who had managed to find a stick washed up by the sea. He gazed up at Rachel's house. Her son would have arrived by now with his special someone. Luke hoped all was going well and the new lady fitted into the family. He hadn't met either of Rachel's daughters yet, or her granddaughters. Perhaps they'd all bump into each other tonight at the carol singing. He was sure Josh and Abby would be happy to attend, though he'd leave Nelson at home.

Luke checked his watch. Josh and Abby should be leaving Sydney around now. He'd offered to pick them up at the airport, but Josh insisted on hiring a car. He was independent, like his dad. Ness had always told him how much Josh resembled him – not in looks but in personality.

Back home, he made himself a sandwich and gave Nelson a treat, then settled down to read more of the book on Italian immigration. It had been a stroke of luck meeting Agnes this morning, and she'd known his mother. With a bit more luck, she'd remember his grandparents too. He was looking forward to seeing her again – and to checking up on Lady.

Luke had just put a lasagne in the oven and was preparing a salad, when there was a flurry of barking and Nelson bounded to the door, seconds before there was a loud knocking and the door opened.

'Hey, Nelson. How are you, boy?' Josh said, as Luke walked through the hallway to see the dog with his paws on Josh's chest.

'He missed me, Dad,' Josh said, pushing the dog down to give Luke a hug. 'This place looks amazing. How does it feel to be back?'

'It's good,' Luke said, surprising himself with the realisation he really was enjoying being back in Pelican Crossing. 'Welcome. It's good to see you. You, too, Abby,' he said, turning to give her a hug too.

'Thanks, Luke. We drove along past a marina and a long stretch of beach. It looks amazing. I can't wait to go for a swim.'

'You'd have driven past the surf beach and the dog beach. There are steps by the back gate to a more private one. It's mostly only used by a few surfers and Bob's neighbour. It's not patrolled, so you have to take care, but there aren't any rips.'

'Sounds awesome. D'you have a beer, Dad? I'm parched.'

'Sure. Come through to the kitchen. Abby?'

'Water for me, thanks.'

'Do you want to bring your gear in from the car?'

'Later. Beer first.'

'Okay.'

They all trooped through to the kitchen, and Luke poured beer for himself and Josh and a glass of water for Abby, who wandered over to gaze out the window at the ocean while the two men took seats on the high stools by the kitchen bench.

'Do I smell lasagne?' Abby said, turning back from the window.

'You do. I thought you'd be hungry, and we could have an early dinner. There's a carol singing event in town this evening which promises to be good. What do you think?'

'Oh, that sounds like fun. And you have a tree,' she said, as if suddenly catching sight of the Christmas tree in the other room.

'Yeah, thought I'd make a bit of an effort since you two were coming.'

'Thanks, Dad,' Josh said. 'I know Christmas has been difficult for you since Mum died. I think this is the first Christmas we've spent together.'

'Are those the steps down to the beach?' Amy had turned back to the window. 'Have we time for a swim before dinner? The ocean looks amazing.'

Josh rose to join her. 'Wow, Dad!' He drained his beer.

Luke laughed. 'Sure. I can delay dinner, as long as you don't take too long.'

In a flash, Josh went out to the car, returning with two bags which he took to the bedroom Luke indicated. It seemed only a moment later that the two young people re-emerged in swimmers and carrying towels. 'You won't join us?' Josh asked.

'Not this time.' But Nelson, unwilling to be left behind when there was fun to be had, didn't need to be asked twice.

Luke timed it perfectly. By the time Josh and Abby returned from the beach, full of praise for it and the warmth of the ocean, and had dressed, the lasagne was ready to be served, and Nelson was tucking into his dinner.

'What's the practice like?' Josh asked.

'Different to what we've been used to. Still small animal, but not nearly as busy. There have been a few ticks, but nothing major. Though today...' Luke pulled on his beard.

'What?' Josh stopped eating.

'I had a dog in that had been poisoned.'

'That's not good. Were you able to identify the cause?'

'Rat bait, I believe.' Luke realised what was worrying him. Unless… or until… he knew exactly where Agnes's Lady had eaten the poison, there was always the risk of it happening to another animal.

'Not good. Remember that case a few years ago?'

Luke did. The dog had died. It had later been discovered the owner's neighbour had set a bait with rat poison in a piece of meat. But he couldn't imagine anything like that happening in Pelican Crossing and said so.

'You may be right, but you can never tell. Strange things happen all the time, even in a small place like this.'

Luke flinched. He didn't want to think Agnes's dog had been poisoned deliberately. Who would do a thing like that? He could only hope no more cases came to light.

Twenty-eight

Rachel was glad to find the house empty when she returned. It gave her time to wrap Verity's gifts and hide them, along with the red felt stocking which matched those belonging to Gemma, Indie and Emily. Then she started to prepare the salmon which she'd poach for tonight's dinner.

Molly heard Alexander and Verity's return before Rachel and she scampered to the door to greet them. Popping her head out of the kitchen, Rachel was pleased to see Verity looking more animated than she had earlier. 'Did you catch up with your sister?' she asked Alexander, seeing Verity cautiously pat the little dog.

'We did… and the rest. Verity was quite overwhelmed at first, but Gemma and Indie took her under their wing and insisted she join them on the trampoline. She loved it, didn't you, Verity?'

Verity looked up at him, her wide eyes large pools of pale blue – exactly like hers, Rachel realised with a shock.

'The trampoline with Gemma and Indie,' Alexander prompted.

'It was fun,' she said in her cute English accent that sounded so foreign to Rachel.

Rachel felt a warm glow. Apart from the comment about being hungry, these were the first words she'd heard Verity utter. 'Gemma and Indie are a lot of fun, aren't they?' she said with a smile. 'But they never stop. They can be a bit overpowering at times.'

'They said you're their grandma too,' Verity said solemnly, staring at Rachel as if daring her to deny it.

She looked so bereft, Rachel wanted to pick her up and hug her but wasn't sure how she'd react. She appeared to be a very self-sufficient little girl. Rachel supposed she'd had to be, with a sick mother. 'I am,' she replied, 'and I'm thrilled to have another granddaughter. Did they tell you they're coming here to dinner tonight?'

Verity nodded. It seemed she'd used up all her words.

'How about some lunch? I was about to make myself a sandwich. Maybe cheese and pickles for us, Alexander, and I'm betting you'd like Nutella on yours, Verity. It's a favourite with the twins.'

'Yes, please.' Verity's eyes lit up.

Rachel gave a sigh of relief. This might be a breakthrough. Who'd have thought a Nutella sandwich would be the answer?

'Why don't you and your dad go and wash your hands while I fix lunch? We can eat outside, and Molly can have the run of the yard.'

'This is delicious, thank you,' Verity said, as she sat at the outside table with a generously filled Nutella sandwich and a glass of milk.

'You're very welcome,' Rachel said, her heart going out to the girl as she took another bite of sandwich. At least she was eating well.

'May I play with Molly, please?' Verity asked, when she had finished her sandwich and dabbed her milk moustache with a napkin. She was so well-mannered and polite, it almost broke Rachel's heart. She was too young to have gone through what she had.

'Of course you can, sweetheart,' she replied. 'I'm going to be in the kitchen. Let me know if there's anything you want.' She glanced at Alexander and nodded. This was a good step forward. It would take time, but she could predict that, by the time Christmas was over, Verity would be behaving more like others of her age, though perhaps not quite as wild as the twins.

*

As Rachel had expected, dinner was a riotous affair – a prelude to what was to come next day. The house seemed to be overflowing with people once everyone arrived, the twins, excited about Christmas, darting around and getting in everyone's way, while Verity watched on wide-eyed. To Rachel's delight, the little girl gravitated to her side when the two terrors became too noisy.

After dinner, it was time to leave for the carol singing and it seemed they'd never make it as first Gemma, then Indie, disappeared and had to be searched for, then Molly wanted to come with them. Finally, everyone was ready, and Rachel was able to lock the door behind them. They piled into three cars and set off for the marina.

The crowds were already gathering when Rachel, Alexander and Verity got out of Rachel's car. They joined the other family members and made their way to Pelican Plaza where the event was to be held. Pelican Plaza was a semicircle of stone steps close to the marina where every day at two o'clock, volunteers fed the pelicans. It was popular with tourists and locals alike and made a good focal point for the annual carol singing, close to where the town Christmas tree had been erected.

As they approached the area, Rachel felt a little hand in hers and, looking down, saw it was Verity. A bubble of happiness welled up, and she couldn't stop herself from smiling. She was still smiling when they managed to find a spot not far from the front with a good view of the podium and the Christmas tree, decorated with baubles, tinsel and coloured lights.

When the local mayor appeared on the podium to open the proceedings, Rachel felt a presence behind her and turning, saw it was Luke, accompanied by a young couple. The mayor began to speak, so she was unable to say anything, but the smile of welcome on Luke's face sent a warm glow through her. They didn't need to speak; it was enough that he was there.

The mayor finished his greetings, then his place was taken by the musical group and choir from the local high school who proceeded to perform a collection of new and traditional carols, with the audience joining in. Rachel glanced down from time to time to see from Verity's expression that the little girl was enjoying herself, her enjoyment more subdued than that of the twins who were jumping up and down as they joined in with the carols they knew.

When the event finally came to an end with a rendition of *We wish you a Merry Christmas,* and the crowd began to disperse, the twins and Verity were wilting and ready to go home. Jess had brought Emily along in her pram and she was already asleep. Steph and Chloe had snuck away earlier, claiming to be tired.

'See you tomorrow, Mum,' Jess said, giving Rachel a hug. Gemma and Indie raised their arms for a hug too, but they were clearly very tired. Verity had climbed into Alexander's arms during the singing and was sucking her thumb. Rachel couldn't help thinking how cute they looked together.

'Hey!' Luke tapped Rachel on the shoulder. 'Good to see you. That was a stellar performance, a lot bigger than I remember.'

'It's seems to get bigger each year. Hello,' Rachel said to the young couple who were with him.

'This is Josh and Abby,' Luke said. 'Rachel is a friend of mine and my closest neighbour.' They all shook hands, then Rachel introduced Alexander and Verity, seeing Luke's eyes widen at the sight of the little girl. She'd have to explain to him later.

By the time they reached home, Verity was asleep. Alexander carried her into the house and straight to bed, while Rachel poured two glasses of port and cut the Christmas cake. It had always been a tradition with her and Kirk to have a glass of port with a slice of Christmas cake after the carol singing and while they were filling the children's stockings. Rachel had continued the tradition with the grandchildren, and now there were four stockings to fill and hang up.

She had the stockings out and was unpacking the small toys and lollies to fill them with, when Alexander reappeared.

'Thanks, Mum,' he said, taking the glass of port and helping himself to Christmas cake. 'Verity didn't waken when I undressed her to put on her nightie. The port always reminds me of Dad.'

'Me, too,' Rachel said, taking a sip of hers. 'He always loved this time of year.' She gazed into space for a few moments, then gave herself a shake. 'I'm glad Verity seems to be more comfortable with us. It must be very strange for her.'

'She and Anthea were very close. Anthea tried to prepare her for what was going to happen but I'm not sure she fully understood, not until it happened. It was when she started sucking her thumb to go to sleep.'

'The poor mite.'

'Yeah. It's not been easy for me, either. I never expected to have a child… not for ages yet, but…' He shrugged.

'It's a good thing you're doing, Alexander. Not all men would rise to the challenge like you have. Verity's a lovely child. Her mother has clearly taken good care of her, taught her good manners. And spending time with the twins will soon bring her out of herself a bit more. She'll miss them when you both go back to London.' Rachel thought Alexander gave her a strange look but decided to ignore it. She wondered how long he planned to stay but decided not to ask. She'd wait till Christmas was over. She just hoped he didn't intend to dash off as quickly as he'd done on his last visit. She wanted more time to get to know Verity.

The stockings filled and hanging beside the tree, Alexander poured them another glass of port which they took out to the courtyard. Molly was asleep too, snoring away in her bed by the kitchen door.

It was a lovely summer evening, the moon reflected in the ocean the stars twinkling overhead. 'I miss this,' Alexander said, leaning back in his chair and gazing up at the sky. 'The air's so much cleaner here, softer somehow.'

'Mmm.' Rachel didn't want to spoil the moment by speaking. She loved having Alexander here – and now Verity too – and though tempted to comment, to suggest he might come back home to live, knew it was better to remain silent.

It was Alexander who broke the silence. 'Who's that guy you introduced me to? You said he was your neighbour. I thought Bob Reed was your neighbour. What's happened to him?'

'Bob still is. He's off on some course or other, and Luke's looking after the practice for him. We met when Molly got a tick, and I've been helping him settle in.' Rachel mentally crossed her fingers hoping Alexander wouldn't ask anything more and hadn't noticed the spark between her and Luke of which she'd been very much aware.

He didn't, and Rachel gave a sigh of relief which Alexander took to be tiredness. 'You must want to get to bed, Mum,' he said. He had always been the most caring of her children, even when he was little. The girls used to tease him about it, because although he played pranks on them, he was always caring and sweet to his mother.

'Yes,' she yawned, 'it's been a busy day and another one tomorrow. You have got a gift for Verity, haven't you?' she asked, a sudden fear taking hold.

'Of course, and Anthea left a few things she'd put aside for her too.

She knew she wouldn't last till Christmas and wanted it to be special for Verity.'

Rachel felt her eyes moisten. 'We'll have to make sure that it is, then,' she said. 'Goodnight, my darling.' She hugged Alexander, marvelling yet again that she'd given birth to this tall, handsome creature, and wishing he didn't live so far away, and she saw him more often. Then she went off to bed to dream of another tall, handsome man who lived only a stone's throw away.

Twenty-nine

Rachel was wakened on Christmas morning by squeals of delight. For a moment, she wondered if it was Verity who had somehow transformed overnight from the shy little girl she'd been since she arrived into a regular three-year-old. Then she realised the sounds came from not one, but several voices. Jess and the girls were already here. For the first time since she could remember, Rachel had overslept and on Christmas Day of all days.

After a quick shower, she dressed hurriedly in the orange dress she'd hung outside the wardrobe ready for today. A quick application of makeup and a comb through her hair and she was ready.

'Grandma, finally!' Gemma and Indie yelled in unison, then Gemma added, 'Mum said we could open our stockings but had to wait till you were here for our presents. Look what Santa brought us. And Verity got one too!'

Rachel blinked at the sight of three tiny pink bicycles standing on the living room carpet. They had definitely not been there when she went to bed, and although Santa would have visited the twins at their house… She swivelled round to meet Alexander's eyes. He winked. How had he managed it? But it was definitely a success. Verity was more animated than on the previous two days. Pelican Crossing was working its magic on her. Or was it Molly? Verity did love playing with her. The dog was dashing about among the girls and having a good old time.

'Why don't I fix us some breakfast so we can get started?' she said.

'No need,' Alexander said. 'Steph and Chloe have it covered. He had barely finished speaking when Chloe appeared with a platter of French toast, followed by Steph carrying glasses of orange juice for the girls and buck's fizz for the adults.

'I thought we could have it here,' Chloe said, setting the platter down on the coffee table along with a pile of paper napkins.

'Yum,' the twins said in uncanny unison, each grabbing a piece of toast, while Verity followed more sedately.

'Be careful, girls,' Jess said. 'Sit down while you're eating. Verity could show these two how to behave,' she said to Alexander, who beamed.

It wasn't long before the food disappeared, Rachel turning a blind eye when a chunk of eggy toast was fed to a delighted Molly.

'Can we open our presents now?' Gemma asked, clearly tired of waiting.

'Yes, I think it's time.' Rachel said, smiling with happiness. She loved times like this – her whole family around her, everyone full of joy. The only one missing was Kirk. She forced back the tears which threatened as they always did at moments like this. 'Why don't you and Indie start, Gemma?'

As the presents were duly presented to their owners and the floor became covered in torn Christmas wrappings, someone turned on a playlist of Christmas carols and the house rang with music, laughter and more squeals of delight. Even Verity managed to join in the ruckus, competing with the twins to get Molly's attention, the wily dog managing to evade the little girls' hands.

'Look,' Gemma said, 'there's one present left, on the tree.'

She was pointing to the gift Rachel had wrapped for Molly and purposely put out of Molly's reach, certain the little rascal would sniff it out. Rachel could barely speak for grinning.

'I wonder who it's for,' she said, 'why don't you take it down and have a look?'

With the everyone watching on, Gemma shuffled forward on her knees and reached up to dislodge the gift from its perch.

She turned to face her audience and read from the gift tag. 'It says, *For good girl Molly. Love from Santa.*'

Molly barked upon hearing her name and the twins cheered.

Seconds later, Molly was tearing at the loosely wrapped gift, soon revealing a new multicoloured tugger rope.

'Santa is so thoughtful,' Verity said, playing tug with Molly as the twins cheered them on and Emily giggled at the spectacle.

Buzzing with joy at their antics, Rachel left them to their fun, and went into the kitchen to make a start on lunch, glad she'd already done a lot of the preparation the day before.

'We're all going for a swim, Mum. Do you want to join us?' Steph popped her head into the kitchen. 'Verity's gorgeous. Alexander's very lucky.'

'Isn't he. No news for you on that front?'

'Too early to tell, but Chloe and I have our fingers crossed.' She held up two crossed fingers. 'We'll let you know as soon as we do. Wouldn't it be fun if we had a girl too?'

Rachel chuckled at the thought and hugged her daughter. 'Pandemonium comes to mind,' she said. 'Thanks, but I won't join you. I have a lot to do here.'

'Do you need help? Chloe and I could...'

'No, off you go. Enjoy your brother's company. Who knows when he'll be back now he has Verity to care for.'

'True.' Steph looked as if she wanted to say more. 'See you later, Mum,' she said, hugging Rachel again. 'We'll take Molly,' she added, seemingly as an afterthought.

What was that about? Rachel stared after her daughter, positive there was some hidden agenda, something Steph didn't want her to know. But she'd find out. She always did. None of her children had been able to keep things from her for long.

*

Lunch was almost ready when everyone came in from the beach, the kitchen redolent with the mouth-watering aroma of turkey and all the trimmings of a Christmas lunch which gave no concession to the fact it was close to forty degrees outside. The table in the dining room was set with the plates and napkins which only came out at Christmas and each place was decorated with a piece of artificial holly and a Christmas cracker.

Rachel poured herself a well-earned glass of champagne when the others were showering and changing, knowing it would be her last few minutes of peace that day. Molly, seemingly exhausted by the beach trip, had collapsed onto her bed, only moving when she heard Rachel fill her bowls.

'Wow, don't you all look pretty!' Rachel said, when all four little girls appeared in the kitchen wearing the party dresses which had been in some of the parcels under the tree.

'Thank you, Grandma,' Gemma and Indie yelled together, Emily lispingly joining the chorus.

'Thanks, Grandma,' Verity whispered. She looked lovely in the pale green dress Rachel had chosen for her. It complemented her red curls as the pink dresses complemented Gemma and Indie's blonde locks and the lemon Emily's darker tresses. *They're like a bunch of pretty flowers*, she thought, *my lovely granddaughters*.

The adults appeared as Rachel was taking the turkey out of the oven. 'Let me help,' Alexander said, while the women took the salad makings out of the fridge.

'Thanks, Alexander. You'll need to let it stand for about half an hour. The veggies should be ready by then, and the ham's in the fridge ready to be sliced.'

'I can take charge of drinks, Rachel,' Paul said.

Rachel shot him a grateful look. Paul didn't say much. With a household of four women, even though three of them were children, she supposed he didn't get much of a chance. But he was a good husband and father, and a kind and generous son-in-law.

'Why don't you sit with the children?' Jess said. 'You've been busy all morning. It's time you had a rest.'

'Thanks.' Rachel included both Jess and Paul in her glance, though she wasn't sure how time with the twins would be restful. But it would give her an opportunity to see if Verity had become more outgoing after their trip to the beach.

Rachel went through to the living room with the girls. This time, Molly remained behind, the smell of the turkey too enticing for her to leave the kitchen. 'What shall we do, girls?' she asked, taking a seat on the sofa.

'I know,' Gemma said. 'Can we watch cartoons? Grandma has the

Disney channel,' she told Verity with a sense of superiority. 'What's your favourite?'

Verity appeared puzzled.

'On television,' Indie said helpfully, while Emily played happily with a piece of tinsel which was hanging from the tree.

'I used to watch the nature channel with my mummy,' Verity said at last, making Rachel realise Verity had experienced a very different upbringing to the two terrors.

The twins stared at her for a moment, then Gemma said, 'Our favourite is *Puppy Dog Pals*. Molly likes it too. Can we see that one Grandma? You'll like it, Verity,' she said confidently.

Amused, Rachel turned on the television as requested, while the girls settled themselves on the floor, lying on their stomachs, careless of their new dresses. With her granddaughters engrossed in the antics of the two cartoon dogs, Rachel leant back and closed her eyes, pondering on the fact that this was the first time Verity had mentioned her mother and wondering if it was a good sign. She was almost asleep when Steph came in to tell them lunch was ready.

Verity's eyes widened at the sight of the table when she entered the dining room, and her thumb went to her mouth again, but Rachel was pleased to see her remove it when she caught Gemma staring at her. It was as she'd thought, the twins were good for her.

Lunch went well, the turkey and roast vegetables done to perfection, the ham succulent, and the three women had produced excellent salads. When they had all finished, and even Molly was satisfied with the morsels she'd been fed surreptitiously by the twins, it was Alexander who said, 'Who's up for a game of beach cricket?'

There was a series of groans from all the adults except Paul, who appeared keen, and loud whoops of delight from Gemma and Indie. Verity sent a questioning glance to her dad sitting next to her.

'It's an Australian tradition,' he explained to her. 'After Christmas lunch we all go down to the beach for a game with a bat and a ball. It's a lot of fun. Molly usually joins in and tries to steal the ball.'

Verity's eyes widened again. Rachel could see she was having to learn a lot of new things since coming here, but she seemed to be coping reasonably well. 'You girls had better change from your pretty dresses,' she said. 'You don't want to get them spoiled with sand, and you're most likely going to get wet too.'

As they ran off to change, and the others began to clear the table and load the dishwasher, Rachel thought again how much she enjoyed Christmas, and how lucky she was to have her whole family around her. She just wished… No, she wouldn't get sad about Kirk today. Today was a day for celebration. And she was loving every minute.

Thirty

Lunch in the other house on the bluff was a much more subdued affair. To Luke's delight, the turkey breast Rachel had recommended had been easy to cook and earned compliments from Josh and Abby. He'd chosen to accompany it with roast potatoes and salads which seemed okay too, and to finish with a Christmas pudding he'd bought ready-cooked and served with ice cream. For a first effort, Luke thought he hadn't done too badly, though it was far from Ness's standard.

They'd exchanged gifts before the meal, and Luke was thrilled to receive a year's subscription to a favourite magazine, while both Josh and Abby seemed pleased with Luke's gifts to them, perfume for Abby and a voucher for the craft beer brewery for Josh.

When lunch was over, they took coffee out into the courtyard then, just as Luke was thinking he might take a nap, Josh said, 'Why don't we all go to the beach for a swim?'

Abby was keen, and unwilling to be a wet blanket, Luke agreed too. The young couple were only here for a few days. He should make the most of their time together. Nelson agreed too, emitting a 'Woof'. He'd soon realised that the word *beach* meant *walk* and a chance to play in the ocean. Before long they were all making their way down to the beach.

When they reached the foot of the steps, there were already some people there, and Luke's heart suddenly raced when recognised Rachel and her family.

'Look!' Josh said. 'Isn't that the people we met at the carol singing, the woman you said was your neighbour? Wonder if we can get a game.'

'I don't think…' Luke started to say, but Josh and Abby were already racing across to join the group, followed by Nelson who had no doubt spotted Molly and caught sight of a ball being thrown around.

By the time Luke reached the area where the cricket game was taking place, Josh and Abby had already been absorbed into the group, and Nelson was vying with Molly and the humans to gain possession of the ball. A small child was seated in a pram, and three little girls were building a sandcastle. Rachel was standing to the side watching.

'Merry Christmas!' he said, joining her.

'Merry Christmas!' Rachel smiled and Luke's heart turned over.

Rachel was looking amazing in an orange dress which skimmed her figure. 'You're wearing the earrings,' he said. 'They look good on you.'

Rachel put one hand up to her ear. 'Thanks. I love them. They make me feel like a different person.'

'Not too different, I hope. I like the one I took to dinner.'

Rachel blushed.

'That the rest of your family?' Luke asked, gesturing towards the cricket players and the children on the sand.

'Yes. Alexander and Verity, you've met. The tall man bowling, and the wicket keeper are Paul and Jess, my oldest and her husband. The two women batting are my younger daughter, Steph, and her partner, Chloe. Steph's the one with the short dark hair. She and Alexander take after their father. People say Jess is like me.' She shrugged.

'I can see the resemblance.' Although Jess was younger and slimmer, Luke remembered what Rachel had been like as a teenager. 'And I'm guessing the two building a sandcastle with Verity are the terrible twins you told me about.'

'Gemma and Indie, yes.'

'So, what's the story about Verity? Not exactly the surprise you were expecting?'

Rachel laughed. 'Definitely not, but she's lovely, definitely Alexander's daughter. Her mother died. It's all so sad.'

'Quite a responsibility for your son.'

'Mmm.'

Luke glanced at Rachel who was keeping an eye on her granddaughters while they were speaking. Then he looked across to where Alexander was jumping in the air to catch the ball and shouting, 'Out!' He wondered what the young man was thinking, what his intentions were. It clearly hadn't occurred to Rachel that her son might have a reason for bringing the girl here, other than to spend Christmas with his mother, but he decided not to say anything. It was none of his business. 'I enjoyed the carols last night,' he said. 'I'd forgotten how Pelican Crossing always turned it on for Christmas Eve.'

'It's a very special event. I love it.'

'Thanks for the tip about the turkey, went down a treat.'

'I'm glad. Your son seems like a nice lad and his partner is lovely.'

'Yes, they're only here till the end of the week. What about your crew?'

'Well, Jess and Steph live here. Alexander? Who knows. I haven't been game to ask. But I hope he stays for a bit. I'd like to get to know Verity. She's been through a lot and is very shy with us.'

The game seemed to be winding up. It was time to go back. They hadn't had their swim, but maybe Josh and Abby would be satisfied with the cricket game. Luke wished he could stay here longer with Rachel. Back at Bob's, Josh and Abby would no doubt find something to do, and he'd be left on his own. It would be like it had been in Sydney, feeling awkward in his own home. At least Nelson would keep him company.

'Why don't you all join us?' Rachel asked. 'There's lots of food and a few more people won't make any difference. The more the merrier at this time of year.'

'Are you sure?' Luke couldn't believe his luck. This was a lifesaver… and would give him more time with Rachel too, albeit surrounded by her family. It would give him a chance to see a different side of her – the mother and grandmother.

'Hey, guys,' he yelled to Josh and Abby who were taking their leave of Rachel's family. 'Rachel has invited us back to hers. What do you say?'

*

Rachel saw the astonishment on Jess and Steph's faces. While Alexander had met Luke the previous evening, they hadn't. As far as they were concerned, Josh and Abby were just two strangers who had joined in the game. It happened all the time at Christmas. Luke was an unknown quantity.

'Meet Luke Findlay, guys,' she said. 'He's our neighbour. He's looking after the vet clinic while Bob's off overseas. Josh is his son, and Abby's Josh's partner.' She smiled a welcome to the young couple.

Jess and the others chorused a "hello" to the pair they'd been playing cricket with, and the whole company made their way up the steps to Rachel's house, the youngest members of the party and the two dogs leading the way.

When they arrived home, Alexander took on the role of man of the house and, helped by Paul, poured drinks for everyone, while Jess made sure the children had plastic tumblers of juice. Steph joined Rachel in the kitchen, loading leftover food onto platters which they carried out to the courtyard.

Luke, Josh and Abby were already there, chatting to Chloe with whom Abby seemed to have things in common. It was all very amicable.

As the evening progressed, Luke revealed that he had grown up in Pelican Crossing, leading to the further revelation that he had known Becky – neither he nor Rachel mentioned he had been her sister's boyfriend. This resulted in both Luke and Rachel reminiscing about what the town had been like in what the younger members of the group considered to be the Dark Ages, and everyone had a good laugh at how things had changed – not always for the better.

It was turning dark when Luke and his family rose to leave, the sea roaring on the other side of the bluff, the sky red and orange from the setting sun. Emily had already fallen asleep, and the three little girls were trying hard stifle to their yawns. When Rachel ushered them to the door, Josh and Abby headed off first, leaving Luke to follow with Nelson.

'I'll let you know when they've gone,' Luke said, 'then, maybe…?'

'I'd like that.' Rachel felt her stomach lurch at the prospect of her and Luke alone together. Then he bent his head, and his lips captured hers, more demanding than before, making her wish he didn't have to leave, and her family weren't waiting inside.

Rachel stood in the open doorway waving him off, and when she turned back to go inside, it was to see a small face peering at her.

'Is he your honey, Grandma?' Gemma asked when she joined the others.

Everyone stared at Rachel who felt herself redden. Was that what Luke was? Had the innocent comment of a child revealed what she had tried to hide, even from herself.

Thirty-one

Next day was Boxing Day and, as per tradition, it was Jess's turn to host the family. Rachel awoke early, while Alexander and Verity were still asleep. Pleased the house was silent, she dressed quickly in her swimsuit and a caftan and took Molly out and down to the beach. Once there, she discarded her caftan and leapt into the water, a delighted Molly joining her as she swam out to sea.

The dog soon gave up, returning to the shallows, but Rachel ploughed on, finally turning to float on her back and think about what Gemma had said last night. *Out of the mouths of babes*, she thought. Gemma had seen her and Luke kissing, but even so, it had taken the words of a four-year-old to force Rachel to accept the truth. She was falling for Luke Findlay, for the boy she'd had a crush on at the tender age of fourteen, for her big sister's boyfriend. Of course, it was a long time ago, when they'd been different people. But was the situation any different now? He was only here for a short time. She'd always known that. But she hadn't anticipated the flash of desire that flooded her at his touch, and last night when she'd have given anything to stay in his arms.

The sound of Molly barking brought Rachel back to the present. She turned over and struck out for the beach. Molly was hungry. Alexander and Verity would be awake. It was time to shower and dress, to make breakfast and start the day. There would be time to examine her feelings for Luke – and what to do about them – later, much later.

To Rachel's surprise and delight, Verity was quite chatty over breakfast, asking why Gemma and Indie didn't have a dog. In the short time she'd been there, after her initial strangeness with the dog, she'd become attached to Molly. The feeling was mutual, and Molly was now her faithful follower.

By popular request, Molly accompanied Rachel, Alexander and Verity to Jess's house where she enjoyed the fuss the twins made of her.

Everything went well until lunch was finished, the girls were playing in the yard with Molly, and the adults were relaxing with their preference of wine or coffee.

'Who's Luke Findlay, Mum?' Steph asked.

Rachel felt herself redden. 'What do you mean? I told you who he was.'

'But Gemma's comment last night, about Luke being your honey… That didn't come out of nowhere,' Jess said.

Clutching at straws, Rachel said, 'She may have seen us saying goodbye and misunderstood. Where on earth did she get that term, anyway?' she asked trying to distract her.

'It's my fault,' Chloe said. 'I was trying to describe my relationship with Steph to her and I said Steph was my honey.'

Steph squeezed Chloe's hand and the two smiled at each other.

But Jess wasn't finished. 'It must have been some goodbye,' she said with a grin.

This time, Rachel blushed furiously.

'I thought he was only here for a short time, some sort of locum?' Alexander said.

'That's right. He'll be off back to Sydney at the end of March. So, you see, there's nothing to talk about.'

'A lot can happen in three months.' It was Jess this time, smiling at Paul.

Rachel had forgotten their sudden courtship and marriage.

'There's nothing wrong with your mother having a relationship,' Paul said, much to Rachel's surprise – her son-in-law rarely gave an opinion. 'She's still an attractive woman.'

Rachel didn't know whether to be flattered or insulted at the *still*, but at least he hadn't added *for her age* – though he'd probably thought it.

'I say go for it, Mum.' It was Chloe who spoke next. 'You've been on your own for a long time. It would do you good to have a bit of fun.'

Rachel stared at her. What exactly did she mean? What was she suggesting? Rachel was glad none of the grandchildren were within earshot though if they had been, this conversation might never have taken place.

*

At Bob's house, Luke was experiencing a similar grilling. He had just returned from the clinic where, to his relief, Lady's blood test revealed that the clotting time had improved. There had been no opportunity to question Agnes about his grandparents, but he'd arranged to visit her at her home after the holidays, when she said she'd be happy to chat.

'So, Dad,' Josh said with a grin. 'Looks like you fell on your feet returning to your old stomping ground. Did you and Rachel… back when you were teenagers?' He wiggled his eyebrows.

'Don't be stupid, Josh. Rachel's a lot younger than me. She was only fourteen when…'

'When what?' Josh stared at him.

Luke shifted uncomfortably in his chair, and Nelson rose from where he had been lying at his master's feet, to put his head into Luke's lap. Luke let his hand fall onto the dog's head for comfort. 'When I was dating her sister,' he said with a sigh. They might as well know now. They'd soon find out, Pelican Crossing gossip mill being what it was. According to Troy, there were quite a few still around who were familiar with his history. It wouldn't take much probing for Josh to find out if he tried. And what did it matter now? It was old news.

'Really?' Abby said. 'That's weird. Where's her sister now?'

'In Adelaide… suffering from Alzheimer's sadly.'

'Oh, I'm sorry!'

'Yeah.' Luke sighed. It must be difficult for Rachel. He still hadn't told her that he knew about Becky.

'So, Dad,' Josh said, getting back to his earlier comment, 'you and Rachel. Is it a thing?'

Is it a thing? Where on earth did Josh get a phrase like that? Sometimes he wondered about his son, about young people in general.

'If you mean a relationship, then the answer is "No". Rachel is a neighbour, a good friend. She's good company. We get on well,' he lied.

'Sounds like a thing to me.' Josh grinned. 'I wouldn't blame you. She's not bad looking for someone her age. She must be… what?'

'Fifty-eight.'

'There you go.'

'That's enough, Josh. I don't know how we got started on this.'

'You're too set in your ways, Dad. It's about time you had some fun. Mum's been gone a long time and…'

'Don't bring your mother into this.'

'Josh…' Abby put a hand on his arm. 'Maybe you should let it go.'

Josh looked as if he wanted to say more but seemed to think better of it.

Abby nudged Josh and whispered something.

'Abby and I have something to tell you, Dad,' Josh said, taking Abby's hand in his.

Luke gazed at the pair who were now smiling. Maybe they'd found the money for a deposit, and he could have his home back when he returned to Sydney.

'Abby and I… we're having a baby.'

Luke felt his mouth fall open. He was going to be a grandfather. His first thought was that Ness would have loved to be a grandmother. She'd been denied this privilege.

'Congratulations! When is the happy event?'

Abby glanced at Josh before replying. 'The baby's due in July. We didn't tell you before you left as we wanted to wait till we were sure, but it means…' She looked at Josh again.

Josh cleared his throat. 'It means we may need to stay at the house for longer than we'd planned, Dad. A baby costs money. We had intended to save for a one-bedroom apartment. Now we'll need more room and…'

He didn't need to finish. The family home would be perfect for a young family with a baby. But how would Luke adapt? He tried to hide his shock at this bombshell, knowing that if Ness was alive, she'd be delighted. But she wasn't, and Luke had visions of all the challenges of living with a young baby. He'd done it once, but he'd been younger then, more able to cope with the broken nights and everything else involved. He'd never expected to face it at sixty-two. 'Of course you must stay,' he said.

Thirty-two

The day after Boxing Day, it was as if Christmas had never happened, the only reminder was the large Christmas tree still sitting in the window of the living room, looking very out of place amid Bob's austere furniture.

Luke was still trying to come to terms with the news of the new baby, but neither Josh nor Abby seemed to notice they'd thrown his world into chaos. They were heading back to Sydney today, and although Luke would be sorry to see them go – and sorry they hadn't had the chance to take up Troy's invitation to go sailing – he'd be glad to be alone with Nelson again to digest the news.

The clinic was closed today, and Luke wanted to use his time to visit Agnes. He needed to fulfil his promise to check up on the spaniel… and he wanted to ask Agnes about his grandparents. He was still puzzled as to how they came to be living in Pelican Crossing. Bob's book hadn't provided him with any answers.

Josh had picked up the book and asked why Luke was reading it. On being told he was checking out some family history, the younger man merely shrugged. Luke suspected he'd have had the same reaction at Josh's age. He wished now that he'd asked more questions when he had the chance, before his mother passed away.

Soon after breakfast, the young couple packed up their car and headed off, leaving Luke and Nelson gazing after them.

'How about we go to visit Lady and her mistress?' Luke asked the dog who barked his agreement, sensing an outing was on the cards. A quick call confirmed Agnes was home, and they set off.

Luke entered Agnes's address into his car's satnav. His memory wasn't good enough for him to find his way there unaided, though he remembered spending time by the river as a teenager not far from where she lived. As soon as he reached the gate, he remembered it, remembered how he and his mates had hassled the old woman who hadn't done them any harm. Now he was ashamed of his behaviour. He hoped Agnes hadn't recognised him back then.

Agnes must have heard the car, because she came out to greet them, her white hair streaming out behind her, her skirt trailing in the dust.

'How's Lady?' Luke asked.

'She's good. I've been giving her the tablets, and she seems to be recovering. But she's still a little weak.'

'It'll take some time,' Luke said. 'It's lucky she seems to only have ingested a small amount of the poison.'

Agnes turned pale, the implication of his words clear – a larger dose could have proved fatal. 'So, no more cases?'

Luke shook his head. Another case of poisoning was the last thing he needed.

'That's good. Come on in and you can see Lady. I've been keeping her inside. Your dog can come in too, if he behaves himself.'

Seeming to understand the old woman's words, Nelson stayed close to Luke's side as they entered the old house. Agnes took them into the kitchen, a room which reminded him of Rachel's kitchen, but this one looked as if it hadn't been changed for the past fifty years. Lady was lying in a dog bed beside an old Aga stove. She made an effort to rise when she saw Nelson, who went across to sniff her gently.

'Hey, Lady,' Luke said, crouching down by the dog to examine her. He pushed Nelson away. After a few minutes he got up again. 'You're right,' he said to Agnes. 'She'll be fine now. Just continue to do what you've been doing, and I'll see you both in three weeks' time.'

Agnes beamed. 'I know my birds,' she said. 'Dogs aren't too much different. All creatures need tender care when they're sick. Lady and I have been together for a long time, haven't we, girl?' She leant down to ruffle the dog's ears. 'Now you wanted to have a chat?'

'You said you knew my mother.'

'Sonja? Yes. We went to school together. I travelled in from here and she came from out of town.'

Luke's ears pricked up. *Out of town?* 'Where exactly?'

'Why don't I make us a cup of tea while I gather my thoughts. It was a long time ago.'

'Sure.' Luke took a seat at the worn scrubbed wooden table which looked as if it was as old as Agnes herself, and Nelson, seeming to sense they were going to be there for some time, lay down at his feet, his head on his paws.

Agnes handed Luke a cup of tea with an unfamiliar smell and joined him. He took a sip. It tasted like grass, but he was prepared to do what it took to get the information he wanted.

Agnes took her time before she began to speak. 'Sonja's parents were Italian. They'd migrated after the end of the war. I remember this little girl arriving in my class one day – I must have been around eight or ten. She didn't speak much English, and the teacher asked me to be her buddy. I think they had a market garden or worked in one. I do know they ran a market stall on weekends. Sonja used to help there. I'm afraid that's about all I can tell you. The family moved into town when her parents became older. That's probably how you remember them. They were well thought of by then, though Sonja had to suffer a lot of name-calling at first. It took time for people to forget the war, and the Italians had been the enemy. Those who came before the war were interned, some for years.'

That fitted with what Luke had read. 'Do you know which part of Italy they came from?'

'I'm sorry. Sonja was more interested in her new life in Australia than in talking about where she'd come from. She wanted to fit in, not to be seen as *that Italian kid,* or called a wog. I'm sorry I can't be of more help.'

'Okay, thanks.' Luke sighed. Perhaps he'd never be able to discover any more about his family background. He knew his mother had been proud of her Italian heritage. He'd been christened Luca. It was only when he started school, he'd insisted everyone call him Luke. For the first time he wondered how his mother and grandparents had felt about that. He'd looked up the meaning of his name one day. It meant bringer of light. He liked that.

As he and Nelson made their way back to the car, Luke thought that perhaps he should abandon his search. It seemed he'd hit a brick wall.

Agnes had been able to shed a little more light on his grandparents, but he was still in the dark as to where they had come from or why they'd left. From his reading, and now he knew they had worked in a market garden, it was likely they'd come from the south of Italy. Perhaps he should add an Italian trip to his bucket list. But once there, where would he start? His mother's name had been Sonja Russo, and he suspected Russo was a common surname.

Deciding to focus on the present, as soon as he arrived home, Luke made a booking for dinner on New Year's Eve at the yacht club, before picking up the phone to call Rachel.

*

Luke's call had taken Rachel by surprise. She'd still been mulling over the conversation the previous evening and her own realisation on Christmas Day, so his invitation to dinner on New Year's Eve seemed like a sign. She'd tried to suppress the dizzying current racing through her as Luke suggested they could perhaps finish the evening with a nightcap at Bob's. When the call ended, she felt like a breathless girl of eighteen instead of a boring matron of fifty-eight. *If Luke could make her feel like this with one telephone call, what might it be like to spend the night with him?*

But was she ready for the next step in their relationship? No matter how much she might want Luke, how much her body ached for his touch, she still hesitated. Kirk was the only man she'd ever made love with. She was no longer the slim young woman she'd been when she and Kirk got together. In bed, there would be no shapewear to disguise the bulges, no loose garment to hide the ravages of the years. What if Luke didn't find her attractive, or worse, if he was repulsed by her middle-aged body?

She needed to talk to someone, someone who would understand her misgivings. Her mind immediately went to Poppy again, the one friend with whom she could share her worries, Poppy, who had sensed her attraction to him before she'd acknowledged it herself. Alexander and Verity were spending the day with Jess and the twins, so Rachel picked up the phone to call her friend.

'You just caught me. I was about to go out,' Poppy said breathlessly, when she answered.

Rachel's heart sank. 'Oh, I'm sorry. I was hoping we could catch up.'

There was a pause, then Poppy said, 'I've promised to babysit the twins for Amber while she meets some friends. But if you don't mind two babies.'

Relieved, Rachel laughed. 'Not at all. I'm used to having littlies around, and it'll be good to see Amber's two again. They must be getting big now.'

'Double trouble… according to their mother.'

'Don't I know it. Just wait till they're running around.'

'I can't wait,' Poppy said. 'Amber waited so long for those two. Anyway, you know where Amber lives, and she assured me Jack and Andrew would be ready for a nap. Why don't you come straight over? We can have a coffee and chat while they're asleep.'

'Perfect. I'll see you then.' As she ended the call, Rachel realised Poppy hadn't asked why she wanted to see her. Perhaps her friend had an inkling that it was about Luke.

Rachel was feeling nervous as she drove across town to the house in the new development which Poppy's daughter and her husband had purchased when they knew they were having twins. She hadn't visited this part of town before, but there had been a splash about the development in the local paper when it had first been proposed. Not everyone had been in favour of it, but to Rachel's eyes, it appeared to be a positive addition to Pelican Crossing, with its tree-lined streets and neat gardens. The homes had quickly been snapped up by young couples like Amber and Chris. Today there were several small children playing in the front gardens and a few older ones speeding along the footpath on scooters which were no doubt Christmas presents from doting parents. It wouldn't be long before Gemma and Indie would be demanding them too.

'Come in,' Poppy whispered after the two women had hugged and wished each other Merry Christmas. 'They've just gone down. If we go through to the kitchen, we won't disturb them.'

'This is nice,' Rachel said, entering the kitchen. The house was too modern for her taste, but similar to where Jess and Paul lived, a good spot to bring up children.

'Now, why did you want to see me?' Poppy asked, when they had exchanged news of their respective Christmases and were drinking coffee and nibbling the shortbread biscuits Amber had left out for her mum.

Rachel took a sip of coffee. Now she was here, she didn't know where to start.

'I suspect it's about a man,' Poppy said, smiling gently. 'You know you can ask me anything, and whatever you say will go no further.'

'Thanks, Poppy.' This was another reason she'd chosen Poppy to talk to. Poppy was much like herself in that regard, unlike Liz who had the reputation of being a gossip – not entirely unfounded. 'It's difficult.'

'Try me. I have brought up three girls and lived through their doubts and traumas.'

Rachel smiled at this. She'd had similar experiences with her two, but this was different. 'As you've guessed, it's Luke Findlay. Despite what I may have said in our earlier conversation, I do find him attractive – very attractive. And…' she hesitated.

'Go on. He finds you attractive too, doesn't he?'

Rachel blushed. 'So he says. And… I know he's only here for three months. That hasn't changed. But I've thought about what you said. You're not the only one – Jess and Lou said the same. The thing is, Poppy. He's invited me to dinner on New Year's Eve with the implication that afterwards…'

'And you're worried about…?'

'I've only ever slept with Kirk. We grew old together, accepting the changes in our bodies. What if…' She blushed again, unable to put her concerns into words.

Poppy did it for her. 'You're worried your body's not as young as it used to be.'

'Yes.' She heaved a sigh of relief. She knew Poppy would understand.

'None of us have the body we had in our twenties, Rach. I bet Luke doesn't either. I wouldn't worry if I was you. When Cam and I…' It was her turn to blush. 'Well, let's say there were other things on our mind than what our bodies looked like. I'm sure you'll find the same.'

'Other things?' Rachel found herself asking, though she already knew the answer.

Poppy winked. 'Trust me, Rach. Your curves are gorgeous. No

wonder Luke wants you. Once you, you know, get started, you won't want it ever to stop.'

At least Poppy wasn't going into gory detail, but still, Rachel felt herself burning up inside, imagining being in Luke's bed, imagining her arms folded around him as they...

'And you can always keep the lights off,' Poppy added with a chuckle.

But Rachel wasn't laughing. She was smiling. Suddenly, her worries disappeared at the prospect of those *other things*. 'Thanks, Poppy,' she said.

'My pleasure. And be sure to enjoy it.' She grinned. 'Luke's still pretty hot.'

Rachel grinned. He really was!

Thirty-three

It had been five days since the revelation about Abby's pregnancy, and Luke was still reeling from the shock. While he'd been prepared to share the house with Josh and Abby for however long it took them to save a deposit, the news about the baby had thrown him. He knew what Ness would have suggested and agreed the house was big enough for all of them, that it was a perfect spot for their grandchild to grow up… in the same house as Josh had. But… and that's where Luke's thoughts became stuck.

It was as well the clinic wasn't busy in this period between Christmas and New Year because he hadn't slept well and wasn't on top of his form. Nelson realised something was bothering his master and had been hovering around him more than usual, as if wondering what he could do to help.

Maybe Luke could make a start on his bucket list. But, even if he visited all the places on his list, he would still have to return to a house with a baby in it. He couldn't see any solution.

The one bright spot on the horizon was that, now Christmas was over, he and Rachel could get together again. She had accepted his invitation to the New Year's Eve bash at the yacht club and there was the unspoken agreement that afterwards they'd come back to Bob's and… His heart pounded at the prospect of what might happen afterwards.

He was about to take his lunch break when a distraught man, accompanied by a small boy and carrying a black and white spaniel were ushered into the clinic. One glance at the dog told Luke he was looking at another poisoning. His heart sank.

'It's Bluey,' said the little boy through his tears. 'He's sick. Can you make him better?'

'Let me see what I can do,' he said, taking the dog and placing it on the examination table. 'It's Finn, isn't it?' Luke said, recognising the man as the editor of the local paper who Joe Harris had introduced him to at the fundraiser soon after he arrived in town.

Finn nodded. 'He's been like this all morning. We were at the dog beach yesterday and think he may have eaten something that…' he glanced at the little boy, '… disagreed with him.'

Luke understood. Finn suspected the dog had been poisoned but didn't want to say so in the boy's hearing.

'What's your name?' he asked the boy while he gently examined the dog. 'My name's Luke.'

'I'm Sandy and I'm six. Bluey's only little,' the boy said in a tremulous voice. 'Grandy said you'd make him better.'

'That's what I'm here for. The dog beach?' He raised an eyebrow in Finn's direction. This was too much of a coincidence.

'We spent the day there yesterday. Bluey seemed fine when he got home, but this morning we saw he was bleeding. I thought it best to bring him here.'

'I'm glad you did. I had another very similar case before Christmas. Another spaniel, belonging to old Agnes.'

'Is Lady okay?' Sandy asked, sounding worried.

'She'll be fine now. You know Lady?'

'Bluey and her are friends, and Agnes is my friend too. We meet on the beach, and I've visited her pelicans.'

'Right,' Luke said, amused, despite the seriousness of the situation. 'Well, I think your grandad's right, Sandy. Bluey has eaten something that disagreed with him. But I know how to help him.'

Sandy gave a wobbly smile.

'First I'm going to take a sample of Bluey's blood.'

'Will it hurt?'

Lule shook his head, and the little boy watched anxiously as he took the sample.

'You can test it here?' Finn asked, seeing Luke go towards the adjoining room.

'Luckily Bob installed an up-to-date laboratory. Otherwise, at this time of year…' He shook his head.

'So, I was right?' Finn asked, when Luke returned.

'I fear so. But it looks like we got to Bluey in time.' Luke explained what would happen next as Sandy listened intently.

'Thanks, Mr Luke,' Sandy said when Luke had finished treating the little dog, handed Finn the tablets, and arranged for the follow-up appointment.

'Thanks, Luke,' Finn said, shaking his hand. 'It concerns me that this has happened before… and only a week ago. Do you think it's deliberate?'

'I can't say.' He pulled on his beard. 'I can't imagine anyone in Pelican Crossing wanting to harm dogs.'

'You wouldn't think so, but…' Finn glanced at Sandy who was busy stroking his pet, '… there are a couple of guys… No, I don't think even they would go to this length.'

Luke raised an eyebrow.

'Last year, they wanted to restrict dogs on the beach, claimed it was dangerous to have them running free. We did an article on it, there was a motion at the council. It was defeated, of course. There are a lot of dog owners in Pelican Crossing. But these guys weren't convinced, and they're still around.'

'It's a big step from banning dogs on the beach to poisoning them,' Luke said so quietly Sandy couldn't hear.

'You're right.' Finn appeared relieved. 'But we may have to warn dog owners to take care.'

'Good idea. We don't want to start a panic unnecessarily, but it may be a good idea to have a quiet word with those dog owners you know well. It doesn't do any harm to be careful.' Luke could see Finn was a useful person to know. Joe was too. He might only be here for a short time, but he really should make an effort to get to know these guys better. 'Good to meet you again,' he said, 'Sorry about the circumstances.'

'Likewise. I'll publish a warning in the next issue of *The Echo* but try to play down the risk to avoid panic. Will you be at the New Year's Eve bash at the club tonight? Might see you there.'

'I will.' When Finn and Sandy had left, it occurred to Luke that Finn's partner was a friend of Rachel's.

*

Rachel had a huge knot in her stomach at the thought of spending New Year's Eve with Luke. The annual New Year's bash at the yacht club wasn't like having dinner there on a regular evening or even on a Saturday. On New Year's Eve, all her friends would be there with their partners, as would Jess and Steph. It was a big deal and one she wasn't sure she was ready for.

As she surveyed the contents of her wardrobe, she wondered if this was all a mistake, if she'd allowed herself to be carried away with the idea of Luke, rather than the reality.

'That one's pretty, Grandma.' The little voice coming from the doorway was a shock. Rachel had forgotten about Alexander and Verity, forgotten she wasn't alone in the house. She turned, the blue dress in her hand, to see the little girl standing there, ready to flee at the least sign she wasn't wanted.

'Do you think so?'

Verity nodded. 'My mummy had a dress like that.' Her eyes filled with tears.

'Oh, my darling!' Rachel pulled her into a hug. 'I'm going to a special party tonight and trying to decide what to wear.' She picked up the dress and held it against her. 'I think you're right. This is the one.'

'Daddy's taking me to see the fireworks. He said Molly can't come.'

'No, the noise and flashes frighten her. She'll be happier here at home.' Rachel knew Verity was referring to the early fireworks display for families at eight o'clock. There would be another at midnight, then… She knew Luke expected her to go home with him, but she still wasn't sure about it, despite Poppy's reassurance.

Once dressed, and wearing the earrings Luke had given her for Christmas, she headed to the kitchen where Alexander was fixing dinner for himself and Verity. To Rachel's surprise, he was proving to be handy around the house and a fairly competent cook. She supposed he'd had to be, living alone in London.

'You look great, Mum,' he said. 'I've fed Molly, so no need for you to worry. Enjoy yourself tonight. The start of a new year is always a good time to reflect.'

Rachel stared at her son as if by doing so she could discern what he was thinking. But as usual, Alexander was a closed book. He and Verity had been here for over a week now and he'd given no indication of when they planned to leave. He'd already stayed longer than last time.

The knock on the door startled her. Molly hadn't given her usual warning of someone arriving. 'Enjoy the fireworks,' she said hugging both Alexander and Verity before picking up her bag and going to the door.

'You're looking lovely.' Luke greeted Rachel with a kiss on the cheek which sent her heart racing, 'and you smell delicious.'

Rachel glowed. Steph and Chloe had given her a new – and expensive – bottle of perfume for Christmas and this was the first time she'd worn it. The fragrance made her feel confident, attractive, and Luke's words made her feel as if she was walking on air.

When they entered the yacht club, the first people Rachel saw were Poppy and Liz. They, along with Cam and Finn, were standing just inside the door as if they were waiting for someone. They were.

'Here they are,' Liz said, coming over to give Rachel a hug. 'Finn said you and Luke were coming tonight, so we've arranged for us all to sit together.'

Rachel glanced at Luke. From his expression this was news to him too, but it might not be all bad. It would prevent any awkwardness and there could be no intimate *tête-á tête*. 'How lovely,' she said. 'Are Gill and Joe here too?'

'They won't be joining us,' Poppy said. 'They've been caught up with some local dignitaries. The challenges of being mayor.' She grimaced.

Rachel was glad of her friends' company as they took their places, feeling all eyes on her and Luke. She wondered how many knew who he was, besides being Bob's locum. Were those who recognised him, who remembered him and Becky, comparing her to her sister?

'No one cares,' Poppy whispered to her, when they were all seated. 'You'd be surprised how many are more concerned with what's on the menu tonight than with who you're with or who Luke is.'

Rachel gave her friend a grateful smile and hoped she was right.

Since it was a special evening, a local trio had been commissioned to provide background music, setting the mood and making Rachel wish they could dance, and she could feel Luke's arms around her.

Instead she had to be satisfied with his shoulder brushing against hers and the occasional touch of his hand.

It was a happy evening. Rachel had all but forgotten what it was like to be out in company as part of a couple. It reminded of her of when Kirk was alive, but then, both Poppy and Liz had been with different partners too. She wondered if they had similar thoughts. Looking at them, she doubted it. They seemed happy, satisfied with their lives. But she knew life hadn't been easy for either of them, and that reminder gave her hope, though for what she wasn't quite sure.

After a sumptuous seafood meal, followed by individual servings of coconut, pannacotta and raspberry trifle and washed down with a delightful white wine, Rachel glanced around the room to see Jess and Paul, and Steph and Chloe. They were seated at different tables with friends, Steph and Chloe with Denny and Ron from *Books and Coffee*. It crossed Rachel's mind to wonder for a moment which of the two young men had fathered Steph's child, and if she was pregnant. She knew she'd never ask, realising she was becoming good at keeping her curiosity about her children's lives to herself.

She tuned back into the conversation to hear Luke ask Finn about Bluey, and Poppy looking concerned. She knew the spaniel belonged to Finn's grandson. 'Is something the matter with Bluey?' she asked.

Luke frowned. 'I was going to tell you later. Finn and Sandy brought him into the clinic today. It looks as if he's been poisoned.'

'And he's not the first,' Poppy said.

Rachel looked back at Luke.

'Old Agnes brought her spaniel in before Christmas. I thought it was a one-off, but this…' He shook his head. 'They were both on the dog beach. It's best to keep away from it for the time being. I've suggested Finn drop a word to all the dog owners he knows, and he's going to print a warning in the local paper.'

'The paper?' Rachel asked. 'We don't want to start a panic.'

'Luke knows what he's doing, Rach,' Poppy said. 'Let's hope it's only these two… and there's no permanent damage.'

Rachel fell silent, but the shine had been taken off the evening for her. She was glad she never took Molly to the dog beach, but so many others did. What if…?

'Don't worry.' Luke squeezed her hand. 'We're doing what we can, and hopefully there won't be any more cases.'

Rachel felt reassured, but wished she'd known earlier, that Luke had seen fit to tell her about Agnes. Then she realised that this was the first time she'd seen him since then, apart from Christmas Day when they'd been surrounded by both their families.

The music suddenly became louder then stopped, and the countdown to midnight began. Without their being aware of it, waiters had been delivering glasses of champagne to all the tables. Now, everyone stood, glasses in hands, joining in the chant till the room erupted in shouts of Happy New Year.

Rachel found herself enfolded in Luke's arms, his lips on hers, her heart exploding with happiness as there was a burst of fireworks outside.

After this, she didn't have to think twice before agreeing, when Luke slowed the car outside Bob's house. They tiptoed in, giggling like a pair of teenagers, so as not to waken Nelson, and made their way to the bedroom falling onto the bed and into each other's arms.

'You're a special girl, Red,' Luke said, kissing her nose, her lips, her chin…

'Girl?' She chuckled, her heart pounding as he kissed her neck. 'Old girl maybe.'

'*My* old girl,' Luke said, dropping a kiss on her shoulder, her arm, then on her breast through the fabric of her dress. She shivered, amazed at the sparks flying through her. 'Let's get you out of this,' he said.

Rachel didn't object when he helped her off with her dress. And she didn't object that the bedside light remained on. Instead, she revelled in his warm and gentle touch; revelled in the way they moved as one.

Afterwards, Rachel didn't know what she'd been worried about. Luke would still be leaving in three months' time but, as Lou, Poppy – even Jess – had said, a lot could happen in three months, and she intended to make the most of every minute of it.

Thirty-four

Waking up in Luke's bed was a novel experience. At first, Rachel didn't know where she was. Then it came back to her – dinner, the fireworks, Luke's kiss, sneaking into the house then making love. It had been so long – for both of them. So much suppressed emotion, so many lonely nights. She looked at the man sleeping beside her, unable to believe that after all these years, she had made love with Luke Findlay.

It was still early, the sun only just peeping through the venetian blinds. Rachel was tempted to cuddle up again against Luke's warm body, but knew she needed to move. She pushed herself up, only to see Luke's eyes open.

'Where are you going?' he asked in a sleepy voice.

'I can't stay. I...' But she didn't resist when he pulled her into his arms. It felt so right to snuggle up to him. She remembered the previous night, their sense of urgency, the way their bodies had melded into one, how tender Luke had been, how he'd made her feel young again. For a few moments, Rachel allowed herself to sink into his embrace, then she remembered. There was Molly to look after, Alexander and Verity. *What would Alexander think about his mother staying out overnight?*

'I'm sorry, Luke. I need to go home.' She pulled away.

'I'm sorry too, but I understand.' He sat up and dragged a hand though his hair. 'I'll drive you.'

'No need. I can walk across the bluff.'

'In those shoes you wore last night? I don't think so.'

Rachel looked across the bedroom floor to where the high heeled sandals she'd worn to the yacht club were lying, alongside the heap of her and Luke's clothing which they'd discarded hurriedly, overtaken by their need for each other.

'Oh!' she said blushing at the memory.

'Give me a few minutes to get dressed, let Nelson out and fill his bowls, and you might want to do something about…' He ran his fingers through her hair, making her realise how dishevelled she must look. 'I love your morning-after appearance, but your son might get a shock.'

Rachel grinned. 'You're right, I'll have a quick shower too, if I may.' She could imagine what the night must had done to her carefully applied makeup.

'Of course. Help yourself.' He gestured to the ensuite.

When Rachel joined Luke in the kitchen, Nelson was tucking into his breakfast and Luke was dressed in shorts and a tee-shirt, his hair wet from the shower which he must have taken in the other bathroom.

'Good morning again, beautiful. Happy New Year!'

'Didn't we say that last night?'

'In oh so many ways.' He grinned.

Rachel blushed.

'Ready to go?'

She nodded, hoping she'd be back before Alexander and Verity were awake.

It was a forlorn hope. Verity and Molly came running towards Luke's car as soon as she opened the door. 'Did you see the fireworks last night, Grandma? We watched from the beach, but we left Molly inside. They were so many colours. It was like a giant 'splosion and made a lot of noise.

'Sounds lovely, darling. Yes, I saw them too,' Rachel said to Verity with a forced smile, her heart sinking. 'Thanks,' she whispered to Luke.

'Wait,' he said. 'Can I see you tonight?'

Rachel wanted to say "yes" with every fibre of her being, but, 'Oh, Luke, I'd love to, but we're having dinner with Steph and Chloe tonight. I'm sorry.' Her disappointment was mirrored in his face, giving her a frisson of pleasure.

'When then?'

Rachel could see Verity hopping impatiently from one foot to the other as she waited for her to get out of the car. 'I don't know. It's difficult… with Alexander and Verity…'

'Why don't you all come to dinner tomorrow?'

Rachel hesitated. 'Can I let you know?' Rachel had no idea how Alexander was going to react. There was no reason for him to be annoyed, not even surprised, so why did she feel like a teenager about to face a disapproving parent?

'Sure.'

Luke kissed her gently, then Rachel followed Verity and Molly inside and into the kitchen where Alexander was making coffee and pancakes.

'I remembered you always used to make us pancakes on New Year's morning,' he said, 'and Verity loves them. Have a good evening?' He winked.

'Yes, thanks. I'll just go and get changed.' Rachel hurried into her bedroom before she blushed again. She was too old for this – though last night had proved that she wasn't. She smiled as she remembered how good it had felt to be desired by a man again.

When she joined them, Verity was pouring maple syrup onto a large pancake, while Molly was bouncing around her chair – she had certainly recovered from her tick. Alexander was looked frazzled and pouring himself coffee.

'Mum,' he said with relief, 'pancakes are ready. Coffee for you?'

'Yes please.' Although Rachel normally preferred her herbal tea at this time of the morning, today coffee sounded good. She gratefully accepted the proffered cup, took a seat beside Verity and helped herself to two pancakes, after rescuing the maple syrup container from Verity who seemed about to empty it over her breakfast.

Alexander seemed flustered was when he finally joined them.

'What did you have for dinner last night?' she asked.

'Pizza,' Verity said with glee before Alexander could speak.

Rachel glanced at her son. Maybe she'd been wrong in thinking he was a competent cook. She wondered how he was going to cope with Verity when they returned to England. They couldn't live on pancakes and pizza and, while he'd assured her he was accustomed to looking after himself, caring for a three-year-old was a different kettle of fish.

'Luke has invited us to dinner tomorrow,' she said, forking up a piece of pancake. 'I said I'd let him know.'

'Can Molly come?' Verity wanted to know. She had become so

attached to Molly, Rachel could predict she'd be asking Alexander to get a dog when they went back home.

'Yes,' Rachel replied. 'Luke has a dog too. A big dog called Nelson. Remember he was here on Christmas Day? He and Molly are friends.'

'Are you sure he wants us to come, Mum?' Alexander said awkwardly. 'I mean… he's *your* friend.'

'And he wants to meet you again. I'd like you to join us. It was kind of him to invite you.'

Alexander sighed. 'Okay, Mum. You do remember we're having dinner with Steph and Chloe tonight?'

'Of course. They always have the family over on New Year's Day.' She wondered again if there was any news yet, or if it was too soon. Steph certainly hadn't given any indication at Christmas, but Rachel had noted she'd avoided alcohol. She wondered if Steph and Chloe had shared their plans with Jess, and thought it likely they had, but probably not with Alexander. It seemed he'd had as little difficulty in making Anthea pregnant as Jess had becoming pregnant with her three. Hopefully it would be the same for Steph.

'She called,' Alexander said.

'Oh!'

'I told her you hadn't come home yet.'

Rachel flinched. Now Steph knew, Jess would too. She shouldn't have stayed overnight at Luke's while Alexander and Verity were still here, but last night had been so…

'She wants you to call her.'

'Right.' Rachel flinched. Was this going to about her staying overnight with Luke?

She waited till breakfast was over and Alexander and Verity had gone to the beach with Molly, before calling Steph.

'Oh, Mum, I'm so glad you called,' Steph said, then instead of commenting on Rachel and Luke, said excitedly, 'We plan to announce it tonight, but wanted you to be the first to know…'

Rachel felt a bubble of happiness well up.

'We're pregnant! I did the test last night after we got home from the club. We're going to have a baby!'

'Oh, my darling. Congratulations! I'm so happy for you,' Rachel said, again overcome with emotion. She patted her eyes which had filled with tears.

*

When Rachel, Alexander and Verity arrived at Steph and Chloe's townhouse, Jess and her family were already there. The twins were running around as usual and were disappointed Rachel had left Molly at home. Verity had wanted her to bring the dog, but Rachel decided four children and a dog would be too much for Steph and Chloe's townhouse, which was a lot smaller than Rachel and Jess's homes.

Before leaving home, Rachel had popped the baby gift into her bag. It was a tiny koala onesie complete with hood and ears. She'd been keeping it till there was news. Steph's eyes were bright with excitement as she greeted her mother with a hug. Chloe wasn't far behind her. 'Isn't she clever,' Chloe whispered to Rachel. 'First time!'

The others came forward to greet the newcomers before Rachel could respond, any reply she might have made drowned out by the twin's exuberant welcome. She was pleased to see Verity allowing herself to be dragged away by them, with only a slight backward glance at her dad.

Steph and Chloe waited till the meal was over – a vegetarian korma of sweet potato, cauliflower and chickpeas, served over cauliflower rice, accompanied by a green salad and followed by a delicious pavlova. Then, having filled everyone's glasses with prosecco, the two women stood up. 'We have news,' Chloe said, before turning to Steph who clasped her partner's hand. 'We're having a baby,' Steph announced.

'Congratulations, what a wonderful start to the year, 'Rachel said, her eyes moistening again.

'Congratulations,' said Jess and Paul together. 'That'll slow you down,' Jess added, 'but what wonderful news.'

Rachel fished her gift out of her bag. 'Baby's first gift,' she said with a smile.

'You knew!' Jess accused her.

'Only today,' Rachel smiled. 'I do believe I was the first to know about your pregnancies too.'

'Apart from Paul,' Jess said, giving her husband an affectionate glance.

'Oh, this is so cute,' Steph said, holding up the tiny outfit so everyone could see.

'We're going to have another cousin,' Gemma said, the twins realising the implication of the news. 'When will it be born, and will it be a boy or a girl?'

'We don't know yet, Gemma. I only did the test yesterday,' Steph said, turning to the others. 'I didn't really expect it to be positive.'

'The father?' Jess asked, when the younger members of the group had lost interest.

Steph and Chloe glanced at each other, then Steph said, 'Denny from *Books and Coffee*.'

Rachel nodded. He was a good choice with his blond Scandinavian looks. He and Steph would make a beautiful baby.

'Let's drink to the new member of the family,' Paul said, reminding everyone they had been so busy talking they had forgotten to raise their glasses. 'To Steph and Chloe's baby, to the new year, and to new beginnings,' he said, as they all raised their glasses in a toast.

'And how about you, Mum?' Steph said, when their glasses were empty, and Chloe had disappeared to make coffee.

'Me?' Rachel pretended ignorance, but she knew what was coming.

'Where were you when I called at seven o'clock this morning? As if we didn't know.' She grinned and winked.

Rachel had no idea what to say, so she said nothing.

It was Jess who rescued her. 'It's okay, Mum. We approve. It's time you did something for yourself. You've kept so busy since Dad died – and I haven't helped, dumping the twins and Emily on you so often. No,' she said as Rachel opened her mouth to object, 'I know you love having them, but it was an imposition. I knew you'd always be available. And, even if nothing comes of this thing with your old flame. Sorry, he was Aunt Becky's old flame, wasn't he?' She chuckled. 'If nothing comes of it,' she repeated, 'it will give you something to look back on in your old age.' She chuckled again.

Rachel wanted to throw something at her daughter, at both of them, as Steph chuckled too.

Rachel looked at Alexander for support, but he was busy organising the children who, tired of the adult talk, wanted to watch something on television.

'Leave it, Jess,' Paul said, coming to Rachel's rescue. 'They're only teasing, Rachel. We're all pleased you have a man friend who…' He ran out of words.

'We're happy for you, Mum,' Steph said. 'We want you to know that, and to know that whatever you do, we love you.'

'Thanks… I think,' Rachel said. She picked up her glass to hide her confusion, but it was empty.

Luckily, Chloe appeared with coffee for everyone, and the conversation changed. But, despite the teasing, her daughters' words had left Rachel with a warm glow. It was true she'd been on her own for a long time and had managed to fill her life, but there had always been an empty space – a man-sized empty space. And if Luke could fill it, even for a short time, she knew she'd be a fool to reject the happiness he could offer.

Thirty-five

Despite spending his days in the clinic, for Luke it was as if every day was Christmas, as he and Rachel managed to spend more time together and became closer. To his surprise the clinic hadn't become busier after Christmas and New Year, and to his relief there had been no further cases of poisonings. As a result, he'd been closing up at lunchtime and meeting Rachel on the beach for a swim or a walk, or sometimes just to talk before heading back to Bob's. But after New Year's Eve, she'd been careful not to spend the night there. He knew it would be hard to leave her when the time came for him to return to Sydney. But they had both decided not to discuss that and to enjoy what time they did have together.

Today, he'd made arrangements to meet Finn and Joe for lunch at *The Grand*, as part of his decision to get to know them better. Finn had been as good as his word and his warning about the beach in *The Echo* had been worded in such a way as to avoid any panic while, hopefully, ensuring dog owners took more care and kept an eye on their animals on the beach.

The two men were already there when Luke arrived. He ordered one of the craft beers he'd developed a taste for and joined them to discover they were discussing the poisonings.

'I've been having a good look around when I take Coco to the beach,' Joe said, 'but haven't seen anything out of the ordinary.'

'Coco?' Luke asked, taking a welcome sip of beer.

'My chocolate lab. We go to the beach a lot, but since Finn told me about Lady and Bluey, I've been a lot more careful. Do you think it may have been something that washed up?'

'It was definitely rat poison,' Luke said, 'but we may have seen the last of it. If it was done deliberately, your article may have scared off whoever was responsible.'

'Coatts and Small?' Finn asked Joe.

Luke was puzzled.

'Two councillors who tried to ban unrestrained dogs on the beach last year,' Joe said. 'But I don't think even they would go as far as to poison them.'

Luke remembered Finn mentioning something about this. He shook his head. 'The courts take cruelty to animals seriously. I seem to recall the penalties in Queensland can amount to jail time.'

'Let's hope it doesn't come to that, much as I'd like to be rid of them from the council,' Joe grimaced. 'Now, pie and chips for everyone? My treat.'

After a bit of disagreement with both Finn and Luke offering to pay, Joe made his way to the bar to order.

'Good to see you again, under more favourable circumstances,' Finn said. 'Sandy was relieved the second blood test showed a good result. He's very attached to Bluey. The little dog managed to help him recover from his grief after his dad died. Sandy saw him drown and it made him terrified of the sea. It took Bluey to give him the confidence to take his first few step… him, old Agnes, and Lady.'

'Wow. I saw Agnes and Lady this morning, by the way. She's going to be fine. I expect Bluey to be the same when you bring him in next week.'

'Good man.'

Joe returned, a waiter following him with three plates of food.

'This takes me back,' Luke said. 'Pie and chips in *The Grand*, washed down with beer, though back in the day it wasn't craft beer we'd be drinking.'

'Still not for me,' Finn said, holding up his glass of the more traditional brew.

'So,' Joe said, 'How are you enjoying being back in Pelican Crossing, Luke? You've had time to get used to it now.'

'I'm enjoying it more than I expected,' Luke said, surprised to realise it was true… and not only because of Rachel. He had slipped back into the more laid-back lifestyle of the small coastal town and some days it felt as if he'd never been away.

'You'd not think of staying?' Joe asked. 'I hear that you and Rachel…'

'No, mate. This is a temporary thing, a favour for a colleague. My life's in Sydney these days. Rachel understands that.'

'Hmm,' Joe said. 'I'll never understand the way women think but I do know one thing, they don't comprehend the meaning of temporary.' He chuckled.

Luke took another sip of beer and forked up a couple of chips. Was Joe right? Had he misinterpreted Rachel's acceptance that what they had was only for the time he was here? It had never occurred to him she might be hoping for more. He couldn't uproot his life, move here, return to this place he'd been so happy to leave. Then he thought about what waited for him in Sydney. He sighed. 'Hope you're wrong, mate.'

*

While the three men were having beer with pie and chips at *The Grand*, Rachel and her three friends were enjoying a healthier meal. It was Poppy's turn to host the group and, although she was loath to leave Alexander and Verity, Rachel knew she couldn't let her friends down. There was also the risk that if she didn't go, they might talk about her… about her and Luke.

Rachel loved visiting Poppy's house, the one she and Jack had built on the top of the cliff, glad her friend hadn't felt the need to move when she and Cam got together. She wasn't sure how *she'd* feel bringing another man into the home she and Kirk had shared. Stop right there, she told herself, knowing there was no likelihood of that happening. But she knew, deep in her heart, how much she'd miss Luke when he went back to Sydney. She'd allowed herself to become more involved with him than she'd intended. But there were still several weeks left, she reminded herself.

'You're first,' Poppy said, greeting her with a hug, while Poppy's little dog, Angus, a male version of Molly, sniffed at her ankles. 'Wine?' she asked, taking a bottle out of the fridge.

'Thanks, Poppy.' Rachel accepted the brimming glass – no careful measures in this house – and the two women carried their drinks out to the deck where Poppy had set a table for lunch.

'How is everything?' Poppy asked, when they had both taken a sip of the cooling wine. 'Alexander and Verity still with you?'

'They are,' Rachel said. 'I'm afraid to ask him when he's going to leave. It's so lovely to have them both with me. But I have guests booked in from Saturday week so it could be a bit of a crush.' She grimaced and took another sip of wine.

'Have you considered…' Poppy began but was interrupted by a knock on the door and she hurried off to answer it, Angus at her heels.

She returned, followed by Liz and Gill, and in the flurry of greetings and hugs, Poppy's words were forgotten.

As usual, Liz was eager to report the gossip – there had been a break-in at a local pharmacy, the high school had discovered a boy trying to sell drugs, and *The Haven*, the retirement village where Liz's mother lived, was planning an extension. The report in the paper of the poisonings was a concern to all four women. Both Rachel and Poppy were dog owners and, although Liz and Gill didn't own dogs themselves, Gill had become very attached to Joe's dog, Coco, and Liz to Bluey, Finn's grandson's dog.

'What have you heard from Luke?' Liz asked Rachel.

'Nothing more than you've read in the paper. There haven't been any more cases. It looks as if it might have been bits of the same substance both Lady and Bluey have eaten.'

'Let's hope so.' Poppy shuddered. 'Your Molly's safe on your beach, but the rest of us have always used the dog beach. I still go there but I keep a strict eye on Angus and worry all the time.'

'I know Finn does too, and always makes sure either he or Adele are with Sandy,' Liz said.

'Joe, too,' Gill added.

When Poppy brought out the lunch – a large spinach and ricotta quiche with a couple of colourful salads – the topic of conversation moved to children and grandchildren. After Liz proudly reported on the surfing success of the granddaughter she'd only discovered earlier that year, she turned to Rachel. 'Your twins will be starting school soon, won't they?'

Rachel flinched. She'd been trying to forget that she'd no longer have their company several afternoons each week. 'I'll still have Emily,' she said, 'but I will miss their chatter. They're such good company, and Molly loves them.' She thought Poppy gave her an odd look, but decided she was imagining it. 'Anyway, I have no doubt Jess will call on me to pick them up from school on the days I used to look after them. It just means a change to my routine. What about Mandy, Liz? Her baby must be due soon.'

'Any day now,' Liz said. 'I can't wait. I know I now have Tilly, but I didn't know her as a baby. And…' she beamed, 'Gary and Mandy plan to get married. I wish they'd do it before the birth, but I guess we can't have everything we want.'

'Oh, congratulations!' Gill and Rachel said in unison, and Poppy followed suit.

'No news about Freya?' Rachel asked, knowing Gill's daughter was taking up a teaching position in a university in Sydney sometime soon.

'She'll be off in a few days, then…' She threw her hands in the air. 'But at least she's in Australia.'

'Mmm.' Rachel knew that when Freya returned to Pelican Crossing the previous August, Gill had hoped she'd stay, might even have had hopes of her forming a relationship with Rory Whittaker, Gary's brother.

'Aren't we lucky,' Poppy said. 'All of our children are happy. Those who have married have chosen well, and three of us have grandchildren to spoil. I think we should drink to that.'

'Hear, hear,' Liz said, as they all raised their glasses.

Rachel was about to sigh with relief, that nothing had been said about her and Luke, when Liz stared at her.

'What about you and our vet?' she asked. 'Is he still planning to return to Sydney? You've been very quiet about him, but a little bird tells me…' She tapped the side of her nose with one finger.

Rachel felt herself blush. She should have known Liz would make some comment. Despite having curtailed her hurtful comments when she was in a similar situation with Finn, she had quickly reverted to her usual form. 'Yes, we've been seeing each other, and yes he'll be returning to Sydney. I always knew he would, but I decided to take the advice I was given.' She let her eyes wander around the group. 'After all, half a loaf is better than no bread,' she attempted to joke, only to see three pairs of eyes fill with concern. 'I'm fine with it, really. Now, can we talk about something else?'

To Rachel's relief, Poppy steered the conversation in a different direction, giving her time to regain her composure. She drained her glass and pretended to be interested in what the others were saying, but she was glad when it was time to leave. As she drove home, all she could think of was how empty her life was going to be once Alexander and Verity returned to London, and Luke went back to Sydney.

Thirty-six

On Saturday morning, Rachel was checking her bookings and trying to work out what she needed to do before her guests arrived the following week. She wanted to get it done before lunch as Jess was bringing the twins round to play with Verity in the afternoon while she took Emily to a birthday party. They'd miss Verity too, when she left, though school started next week, and they were excited about that.

'Mum, can we talk?' Alexander popped his head into the study where Rachel was struggling with the computer which was refusing to cooperate.

She looked up. This was it. He was going to tell her they were leaving. 'Sure,' she said, glad of a break. 'Why don't we have a cup of coffee? Where's Verity?'

'She and Molly are in the yard.'

'Okay.'

'You're going to tell me you're leaving,' she said, trying to sound calm, when they were seated in the courtyard with coffee and the remains of the Christmas cake. Verity had already had a piece and a glass of milk and had scampered off to play with Molly again.

Alexander pushed back his hair, a habit he'd developed in childhood when he knew he was going to be in trouble. 'It's been great… you've been great, but I need to get back. There's my job, and… I need to earn a living. I've booked my flight for Wednesday.'

Rachel was about to made soothing noises, say it was okay, that she hoped he'd bring Verity back soon, when she realised he'd said "my flight" not "our flights". She stared at him, her eyes widening, a cold chill in her stomach. 'What about Verity?' she asked, looking across the yard to where the little girl was playing happily with the dog.

'Ah…' He looked sheepish. 'Mum. Much as I love her, I can't… My life…' he pushed back his hair again, '… it wouldn't work. She loves you… and Molly, the twins, loves being here. I'll visit…'

'You're her father.' It was all Rachel could think of to say. She'd seen how the little girl clung to him when they first arrived. And, although she had now warmed to Rachel and the other family members, it was Alexander she looked to, his lap she curled up in when she was tired, his arms she wanted around her when she was upset, he who soothed her when she awoke and cried in the night. 'I thought you told ne you'd promised her mother you would take care of her?'

'I promised Anthea she'd have a home, and she will have, here with you. She'll have the same loving home I grew up in, plus aunts and cousins. She'd have none of that in London. And I'll come back more often. I promise.'

In a blinding moment, Rachel understood the strange looks, the half-finished phrases both Poppy and Jess had been guilty of. Had they known… or guessed? 'Who else knew your plan?'

'No one.' But Alexander looked guilty. 'I think Jess may have guessed,' he said, shifting uncomfortably in his seat. 'She wanted to know a lot about my life in London.'

'Well, I certainly didn't expect this.'

'But you will… give her a home?' he pleaded.

Rachel was conflicted, various scenarios playing out in her mind. She loved Verity, would miss the twins when they started school, but she had never contemplated taking care of a young child on a permanent basis. She looked at Alexander, remembering how, as a small boy and a teenager, he'd always managed to get around her objections, always got his own way, and sighed. 'Of course I will.' How could she refuse to take in her own granddaughter? 'Have you told her?'

Alexander looked awkward again. 'I was hoping…'

'No! I'm sorry, Alexander, but Verity is your daughter. You're the one who has to tell her but do it gently. She's still very vulnerable. She only recently lost her mother. Now she's going to lose her father too.'

Alexander flinched. 'It's hard for me too, but I haven't been much of a father to her.' He stared down at the pavers.

'I disagree. You stepped up when Anthea contacted you. Many men wouldn't have taken responsibility. And you brought her here, to a home where you knew she'd be welcomed and loved, find a family.'

'Thanks, Mum.' Alexander's voice was subdued.

'But you can't hand Verity over like a parcel. You need to talk to her, tell her you love her, that we all love her, explain in words she can understand how she can't live with you, why she will be staying here with me, and promise to visit often. And do it today to give her time to get used to the idea before you head off.'

'Thanks, Mum,' Alexander repeated, beaming with the smile that had managed to get him out of trouble for most of his childhood. 'But I need time to prepare what I'm going to say.'

And I need time to come to terms with the fact that I'm about to become sole carer for a three-year-old. Rachel had thought she was past all that, happy to look after the twins and Emily, and equally happy to hand them back to their mother. 'The twins will be here this afternoon,' she said. 'Best wait till after they've gone. Perhaps you could take her for a walk on the beach. Everything always seems easier down there.'

'Okay, Mum. Thanks.' Alexander rose and kissed Rachel. 'Wish Dad was here.'

'I do too.' Suddenly a wave of grief welled up in Rachel for the man who had always been by her side, the man who would have torn strips off Alexander then pulled him into a warm hug, who'd have been here to help her with this unexpected blessing. For, Rachel realised, it was a blessing to have the care and nurture of this lovely little girl at this stage of her life.

*

The afternoon proved riotous at usual, with the girls attempting to dress Molly in some doll's clothes and the wily little dog managing to escape their clutches. When Jess arrived to pick up the twins, she didn't seem to be as rushed as usual, and Rachel was able to persuade her to sit down for a cuppa. Alexander chose this time to suggest a walk on the beach to Verity and, with hugs and promises to see the twins soon, Verity agreed.

When the pair had disappeared down the steps to the beach, and the twins and Emily were happily sitting on the grass with milk and biscuits… and a hopeful Molly, Rachel took the opportunity to talk with her daughter. 'Did you know what Alexander was planning?' she asked.

The tips of Jess's ears turned red. 'Not exactly,' she said, 'but I had an inkling. He's not cut out to look after a little girl like Verity, Mum. She'll be much better here in Pelican Crossing with you.'

'Hmm.' While Rachel couldn't dispute Jess's assessment of the situation, she couldn't help but be annoyed with Alexander, and feel sorry for Verity. She gazed down at the beach to where the two figures were standing at the edge of the ocean, and wondered what he was saying to his daughter, how he was explaining he was about to leave her here. As she watched, she saw the little girl throw herself against his legs, her arms clasping him tightly. It didn't augur well.

Rachel and Jess chatted a little more, then the girls became restless, Molly left them to join Rachel, and Jess rose. 'We need to go now, Mum. It'll be fine. You'll see. Are you going to have a farewell dinner for Alexander?'

'I suppose.' Though she didn't feel he deserved one after his announcement, Rachel knew both Jess and Steph would want to see him one last time before he left. 'Tuesday?'

'Sounds good. Bye, Mum.' Jess gave Rachel a hug, followed by the three girls. The house was quiet when they left, and she felt the sense of relief she always did after an afternoon with the two terrors. While she loved them to bits, it was always good to have the house to herself again. But, she realised, she never would again. Even though Verity was a delight and much more subdued and quieter than the twins, she'd be a constant presence. It was a long time since Rachel had needed to care for a child on a full-time basis. Would she be able to cope? Then she straightened her shoulders. What was she thinking? Of course she would cope. She always did, always had, with whatever life had thrown at her. Look at how she had coped with Kirk's illness, something neither of them had predicted. One never knew what the future would bring.

It wasn't until a very subdued and teary Verity was in bed, and Alexander had disappeared into the study to catch up on his emails, that it occurred to Rachel how having Verity here might prove a stumbling block to her relationship with Luke.

Thirty-seven

Luke wondered what was wrong with Rachel. She'd sounded upset when she'd called the previous evening to cancel the dinner they'd planned, arranging instead to meet on the beach that morning. 'What do you think, boy?' he asked Nelson, but the dog had nothing to suggest.

Rachel was already there when Luke reached the beach, Nelson padding at his heels. She was standing gazing out towards the horizon, seemingly unaware of his arrival. For a moment he stood watching her, stunned by how amazing she looked in a pair of cut-off jeans and a loose shirt, her hair a mass of wild curls.

'Hey,' he said, tapping her gently on the shoulder and turning her towards him, shocked to see her eyes filled with tears. Hoping it was nothing he had done, Luke pulled her into his arms, holding her tightly as he felt the tension in her body gradually lessen. Realising this wasn't the time for passion, he kissed her gently then said, 'What's the matter?'

'It's Alexander,' she said.

'He's leaving?' Luke couldn't understand why the news her son was returning to London would cause her to be so upset.

'Wednesday… and he's going alone.'

'He's…' For a moment, Luke didn't understand what she meant, then the penny dropped. 'Verity?'

'He's leaving her with me.'

'And…'

'The poor little mite can't understand. She's still grieving for her mother, becoming accustomed to having Alexander in her life, to having a father. Now he's leaving her too.'

'But she'll have you.' Luke couldn't think of a better person to care for the little girl. Rachel was such a warm, loving person – as he had discovered. She'd be able to provide the sort of family life her son couldn't.

'Yes, but…' She sniffed. 'I'm sorry, Luke. It was such a shock. I never expected to have to care for a young child at my time of life. I know I spend a lot of time with Jess's girls, but I'm able to hand them back, whereas with Verity… It's a huge responsibility.'

'Which you'll cope with admirably.'

'You think?'

'I do. I haven't known you very long, but one thing I do know is that you'd never shirk your responsibility. Verity's lucky to have you.'

'Thanks.'

'How is she taking it? I presume Alexander has told her?'

'Yesterday.' Rachel sighed. 'She was upset, refused dinner, went to bed in tears.' She gave a watery smile. 'I turned a blind eye when Molly snuck into her room. They were both curled up asleep in her bed when I left.'

'Having Molly around will help.'

'You're right,' Rachel said sounding more cheerful. 'She loves that little dog, and the feeling's mutual. But I could wring Alexander's neck. He should have given us more warning.'

'Our children don't always do what we want them to,' Luke said ruefully, remembering the situation in his own home. At least Rachel wasn't going to have to cope with a baby.

'You too?' she asked.

'Josh and Abby are having a baby, and it seems they're going to be a permanent fixture in my Sydney house.' It was the first time he'd actually put into words what he knew he'd tacitly agreed to.

'Oh, I didn't know. That will be hard.'

Luke pulled on his beard as a vision of his tidy home being filled with baby clothes, nappies and bottles formed in his mind. 'Who was it who said, "What doesn't kill you, makes you stronger"?'

'Nietzsche.'

'Looks like we both have our challenges, and of the two, I think I'd prefer yours.'

'You're right, of course.' Rachel was smiling now. 'Why don't you join us for breakfast? I think Alexander and I might need a buffer this morning.'

'If you're sure…' The prospect of breakfast with Rachel filled Luke with delight but how would Alexander react? And what about Verity?

'I am, very sure. And thanks for listening.' Rachel reached up to kiss Luke on the cheek. His heart leapt. He knew he should be thinking about how this new situation would impact on his time with Rachel, but for now, he was glad to be with her.

When they arrived back at Rachel's house, Alexander was already in the kitchen which was redolent with the aroma of freshly brewed coffee.

'Morning, Luke,' Alexander said, as if it was the most natural thing in the world for him to walk in with Rachel. 'I suppose Mum's told you? It's for the best, better for everyone. Coffee?'

'Thanks.' Luke accepted a mug and took a seat at the table, while Rachel busied herself with eggs and bacon. He wasn't sure what to say, whether to agree with Alexander or suggest it was a selfish move on his part. But was it? As he'd said to Rachel, she'd cope. He had the impression she always did manage to cope with what life threw at her. And the child would probably be better off – and happier – being raised by her grandmother than by her single dad.

At that moment, the object of his thoughts slid silently into the kitchen, Molly padding behind her. She stared at Luke warily before making for Alexander who picked her up in his arms. 'Morning, sweetheart,' he said, giving her a kiss. 'I'm going to miss you when I go back to London, but you're going to have a lovely time here with Grandma.'

'And Molly?' Verity asked, as the dog followed her into the kitchen. Nelson chose that moment to make his presence felt too, moving from Luke's side to join Molly.

'Molly is looking forward to spending more time with you,' Rachel said. 'Shall we give her some breakfast?' She left the stove to hold out her hand to the little girl.

'Can I feed her?' Verity slid out of her dad's arms and took Rachel's outstretched hand.

The sense of relief on Alexander's face was unmistakable. Luke sympathised. It may have seemed selfish, but it must have been a difficult decision. Luke wondered about Alexander's relationship with Verity's mother. Had she really only been a former colleague, or had Alexander had stronger feelings for her, ones which were unreciprocated? He supposed they'd never know, but it was clear he loved his daughter.

Once Molly was fed, and Nelson had licked the empty bowl, Rachel finished cooking breakfast and they all sat down to eat. Luke noticed Verity merely picked at her food and clung to Alexander's side. It wasn't going to be easy for her to let him go.

Breakfast over, Luke wasn't sure what to do. Should he leave or… He was saved from making a decision by Alexander saying, 'What would you like to do today, Verity?'

Verity thought for a moment, her finger in her mouth, then said, 'Can we go to see the pelicans, Daddy, just you and me? The twins told me about them.'

Alexander looked helplessly at Rachel.

'She means the pelican feeding, Alexander. At Pelican Plaza. Don't you remember?'

'Of course!' Alexander snapped his fingers. 'I remember going there with you and Dad. But isn't it in the afternoon?'

'It is. Two o'clock from memory. What about the park in the morning?'

'How about that, Verity? We can go to the swings in the morning, have lunch by the marina, then see the pelicans have their lunch afterwards.'

'Yay!'

Alexander raised an eyebrow in Rachel's direction.

'It's the twins' influence,' she said. 'It's one of their favourite expressions.'

'Hmm. Okay, sweetheart. Why don't you clean your teeth and put on your shoes, then we can go.' He grinned at Rachel and Luke, as if to say what a good dad he was.

When they had gone, Rachel made more coffee and she and Luke took their mugs out to the courtyard where the dogs were already lying in the sun.

'That son of mine!' Rachel said. 'He always manages to come up smelling of roses. I'm willing to bet that by the time they get back, Verity will have accepted that he's leaving and she's staying, and will be looking forward to living in Pelican Crossing. I don't know how he does it.' She shook her head.

'Difficult to imagine, but you know your son.'

'One thing I'm sorry about…' Rachel put her hand on Luke's. 'It's going to mess up our time together. Once Alexander leaves, I won't be able to sneak over to Bob's. You can come here, but…'

'It's okay. I understand.' Luke turned his hand to clasp hers and squeeze it. 'We're not young kids. We don't need to…' He cleared his throat. 'We can pretend we're teenagers again on our first dates.'

'Some teenagers,' Rachel laughed.

Luke laughed too. 'Anyway, since it seems we've been left alone for the day, why don't we do something special too?'

'Do you have anything special in mind?' she asked.

'As it happens, I do. And I can't think of anything more special.' Still holding Rachel's hand, Luke rose.

'Oh,' Rachel said. 'You don't mean…'

Luke smiled at the beautiful woman gazing up at him. 'Yes. That's exactly what I mean.'

He pulled a blushing Rachel to her feet and led her to the bedroom.

Thirty-eight

It had been sad to watch Alexander leave. Verity had clung to him as if she would never let him go, but eventually he'd managed to prise her arms from around his neck and hand her over to Rachel. Then she'd clung to her, sobbing.

Rachel had foreseen this and had made arrangements for Jess to drop off the twins. It was difficult for anyone to remain sad with the two terrors around, and with Molly dashing around excitedly. But today, Verity wasn't so easily enlisted into the twins' games, preferring to stay around Rachel in the kitchen.

'Why don't we decide on your birthday cake?' Rachel said finally to the twins, after having tried everything she could think of. It was fortunate their birthday fell on a weekend, only days before school started. Her words managed to elicit a spark of interest from Verity, and a whoop of delight from the twins who immediately made for the bookshelf where Rachel kept her recipe books and pulled out the now somewhat battered copy of *The Women's Weekly Children's Birthday Cake Cookbook*. Rachel had bought it when her three were little, and it had had seen a lot of use over the years as she produced cakes for Jess, Steph and Alexander, and now Gemma, Indie and Emily.

Rachel smiled as all three girls pored over the book, Gemma and Indie arguing over which cake to choose before finally settling on the Alphabet cake because, 'We're starting school,' Gemma said.

It was a good choice, and an easy one for Rachel with only the purchase of two packets of round caramel mud cake mix, a tub of vanilla frosting, six packets of jumbles biscuits, some coloured icing and packets of M&M's. She'd already made that one when Jess was little, though it hadn't been Steph or Alexander's choice. One thing she liked about the Women's Weekly cake recipes were how easy they were to make.

The twins were excitedly discussing the party they were having on the Saturday, and Rachel was writing the shopping list when Verity sidled up to her. 'Can I have a party for my birthday too, Grandma?' she asked in a tiny voice. 'I'm going to be four.'

'Of course you can, honey. Your daddy said it was in March. I'll check with him on the date. Would you like to choose a cake too?'

'Can I have the one that looks like a chocolate dog?'

Rachel chuckled. The sausage dog cake had been Alexander's choice one year too. 'You surely can. Your daddy chose that cake too when he was about your age.'

Verity's lower lip trembled. 'Will my Daddy be here for my birthday?'

Rachel's heart dropped. How could Alexander have been so heartless as to leave his daughter here? 'I hope so,' she said, crossing her fingers and deciding to do everything in her power to ensure he was.

'Can we go for a swim now?' Gemma asked, now the cake was decided on.

As it was past the worst of the day's heat, Rachel agreed and, only a few minutes later, she and the three girls made their way down to the beach with Molly.

As usual it was deserted. Today, there weren't even any surfers sitting out on their boards or riding in on the waves. Wearing only a shirt over her one-piece swimsuit, Rachel joined the girls in the shallow water. They were protected from the afternoon sun by their rashies and a liberal application of sunscreen and were all enjoying holding hands and jumping the waves when Molly dashed off.

'Molly!' Gemma shouted, dropping Rachel's hand and staring after the little dog who had been joined by another.

'It's Nelson,' Verity said, and when Rachel shaded her eyes, she saw the boxer, followed at a more leisurely pace by his master. She began to tremble. She hadn't expected to see Luke today.

By the time he reached the group, the girls had decided they'd had enough of the water and had moved to the dry sand where they were attempting to build a castle. The dogs immediately joined them leading to chaos, which they all seemed to enjoy.

'Your son's left?' Luke asked.

'This morning.'

'How's Verity?'

'She's been very clingy since he left, until the twins arrived. I'm not sure how she'll cope tonight.' She sighed, silently cursing her son, while aware it was probably the best solution for Verity in the long run.

'Remember I'm not far away if you need anything.'

'Thanks.' Rachel's eyes met his, comforted by the warmth she saw there. She could scarcely believe how short a time it was since she'd taken Molly into the vet clinic and met Luke again. He had become an important part of her life so quickly. And, while they both knew his time here was limited, it was something they never talked about, as if by refusing to mention it, it didn't exist. 'I'll let you know how I go,' she said, 'but I'm going to be busy. I'm going to need to spend time with Verity, and my next group of guests arrive soon too.' She gave a rueful grin, blinking as the sun shone into her eyes.

'Not too busy, I hope.'

Rachel's heart turned over at the memory of the last time they'd been together. She couldn't imagine how they'd manage to find time to be alone with each other now she was responsible for Verity... and with a houseful of B&B guests. 'I hope not,' she said.

'Call me.' Luke stroked her cheek with one finger and for a moment, Rachel thought he was going to kiss her. Instead, he called to Nelson and strode off, leaving her staring after him and wishing...

'Grandma, can you help us?' Indie's voice brought Rachel back to the present. She was on the beach. She had responsibilities, and her own desires must be put aside... for the moment.

That evening, as she bathed Verity and put her to bed, reading her a story and staying with the little girl till she fell asleep, Rachel had a sense of déjà vu. It was as if she was back when Jess was Verity's age, when there was so much to look forward to, when... But this time, there was no Kirk to share the burden, waiting for her with a glass of wine, there to curl up with at the end of the day... and Luke was in Bob's house on the other end of the bluff.

Rachel stifled the burst of anger with Alexander, one of the many which had regularly tortured her since he left, and tried to suppress her doubt that she could cope with Verity on her own. She was a survivor. She'd managed to cope with Kirk's illness, with being left alone. Surely she could cope with a three-year-old child?

Thirty-nine

To Rachel's relief, the guests who arrived to spend two weeks with her were older couples who had stayed there before and didn't require any special attention, leaving her free to concentrate on Verity.

Since that first evening, on the day Alexander had left three weeks earlier, the little girl had snuck into Rachel's bed in the middle of the night to cuddle up to her, sobbing, only to fall into a fitful sleep. Rachel hadn't had much sleep either and had to rise early to prepare breakfast for her guests.

Glad she had a week's respite before her next lot of guests arrived, Rachel glanced at the sleeping little girl and slid out of bed. Molly would be wanting to go out and she had a birthday cake to make. Today was the twins' birthday, and even Verity seemed to have become caught up in the excitement.

Rachel let Molly out and filled her bowls, before taking the ingredients out of the pantry. Maybe she could get it all done before Verity was awake. She turned on the radio at low volume and started to make the cake, barely needing to glance at the recipe, as she hummed along to the old favourites being played on the local channel.

The two cakes were out of the oven and had cooled. Having carefully stuck the two layers together, Rachel had just finished adding the remaining frosting to the top and sides of the cake and was about to stick the biscuits around the outside, when there was the patter of tiny feet and a little voice said, 'Can I help, Grandma?'

Turning quickly, Rachel saw Verity standing there, a pleading expression on her face. 'Of course you can, darling,' she said. 'Watch how I do it, then you can stick some on too.'

Verity watched solemnly as Rachel began placing the alphabet biscuits around the cake. 'That one's for Verity,' she said, when Rachel picked up the biscuit with V on it.

'Well done. Can you find one for Gemma, and for Indie?'

Verity stared at the biscuits for some time before finally selecting the ones with G and I.

'Good girl!'

'My mummy showed me how. She gave me a book with all the letters in it.' Verity's eyes misted.

Rachel felt guilty. It had never occurred to her to ask if Verity knew her letters. Anthea must have spent time teaching them to her before she became so sick. 'We'll get you another book like that, sweetie,' she said.

'It's okay, Grandma. I like the books I got for Christmas, and the stories you read to me.' She picked up the biscuits she'd chosen and carefully stuck them into place. 'Shall we put some on the top too?' she asked, looking at the picture in the recipe book.

'Well, I thought we could make a five with M&M's on top along with five candles.'

'Yes!' Verity said, sounding more cheerful.

The party was due to start at eleven, and Rachel had promised to go to Jess's early in order to help her daughter prepare. When she and Verity arrived, having left Molly at home, the twins were in a state of high excitement, chanting, 'We're five, we're five!' and managing to get in everyone's way, only stopping wide-eyed when Rachel placed the cake on the kitchen bench, and saying, 'Thanks, Grandma,' before grabbing a bewildered Verity's hand.

'Am I glad to see you, Mum,' Jess said, hugging Rachel. 'These two have been up since the crack of dawn and I haven't been able to get anything done.'

Rachel quickly took charge, dispatching the twins and Verity into the backyard with Paul who was happy to supervise them, before making a cup of tea for her and Jess, to calm her daughter down.

By the time the party was due to start, the table in the dining room was covered with plates of fairy bread, slices of watermelon, bowls of chips, little cups of crackers and cheese, and fruit juice poppers. Tiny hot dog nuggets and individual quiches were waiting to go into the oven, and the cake was ready to be produced at the appropriate time. Rachel and Jess were exhausted, much to the amusement of Steph and Chloe who had arrived too late to be of any help.

And I'm going to have to do this all again for Verity, Rachel thought, as a steady stream of small children began to arrive carrying gifts, causing the twins to squeal with delight, and sending Verity to take refuge with Rachel.

*

Luke was preparing to go to the school reunion, already regretting agreeing to attend. 'What do I want with seeing a lot of old people I used to go to school with and haven't spoken to for years?' he asked Nelson, while staring in the mirror. Some days, he felt older than others and this was one of them. There had been another case of poisoning at the clinic today, and he was worried it might not be the last. He'd have preferred to spend the evening at home, rather than with a group of people he barely knew. At least Troy would be there, and Phil Cook. But, so far, he hadn't come across any others he'd been close to. Troy had told him many of their classmates who had left town intended to return for the weekend, and had planned a barbecue next day, one which Luke had declined to attend, citing a previous engagement. He expected he'd have had enough of socialising with his old schoolmates after tonight.

When Luke arrived at the hall where the event was being held, in a sports centre which hadn't existed when he lived there, the first person he saw was Lou Chalmers. She was chatting with a group of women and, from the way they turned to stare at him, he got the impression he had been the topic of their conversation. He remembered Troy telling him she owned a bookshop, and he seemed to recollect Rachel mentioning her too. She'd been Becky's best friend, back in the day, and hadn't changed much. He didn't recognise the other women.

'Hey, mate. Glad you made it.'

Luke turned with relief as Troy slapped him on the shoulder.

'Let's get you a beer and you can meet some of the guys.' He led Luke across the room to where a bar had been set up and where a few faces Luke recognised were standing chatting with glasses in their hands. He'd been right. They'd all turned into old men, some in better shape than others. What was he doing here?

Luke accepted a beer and joined in the conversation, surprised to discover an interest in what they had all done with their lives in the decades they'd been apart. Only a few still lived in Pelican Crossing, and those were the ones who seemed most satisfied with their lives. It gave Luke food for thought. The idea of moving back here had been simmering in the back of his mind ever since he'd met Rachel, but he'd dismissed it as a pipe dream. Maybe it wasn't such a crazy idea. Maybe… His thoughts were interrupted by Troy calling everyone to be seated and he moved with the others to where tables had been set up. There was a name card at each place. Finding his name, Luke discovered he was seated between Troy and Lou, and wondered if his old friend had been in charge of the seating plan and, if so, why he had chosen to place him here.

During the meal, the conversation at the table was general, focussing on changes to Pelican Crossing since their schooldays and reminiscences of their time there. It was when they had progressed to coffee, that Lou said quietly, 'I hear you've been seeing a friend of mine.'

'You mean Rachel?'

'Yes. She's a good soul, been through a lot. I'd hate to see her hurt.'

'It's not my intention to hurt her. We're…' Luke paused. How did he describe his relationship with Rachel? They were more than friends, sometime lovers, though, since Rachel's son had left, there had been few opportunities for them to get together. He was beginning to wonder if he'd dreamt the blissful moments in his bed.

Lou hadn't finished. 'I've watched Rachel over the years,' she said, 'while she brought up three children, cared tirelessly for her husband during his illness, then set up her B&B business. She gives the impression of being full of confidence, able to cope with whatever life throws at her. I know many of her friends seek her help and advice when they're worried or in trouble. But underneath is a vulnerable woman who has no one to turn to when she's in need. She's lonely,

Luke, has been since Kirk died, even though she fills her life with B&B guests, grandchildren and her little dog. I'd hate to think you're taking advantage of her vulnerability.'

Luke shifted uncomfortably in his seat, glad when Troy pulled him into an argument about the old days. But Lou's words had made their mark, making him wonder if he was being fair to Rachel and to think again about the possibility of staying on in Pelican Crossing.

Forty

Luke didn't have the opportunity to ponder much on staying in Pelican Crossing as, in the next week, there was a spate of animals arriving at the clinic with signs of poisoning, culminating in him being unable to save the chihuahua belonging to a distressed tourist. Following on from the earlier cases with Lady and Bluey, this appeared to be a deliberate attempt to harm dogs on the dog beach. It was where all of the incidents had taken place.

As soon as he closed the clinic, Luke contacted the police and called Joe to ask him to close the dog beach till further notice. He was glad there had been no cases on Pelican Crossing's main beach or on the secluded beach below his and Rachel's homes.

They couldn't risk more cases. At Joe's request, he agreed to meet with him and Finn at the council chambers later that day.

'This is a bad state of affairs,' Joe said when the three men met. 'How many did you say?' he asked Luke.

'Four cases today, all belonging to tourists, one fatal. They wouldn't have been aware of the warnings.'

The three men stared at each other, a chill entering the room despite the temperature being in the high twenties.

'Can't be by chance,' Joe said at last. 'You contacted the police?'

'Yeah. Not much they can do without evidence. You don't think…?' Luke remembered Joe's earlier reference to two councillors who wanted dogs banned from running free on the beach.

'I hope I'm wrong, but…'

'Well, we need to find evidence,' Finn said. 'What should we be looking for?' He met Luke's eyes.

'Rat poison tends to be in green pellets, easy to detect if you know what you're looking for, and easily obtainable from most hardware stores. It appears the cases I've had to deal with all spent time on the dog beach, hence my request for the council to close it.' He looked across at Joe, who nodded.

'It's done,' Joe said. 'The notice should already be up warning that the beach is closed till further notice and that there may be poison, and we've erected barricades to stop people from wandering from the main beach. It's not only dogs who might be tempted to eat it, though I doubt it tastes good.'

'Is anyone searching the beach?' Finn asked.

There was a charged silence, then, 'There's still an hour of daylight,' Luke said. 'We could make a start.'

The next hour saw the three men searching the beach for any sign of green pellets, to no avail. As the sky darkened, they finally gave up and retreated to *The Grand*. Over several glasses of beer they discussed their options, frustrated till Joe said, 'Tomorrow's Saturday. Let me see who I can round up and we can do a thorough search of the area. If someone has dumped rat bait on or near the beach, enough to poison several animals, there must surely still be some lying around.'

'Sounds like a plan,' Luke said, and Finn nodded, all three agreeing to meet again at daybreak to conduct a thorough search with as many others as they could manage to round up.

Exhausted, Luke drove home, worried that some bait might still be out there and that despite the warning notice, some tourists might decide to ignore it and allow their dogs to run on the beach. He could scarcely believe the poison had been set deliberately, but what other explanation could there be?

He was slowing down at the gate to Bob's house, when he saw the lights of Rachel's in the distance and, in need of the comfort he knew her presence could offer, drove on to her gate.

*

Rachel had been so busy with Verity and a new batch of B&B guests that she and Luke had only managed to get together briefly in the past week and she was beginning to wonder if she'd imagined their closeness. So it was a shock to see him standing at her door looking exhausted.

'Luke, is something the matter?' she asked, glad she was wearing one of the new outfits, a pair of white wide-legged pants with a multicoloured tunic.

'Can I come in?'

'Of course.' Rachel stood back to allow him to enter, as Molly frolicked around his ankles.

'Coffee? Wine?' she asked when they reached the kitchen. In the bright light there, she could see shadows under his eyes and what looked like a new network of wrinkles around them.

'Thanks. Coffee would be good.' Luke dropped into a chair, making no move to hug her.

Something must really be wrong.

Rachel waited till she had made coffee for Luke and a cup of camomile tea for herself, then joined him at the table. Molly, realising no one was interested in her and there was no food to be had, had returned to her bed by the door. 'Now, what's happened?'

'We've had more poisonings. Four today, and one dog died.'

'Oh no!' Rachel's hand went to her mouth. She knew this was what he'd been afraid of, what they'd all been afraid of. 'What happens now?'

Luke took a sip of coffee and sighed. 'Joe's closed the dog beach, and a few of us have been out searching for evidence but with no luck. Joe and Finn are calling in reinforcements, and we're going out again tomorrow.'

'Oh, I wish I could help.' If she hadn't Verity to take care of, Rachel would have been glad to go with them.

'It's okay. You have responsibilities. I just hope we can find something tomorrow, something to prove this is a deliberate attempt at sabotage. Joe and Finn think it may be the same guys who tried to ban dogs from the beach last year.'

'Surely not!' Rachel was horrified to think anyone in Pelican Crossing would set out to deliberately harm animals, but with so many cases, what else could it be? She looked across to where Molly was lying happily in her bed, glad she never took her to the dog beach, but so many others did.

'I'm afraid so. But first we need to find the evidence, find the bait… then comes the difficult part – to prove who is behind it.'

'Oh, Luke!' Rachel wanted to comfort him. She put a hand on his shoulder, and he turned to meet her eyes.

'Thanks, Red. It helps me, being here with you. I couldn't face going back to an empty house, to Nelson who'd remind me…' He shook his head.

Rachel felt the familiar warm glow at his use of her nickname and moved closer till her forehead touched his. She wished she could cuddle up with him in bed, but she had two lots of guests in the house, and a granddaughter who was likely to sneak into her bed at any time. 'I'm sorry,' she said, not knowing exactly what she meant, sorry for Luke, sorry for the affected dogs, their owners, or sorry they couldn't make love. Probably the latter, she thought as she experienced a now familiar rush of desire. Did Luke feel it too, or was he too worried about the poisonings?

His next words didn't help. 'I'm sorry too, Red. It's all such a mess.'

They didn't speak for the next few minutes. Luke took a few sips of his coffee and Rachel her tea. Then he said, 'I should go and let you get to bed. Thanks for listening. It helped.'

Rachel accompanied him to the door, feeling helpless and wondering what more she could have done to help. At the doorway, Luke pulled her into a warm hug. 'Thanks,' he said again.

'Good luck tomorrow. You will let me know how you go? I'll be here if…' she gazed into his handsome face, now etched with worry.

'I will. Take care.'

'You, too.' Rachel reached up to kiss him, but tonight there was no passion in his response. She watched him as he made his way to the car, the slump of his shoulders a sign of his distress, and wished again she could make things better for him.

Forty-one

Next morning was Saturday, and a changeover in guests for Rachel, making it a busy day as she had to clean the rooms and change the beds ready for the new arrivals. She hadn't slept well, thoughts of the poor dogs being poisoned going around and around in her head, and the arrival of Verity to cuddle into her in the middle of the night hadn't helped.

Rachel rose carefully, taking care not to disturb the little girl who was now sound asleep, after having tossed and turned for what had seemed to be half the night. After a shower, she felt better and pulled on the same outfit she'd worn the previous day, before going to let Molly out and begin breakfast.

Verity appeared as Rachel was farewelling her guests, the two couples thanking her and promising to return. 'Why do you have all these visitors, Grandma?' she asked, as Molly licked her bare feet, making her giggle.

'This house is too big for me and Molly,' she said, 'and these people need somewhere to stay when they come to visit Pelican Crossing.'

'But you have me now.'

'I certainly do.' Rachel picked up the little girl and whirled her around. And she was good company. Maybe it was time to make changes, to reduce the number of paying guests. She no longer needed the extra money. Alexander had been very generous in providing for Verity's keep, and she'd received a small inheritance from a distant relative. It was worth considering.

'What are we going to do today?' Verity asked, when they had returned from walking Molly on the beach. 'Are we going to see the twins?'

'I'm going to be busy here, but I can drop you off at your Aunt Jess's first. She called last night after you were in bed, to say the twins wanted to tell you all about school.'

'When can *I* go to school?'

'When you're five, but… maybe we can enrol you in pre-school this year. Would you like that?' Rachel didn't know why she hadn't thought of this before now. Verity was a bright child who would love the activities and the interaction with other children, and it would give Rachel some time to herself, something she'd been missing.

'Yes, I went to *Kindy Korner* with Mummy back home.'

'Oh, sweetheart, this is your home now.' Rachel pulled her into a hug, swamped with guilt. She should have thought of asking Alexander and done something about this before now, but she had been so intent on trying to make sure Verity felt at home here. 'Here in Pelican Crossing we have *Pelican Pals*. We'll go on Monday, and you can decide if you'd like to start there.'

'I'd like that. Are there pelicans?'

'Maybe not real ones there, but we can see if we can find some by the river on our way home.'

'Yes please. I loved it when I went to see them feeding with my daddy.'

Once she had dropped Verity off at Jess's, Rachel went home to start on her chores. Turning on the radio to the local channel, she heard the announcement about the dog beach being closed and the news of the poisonings. She hoped they'd find the evidence needed… and the culprit, though she could understand that might be more difficult. 'We're lucky we have our own special beach, Molly,' she said to her little dog who always accompanied her as she moved around the house.

Rachel was smoothing down the bed in the bedroom which would house her next lot of guests when her phone pinged with a text. Scanning it, she felt a sense of relief. The couple who were due to arrive today had been forced to cancel due to a family emergency. There was another message. This one from Jess asking if Verity could have a sleepover with the twins as the three girls wanted to watch a movie together. Rachel quickly agreed, wondering what Luke was doing this evening. Now she was going to have the house to herself, it might be the perfect opportunity for them to make up for lost time.

*

'Over here!'

The shout came just as Luke had given up hope. He and a band of others, including members of the local scout troop, had been searching all morning with nothing to show for it. When he looked over to where the voice had come from, he saw one of the scouts in the rough grass at the edge of the beach, his hand in the air. Luke, Joe and Finn hurried over to where the boy was standing, to see a few green pellets of rat bait, hidden in the grass.

'Is this what we're looking for?' the boy asked.

'It is. Well done!' Luke said.

'We should keep looking,' Joe said, 'there may be more. But it's proof it's been a deliberate act.'

Luke collected the pellets, sealing them in a plastic bag and dropping it into his backpack, ready to hand over to the police. They'd been happy to allow the group of locals to conduct the search, only interested if they discovered any evidence. Though it was doubtful they could take any action on the basis of a collection of pellets of rat poison, and there was no guarantee that whoever was responsible wouldn't do it again.

'It'll be on the front page of the next edition of *The Echo*,' Finn said, when they had retired to *The Grand* for a quick bite of lunch. 'Someone must know something.'

'Hmm. But will they be willing to talk, to dob in a mate?' Joe said. 'Pelican Crossing is a small community. People are loyal to their mates.'

'But would they keep quiet when they knew a dog had died?' Luke asked. He couldn't believe anyone would.

Joe shrugged.

It was hot on the beach in the afternoon as the search continued, but there was no sign of any more pellets. Joe offered to drop those they'd found into the police station, saying that as he knew one of the officers there, it might help them take action to find the culprit. Luke wasn't optimistic. Even though Joe and Finn had their suspicions, it would be difficult to prove. He was on his way home when Rachel rang.

'Great news! I'm on my own tonight. Can I tempt you to join me for dinner?'

'On your own? What's happened?'

'My guests had to cancel because of an emergency, and Verity is having a sleepover with the twins.'

Luke felt like shouting out loud, whooping like a teenager. An evening – and perhaps overnight – with Rachel was exactly what he needed after the day he'd had. 'On my way home now. Give me time to shower change and take Nelson for a walk, and I'll be with you.'

'Why don't you bring Nelson, and we can walk the dogs together? Molly needs a walk too.'

'Perfect,' he said, his heart racing at the prospect of the evening ahead.

Forty-two

Luke was feeling good by the time he and Nelson made their way across the bluff to Rachel's. The cool shower had rejuvenated him, combined with their success in finding the bait. He'd let Joe and Finn – and the local police – worry about identifying the culprit. He had the evening ahead to look forward to.

Rachel and Molly were in the front yard when he reached the gate, the little white dog's tail wagging when she glimpsed Nelson, who while also pleased, was much better at hiding it. Rachel was wearing white pants and a bright top and looked amazing. She came out to greet him, Molly at her heels.

'Hey,' he said, as he pulled her into an embrace before kissing her. 'You're the best thing I've seen today.'

'How was it? Find anything?' Rachel asked, slipping out of his arms.

'We found some bait pellets. Joe's taking them to the police, but…' he shook his head, '… it doesn't help find who put them there. But it's out of my hands now.' Though he knew he couldn't put it out of his mind as easily. 'Let's go down to the beach.' He reached out to grasp Rachel's hand.

Once on the beach the two dogs gambolling in the water, while Luke and Rachel kept to the hard-packed sand, Luke felt the troubles of the day fall away. There was something about the sea air, the scent of the ocean, the sand beneath one's feet, that made everything seem better.

'Have you done any more about checking out your grandparents?'

Rachel asked, when he had told her all about the day's events. 'You said Agnes wasn't much help.'

'Well, she was able to tell me my grandad worked on a market garden, which helped me work out they'd have come from the south of Italy. But that's about it. You mentioned something about a retirement village?'

'*The Haven*. It's an over-fifties resort style community and has an aged care home attached for residents who are unable to cope with looking after themselves. My friend Liz's mother lives there – in a villa. She'd know if there was anyone there who might be able to help. I think there may be a couple of residents who'd be in their late nineties.'

'Really?' Luke had almost given up on his search for information, but it was worth this one more try. 'When could we visit it?'

Rachel chuckled – probably at his use of *we* – but she was the one with the contact. '*We* could drop in tomorrow. I'd just need to give Joan a call first. But I'm sure it won't be a problem. She loves company.'

Back at Rachel's, when both dogs had been fed, and Luke and Rachel were sitting in the courtyard, Rachel with a glass of wine and Luke with a beer, he found himself relaxing, his mind returning to the possibility of staying on in Pelican Crossing when his locum was over. He glanced at Rachel, wondering how she would feel about it. While passionate in bed, and always pleased to see him, she never gave anything away about her emotions. He knew it was some time since her husband had died, and she'd been on her own since then. Did she consider what they had together as merely a fling or was she looking for something more permanent? He could never work out women.

While he'd been very clear at the start that he was only here till March, and they'd both agreed to accept the temporary nature of their relationship, he was beginning to have second thoughts. He remembered what Joe had said, how women didn't understand the meaning of temporary. But what if Joe was wrong, what if Rachel was satisfied with a short-term fling?

*

She was getting too used to this, Rachel thought, as she sipped her wine and gazed up at the sky where the stars were beginning to appear, *too comfortable in Luke's company*. Although they hadn't managed to have much time together since Verity's arrival, tonight they'd slipped back into it like an old married couple. Luke was so easy to be with, like Kirk in some respects, and Kirk would have liked him. She pulled her thoughts away from the direction in which they were heading. Nothing could come of this, there was no future for her with Luke. She'd known that from the start, so why did she now wish things could be different?

Rachel jumped up, startling the two dogs who had been lying happily at their feet. 'I'll get dinner organised,' she said. 'I made a chicken casserole earlier. I just need to heat it up and throw together a salad.'

'Sounds good. Need any help?'

'No, you can stay here with the dogs for now. I'll call you when it's ready.' Rachel knew she must sound odd, especially after the perfect time they had on the beach, wandering along hand-in-hand, stopping now and then to kiss. But she needed time by herself to work out her feelings.

By the time dinner was ready, and she'd gulped back another glass of wine, Rachel was feeling calmer. She was being silly. Nothing had changed. She could still enjoy Luke's company for a few more weeks, then… then she'd manage to survive. She had before, she could again. And now she had Verity to care for.

During dinner they shared their memories of growing up in Pelican Crossing, laughing to discover to their surprise that they remembered things differently. Rachel thought it was probably the result of the four years difference in age, and the fact Luke had been a football hero, something he denied vehemently.

Afterwards, they sat out in the courtyard again with coffee and some leftover Christmas cake enjoying the sound of the ocean and the occasional snoring of the dogs. When Luke pulled Rachel into his arms, and their lips met, all her earlier doubts were forgotten in the magic of his kiss.

But next morning these doubts returned, as she gazed down at Luke's face on the pillow beside her. She dropped a kiss on his forehead, wishing he wasn't planning to return to Sydney, envious of her three friends who had found their second chance with men who lived right here in Pelican Crossing. What was she doing mooning over this Sydneysider, wishing for the impossible, just as she had when he was Becky's boyfriend?

Thinking of Becky made Rachel wonder how her sister was doing. She hadn't seen her since some time before Christmas and according to Andy, she was deteriorating rapidly. It was so unfair. Becky had been so bright, so full of life. It had been hard to see her on her last visit, and now… Now, Andy was checking out nursing homes, unable to cope any longer. She should visit before the inevitable happened, while Becky might still be able to recognise her.

Still thinking of Becky, Rachel slipped out of bed and was making her morning tea when Luke appeared in the kitchen. She had already fed the dogs, and they were playing happily outside. *This is what life could be like if she and Luke were a married couple.* Quickly stifling that thought, Rachel asked, 'Coffee?'

Luke wrapped his arms around her and gave her a kiss. 'Good morning, lovely lady. Sleep well?'

Rachel felt the defences she'd been trying to erect begin to crumble. Even if it was only for a little longer, what did it matter? Maybe she should just forget he was leaving and enjoy what they had together. 'I did,' she lied. 'You?'

'A man with a clear conscience always sleeps well. And yes please to coffee, but I can make it.'

'Okay.' Rachel took some eggs out of the fridge and proceeded to scramble them with baby spinach, dried tomato and goats cheese. It was a recipe she'd found in a novel by Barbara Hannay and had become a favourite with her.

While she was cooking, Rachel turned on the radio to the local news channel. This morning, along with the usual surf report, there was the added warning about the dog beach, plus the news that rat bait had been found near the beach and police were eager to receive any information about people behaving suspiciously in the area.

'Fat chance,' Luke said, his brow creasing. 'Whoever did this would have done it when there was no one around. Joe said they'd be checking who had purchased rat bait recently, but…'

'It will be like looking for a needle in a haystack. A lot of folk would fall into that category… and it may be someone who's had the bait in their shed for years.'

'Mmm. This is seriously good,' Luke said, forking up some scrambled egg. 'Why does mine never taste like this?'

'Secret recipe.' Rachel grinned.

'So, are we going to visit this retirement village this morning?'

'I'll call Joan after breakfast to see if it works for her. Then I need to pick up Verity.'

'Verity, of course. How's it going with her?'

'Better. She still likes to crawl into my bed in the night, but she's not sobbing herself to sleep anymore. She's proving more resilient than I anticipated. I aim to enrol her in *Pelican Pals* tomorrow.'

'*Pelican Pals*? Don't tell me, let me guess. It's a playgroup for pelicans?'

'Good try. It's an early learning centre. They take children from to zero to five and the three to five group focuses on school readiness. I think it would be good for Verity. She says she was enrolled in one in London.'

'Good idea. It will free up your time too.'

'Yes, but that's not the reason.' Though it had occurred to her.

When they finished eating, Luke insisted on clearing up and loading the dishwasher while Rachel called Liz's mother. Joan was delighted to hear from her and readily agreed to her and Luke paying her a visit, telling her to come for morning tea.

Seeming to realise their people were now available, the dogs appeared in the doorway, their tongues hanging out.

'Must be time for a walk,' Luke said. 'When are we expected at *The Haven*?'

'Not for another hour. Plenty of time to take these two to the beach.'

Once on the beach the scent of the ocean, the sound of the waves lapping on the shore and the feeling of the sand underfoot all worked their magic again, as the dogs ran free, splashing in and out of the waves, and Luke and Rachel ambled along hand-in-hand. *If only it could always be like this*, Rachel thought. But life was seldom so easy.

Forty-three

Luke gazed around with interest as Rachel drove into *The Haven*. It was the first time he'd been in one of these places, though he'd seen the advertisements for over-fifties communities on television. A couple of the old schoolmates he'd met at the reunion even lived in them, but that sort of lifestyle wasn't for him.

However, it did appear pleasant, the neat villas sitting apart with well-tended gardens, and a large building which he assumed was the aged care centre or some sort of common facility.

'Liz's mother loves it here,' Rachel said as she pulled into a parking spot. 'She's even found a gentleman friend.' She smiled.

They got out of the car, and Rachel led the way to where an elderly woman was standing in the open doorway of one of the villas.

'Thanks for seeing us, Joan,' Rachel said. 'This is Luke Findlay. He's acting as a locum for Bob Reed while Bob's overseas. Luke, this is Joan Ellis. Liz's mum.'

'You're a friend of Liz's?' Joan asked.

'Not really, but we've met.'

'Hmm. Well, come in both of you. I've just taken some date scones out of the oven and the kettle's on.'

Luke followed the two women into Joan's tidy home which was redolent with the aroma of freshly baked scones, making his mouth water and reminding him of his mother's baking.

When they had all been served with the delicious looking scones and tea in china cups which also reminded Luke of his mother, Joan fixed him with her gaze and said, 'I remember you. You're Sonja Findlay's boy, aren't you?'

Luke's stomach lurched. She knew his mother. 'That's right. I grew up here, left to go to university.'

'And now you're back.'

'Temporarily.' Luke felt Rachel flinch.

'I was a lot younger than Sonja of course, but I remember when her family arrived in the area. There had never been Italians living here before that. It was quite an experience. Of course, now there are lots of families from various different countries. But it was just after the war and some people had trouble forgetting…' She sighed. 'What is it you want to know?'

Luke put his cup and saucer down on the coffee table and leant forward, hands on his knees. 'It's about my grandparents. I want to know more about them. Where they came from, and why here? I've heard my grandfather worked in a market garden and had a market stall, so I'm assuming they came from the south of Italy, but that's all.'

'Oh dear, I'm really sorry. I can't help you there. I do remember the Russos' market stall. I used to accompany my mother there every Sunday. But as for anything else…' She shook her head.

'Okay, thanks. It was a long shot.' Luke's hopes crashed.

'But there is someone who might be able to help you. There's a lady here. Ines Ferrari lives in the aged care centre now but is still quite alert. She's Italian too, came later than your family. She plays mahjong with us on occasions. She'd be about the right age and might remember more than I do.'

'Would I be able to talk with her?'

'I don't see why not. Like many others in the centre, I don't think she gets a lot of visitors, and she'd enjoy seeing a good-looking young man like yourself.'

Luke tried to hide his amusement at being called *a good-looking young man* and he could see Rachel suppressing a smile too.

'It may take a little while. How are you fixed for time?' Joan looked at both Luke and Rachel.

'I…' he began, then glanced across at Rachel who was looking awkward.

'I need to pick up Verity – my granddaughter,' she said to Joan, 'but if Luke wants to do it now, I can come back for him later.'

'Are you sure?' Luke asked. He didn't want to inconvenience Rachel who had been good enough to set this up and drive him here, but he didn't want to miss this opportunity.

'I'm sure. Thanks, Joan,' Rachel said, 'and thanks for the tea and scones. I wish mine always turned out like that.'

'I'm sure they do, and it's no trouble. I'd be interested to know more about Sonja myself.'

'Can you call me when you're ready to leave?' Rachel asked Luke.

'Sure, Red.' He grinned, happy that this might prove to be the breakthrough he'd been hoping for.

*

Rachel was pleased she'd been able to help Luke. It sounded as if this Italian woman might be the key to him unlocking his family history. Family was important, more so as one grew older. And Becky was her family.

She stopped the car on the way to Jess's and called Andy. 'How's Becky?' she asked as soon as he answered.

'Give me a minute.'

Rachel heard a door open and close, then her brother-in-law's voice again. 'She's not good, Rach. I'm…' His voice broke. 'Sorry. It's one of her bad days.'

Rachel felt her heart drop. This was her big sister, who she'd looked up to for as long as she could remember, who she'd wanted to be like when she was a teenager and Becky seemed so grownup. 'Last time we spoke you said you were looking at nursing homes.'

'Yeah. I put it off for a while trying to handle things myself, but in the end… It's a nice place. Becky has her own room with a view of the gardens.'

'You have to do what's right for you… and Becky, Andy. Last time I saw her…'

'She's gone downhill a lot since then. Some days, she doesn't know who I am. It's…' He stifled a sob. 'Sorry,' he said again. 'I visit most days, and when I leave, we do this rapid kissing thing we always used to do. It's my way of knowing she recognises me, but…'

'I wish there was something I could do to help.'

'Maybe… if you could see yourself able to come down for a visit, for a few days. Seeing you might bring some things back… Oh, who knows? I certainly don't.'

A wave of compassion flowed over Rachel, for Andy, for Becky. It was such a small thing to ask, and Becky was her sister. She had no guests until next weekend. There was Verity but… maybe… 'Let me get back to you,' she said. She started the car and drove straight to Jess's.

When she arrived, the three girls ran out to greet her. For the first time, Verity seemed as full of energy as the other two. 'Gemma and Indie told me all about *Pelican Pals,* Grandma,' she said, grabbing Rachel's hand and swinging on it. 'They used to go there when they were my age, and they said…' Rachel stopped paying attention. She'd all but forgotten Jess had sent the twins there… until they'd become too rowdy for the other children. That's when Rachel had started taking care of them more frequently, and she loved it. She tuned back in to hear Verity ask, 'Can I really go there tomorrow?'

'That's the plan,' Rachel said. 'You had fun with the twins today?'

Verity nodded happily.

An idea began to form in Rachel's mind. 'I need to talk to your Aunt Jess for a few minutes. 'Where's Mummy?' she asked the twins.

'She's inside with Emily,' Gemma said.

'Thanks. I won't be long,' she said to Verity.

Rachel found Jess in the kitchen fixing a band aid with the picture of a dinosaur onto Emily's knee. 'All done,' she said, lifting the little girl down from the table where she'd been seated. 'Take care now,' she called after her as she ran off to join her sisters and cousin. 'Sorry, Mum.' She gave Rachel a hug. 'Good to see you. Did you enjoy yourself last night?'

Rachel gave her daughter a wary look. Did she know… or guess how she'd spent it? No, she couldn't, though she might suspect. 'It was lovely, thanks. How was Verity?'

'Good. We made up another bed in the twins' room and she went to sleep with them and slept right through. She's such a lovely kid. Alexander doesn't know what he's missing.'

'Oh, I think he does.' In the time she'd spent with Verity, listening to her prattle on about her daddy, Rachel had got the impression that Alexander cared more about his daughter than he'd been willing to admit. He must have realised his lifestyle was completely unsuited to bringing up a child and that his mother was better placed to do so. For that, she was grateful, and she suspected they might see a lot more of him in the months and years to come.

'I need to talk to you, ask a favour,' Rachel said.

'Tea first. I was about to make some. Peppermint do you, Mum?'

'Fine.' Rachel resigned herself to wait while Jess boiled the water, then called the girls in and sent them out again with poppers of juice and Oreos, shrugging at Rachel's surprise. Jess was normally so health conscious. 'Sometimes it's easier to give in,' she said.

When they were seated with their peppermint tea – and more Oreos – Jess said, 'Okay, Mum. What's the favour?'

'I wondered if you'd be willing to have Verity for a few days – three or four.' She waited, seeing Jess's eyes widen with disbelief.

'You…?'

'No!' Rachel blushed as it suddenly occurred to her what Jess might be thinking. 'It's your Aunt Becky. I spoke to Uncle Andy earlier. She's not so good, and he thinks maybe if I visited…' Rachel's eyes began to moisten. She blinked away the tears.

'Oh, Mum. I'm sorry. Poor Aunt Becky. Is she in a nursing home now?'

Rachel nodded, suddenly unable to speak, remembering what Andy had told her.

'Of course Verity can stay here. She can stay now, if you like. She'll be company for Emily when the twins are at school.'

'No, not today. I need to make sure she's happy with it. And I've promised to enrol her in *Pelican Pals* tomorrow, so she'll be there for a couple of the days. It means you'll have to drop her off and pick her up.'

'No problem. I've been thinking of enrolling Emily there anyway. She'll be easier for them to handle than the twins were.' She chuckled.

'How are they liking school?'

'They love it. They've put them in different classes which is probably a good thing, so they can't stir each other up like they did at *Pelican Pals*.' This time she grinned. 'Not everyone has your patience, Mum.'

Rachel smiled. She'd loved having the twins so often, would really miss them.

As if realising they were being talked about, the twins appeared, wanting to show off the drawings and worksheets they'd brought home from school, and the remainder of Rachel's visit was spent listening to their stories and admiring their work.

It was past lunchtime when Luke called to say he was ready to be picked up, and Rachel left with hugs and kisses and promises to return soon, relieved at Jess's response to her request. Now, she just had to check Verity was okay with it, and she could book her flight to Adelaide.

Forty-four

Luke was ebullient. Despite his fears – Ines Ferrari must be close to one hundred – the old woman had been extremely lucid. Not only did she remember his mother, but also his grandparents who had been friends with *her* parents. Her family had immigrated several years after his grandparents and they had come from the same village, located, as he suspected, in the southern part of Italy, a small village outside the city of Palermo. Now he knew where to go, it shouldn't be too difficult to trace any remaining family members.

'You look pleased. A successful visit?' Rachel asked, when he got into the car.

'Very.' He proceeded to report what he'd learned, finishing with, 'I intend to go there as soon as I can arrange it.'

'Oh!' Rachel didn't appear to share his enthusiasm. Come to think of it, she had seemed very down since she picked him up.

'Something up?' he asked in a low voice, conscious of Verity in the back seat.

'Tell you later. All okay back there, Verity?' she asked.

'Yes, Grandma. Can we go to the beach when we get home? I think Molly will want a walk.'

'Good idea, but we'll have some lunch first. Hungry?'

'Yes, please.'

Luke and Rachel both laughed.

The two dogs were waiting for them at the front gate, tails wagging.

'I'll leave you to get on,' Luke said, though he was keen to know what was bothering Rachel.

'No. Stay for lunch… if you're happy with a sandwich.'

'Sure,' he said, relieved he didn't need to rush off.

Once inside, the dogs retired, happy with a couple of treats, and Rachel made them delicious ham, cheese and tomato sandwiches on rye bread with a beer for him and water for her and Verity. When she had finished, Verity slid down from her seat to join the dogs in the yard.

'Now, are you going to tell me what's bothering you?' Luke asked.

Rachel took a long drink of water before replying. 'I didn't tell you about Becky,' she said. 'She developed Alzheimer's a few years ago, a type with a particularly rapid progression.'

'Oh, I'm sorry.' Even though Troy had told him, it was still a shock to hear it from Rachel.

'She's in a nursing home now and… I spoke to Andy, her husband, after I left you. She's deteriorating rapidly, losing speech and much of her movement, and he thinks it might help if she could see me.'

'Oh!' Luke wasn't familiar with Alzheimer's or how it could progress. It was difficult to imagine the bright, active woman he remembered reduced to this state. 'Where does she live?'

'Adelaide.'

'Oh!' he said again. 'Will you go? What about Verity?' He knew the little girl was still getting used to being in Pelican Crossing and to living with Rachel.

'I talked with Jess. She slept through last night… with the twins. She can stay with them while I'm gone. I don't have any guests this week.'

'When will you go?'

'Well, I want to get Verity enrolled in *Pelican Pals* first, so probably in a couple of days, if I can arrange a flight.'

'If there's anything I can do… look after Molly?'

Rachel smiled, and Luke could see the worry lines around her eyes ease. 'Would you? That would be good. Jess is happy to have her, but… with Verity plus her three, it's a lot to ask.'

'No problem. She and Nelson get on well together, and one more dog is nothing.'

'Thanks.'

'Come here. You need a hug.' Luke pulled her into his arms and gave her a warm hug, without any of the passion of his usual embrace. She felt so warm and soft in his arms, he wanted to keep her there for ever.

*

Rachel sank into Luke's embrace wishing she could stay there for ever. 'Thanks, I needed that,' she said.

'Grandma, can we go to the beach now?' Verity came back inside, the two dogs at her heels.

Rachel pulled away from Luke and patted her hair which had become dishevelled in the hug. 'Of course we can. Luke?'

'I should get back. I want to check with Joe if there have been any developments, and I have a few animals in the hospital I need to check on too. See you later?'

'Maybe. Call me.' Rachel wasn't sure about continuing to see so much of Luke. Nothing had changed. He would still be leaving in a few weeks' time, and now he was talking about going to Italy… Maybe this trip to Adelaide was a good opportunity to finish things between them before her heart could be broken. But surely one more time wouldn't hurt?

She thought Luke gave her a strange look, but he kissed her on the cheek, then he and Nelson headed off across the bluff.

'Can we go now, Grandma?' Verity pleaded, Molly dancing at her feet.

'Okay,' Rachel laughed. It was hard to remain worried or upset with this sweet little face looking up at her with such trust. 'Let's get your hat and sunscreen.'

As always, being on the beach lightened Rachel's mood. 'Did you enjoy staying at Aunt Jess's?' she asked, when she and Verity were seated on the sand watching Molly playing in the waves.

'Yes. I like Gemma and Indie. It's like having two big sisters. Do you have any sisters, Grandma?'

It was the perfect opening. 'Yes, I do, an older sister, Becky. She lives in a place called Adelaide, a long way from here.' She took a deep breath. 'There's something I want to talk to you about, Verity. My sister's sick and in hospital, and I need to go to visit her. How would you like to stay with Aunt Jess, the twins and Emily while I'm gone?'

Verity's eyes widened and filled with tears. 'You're going away?'

Rachel saw the fear in her eyes. Was one more person going to leave her? 'Only for a few days. I'll be back before you know it.' She hugged Verity. 'And we'll get you enrolled in *Pelican Pals* tomorrow, before I go.'

'Okay. I'm going to play with Molly now.' Verity got up and raced over to join Molly, skipping over the incoming waves.

Rachel watched the pair. She hated to see Verity crying again, to feel responsible for her tears, but she'd enjoy spending more time with the twins, and Emily looked up to her. And Molly would be happy with Luke and Nelson. She only had to worry about herself... and her annoying tendency to overthink things, especially her relationship with Luke. She'd leave it for tonight, she decided, but perhaps see him again tomorrow, one last evening together before she left.

Forty-five

Rachel tried to relax as the plane took off, but the thought of what was waiting for her in Adelaide refused to go away. Last time she'd seen Becky, her sister had at least known her. Could she have gone downhill so quickly? But Andy had no reason to lie.

She turned her mind to Luke, and the previous evening when she'd invited him round. She had already dropped Verity off at Jess's, the little girl full of the day she'd spent at the childcare centre and the activities she'd enjoyed there. She seemed to have forgotten her upset when Rachel told her she was leaving, but the tight arms around Rachel's neck when she said goodbye told another story.

'She'll be fine,' Jess had reassured her mother when they stood at the door. 'The twins won't give her time to miss you, and she'll have Emily and *Pelican Pals*. It'll go quickly, and you'll be back in no time.'

'I hope you're right.' Rachel sighed.

'Give Aunt Becky a hug for me. I hope…'

'I do too. I'll keep in touch, and if there's anything…'

'I'll be sure to let you know.' Jess chuckled.

'Sorry, I'm being silly.'

'No, you're being what you always are… a caring sister, mother and grandmother.'

Rachel felt a warm glow. She'd done something right for Jess to say this.

Being alone in the house with Luke, Rachel had felt on edge, only relaxing when, after they'd enjoyed dinner with a couple of glasses of wine, Luke pulled her into his arms and kissed her as if he never wanted to let her go. Making love afterwards was bitter-sweet, given her decision to end things between them. But despite her resolution, she couldn't bring herself to say the words which hovered on her lips, and Luke had left, none the wiser. When she got back, she'd vowed.

The flight of two hours and twenty minutes was over before Rachel had time to gather her thoughts, and Andy was waiting for her in the airport, an older, more lined version of her brother-in-law. He was suffering too.

'Thanks for coming,' Andy said, hugging Rachel. 'I told Becky you were coming to visit, but I'm not sure she understood.'

Rachel's heart sank.

'How about we go home for a bite to eat, then visit the nursing home? Becky's sometimes brighter in the afternoon.'

'Suits me.' Andy led her to his car and they drove to the modern villa he and Becky had bought, planning to spend their retirement there, never imagining what was going to happen.

It was a few hours later, when Andy drove Rachel to the nursing home, a large blond brick building set in well-manicured grounds.

'Ready?' he asked when he had parked the car.

'As ready as I'll ever be.' Rachel took a deep breath and got out of the car.

When they entered her sister's room, Rachel tried to control her shock at the sight of Becky sitting in a wheelchair staring blankly out the window. Despite the heat outside, it was cool in here. She went across to kiss her sister on the cheek. Her cheek was cool too.

'Hello, Becks. It's me, Rach.' She waited, but there was no response.

'I'll go and see if I can rustle up some tea,' Andy said before disappearing. Rachel had an inkling of what it must be like for him coming here day after day, hoping for some sign of recognition.

She took a seat beside her sister who turned her gaze from the window to look at her. After a few moments Becky said, 'Rach?'

'Yes, Becks, it's me.' Rachel's eyes moistened. She clasped her sister's hand. Becky's eyes were blank again. Not knowing what to do, she began to chat aimlessly, telling Becky about Alexander, Verity, then saying, 'Oh, you'll never guess who's back in Pelican Crossing. Luke Findlay. He's acting as locum for the local vet, so he's my neighbour.'

There was no glimmer of understanding so, not clear why she did, Rachel added, 'We've been seeing each other.'

This time there was a glimmer of something undefinable in Becky's eyes. She tightened her grip on Rachel's hand. 'Luke's hot. Go you!' she said, before disappearing into herself again.

'Here we are.' Andy reappeared, accompanied by a staff member with a trolley containing three cups of tea and a plate of biscuits. 'Anything?' he asked, when the staff member had left.

Rachel was still in a state of shock at Becky's outburst. Had she heard correctly? Was her sister telling her to… what? For that brief moment, she'd sounded like her old self, then it was as if a shutter had come down and she was gone again. 'There was a moment… when she recognised me, seemed to understand what I was saying, then…'

'It sometimes happens like that. I'd hoped… seeing you… Tea, Becky?' he said, holding out a cup which Becky, letting go of Rachel's hand, grasped in both of hers.

Rachel picked up one of the other cups, taking a gulp to hide her confusion. Had she heard Becky correctly? Was the real Becky inside the woman sitting there like a statue? Did she understand everything they were saying? Was she as frustrated as they were trying to get through to her? Rachel didn't know how Andy could cope with coming here every day. He must love her so very much.

Rachel and Andy left soon after, planning to visit again next day. They spent the evening quietly, looking at photo albums of Becky in happier times and reminiscing about the woman who was now confined to a wheelchair in a nursing home. It didn't seem fair.

*

Luke was missing Rachel more than he expected. She'd been gone barely twenty-four hours, but he was very aware of the empty house at the other end of the bluff. Molly was missing her too, wandering around and whining from time to time. It was lucky she had Nelson for company, and that Luke had the clinic to keep him occupied.

There had been no further news from Joe, but yesterday's copy of *The Echo* had devoted the front page to an article about the poisonings, requesting anyone with information to come forward. It was a repeat of what Luke and Rachel had heard on the radio, but somehow had more impact in print. He hoped it would produce some results.

Luke had arranged to meet Joe and Finn at *The Grand* for a beer after work. He was glad he'd become friends with the two men and enjoyed their company. He would miss them when he left town – *if* he left. He was feeling more and more like he wanted to stay, but it would all depend on Rachel, and he wasn't sure of her feelings. She had seemed cooler last time they were together, but it may have been the prospect of seeing Becky. He couldn't imagine what that would be like.

And, while he still intended to visit Italy, when he had researched the trip he'd discovered it would be best to travel there in the Australian winter… and the Italian summer. He was in no hurry. Whatever was there would keep. It was enough that now he had a starting point.

After taking the dogs for a run on the beach, he took a quick shower, changed into fresh clothes, and checked his phone before leaving. To his disappointment, there was no message

from Rachel, but he assumed she might be too busy with her sister and brother-in-law to make time to call or text.

Luke was first to arrive at the hotel. He ordered his usual craft beer, an IPA he'd become fond of, and took a seat.

Joe and Finn arrived together, engrossed in conversation. They ordered and joined Luke. He could tell from Joe's expression there was news.

'I had an interesting visitor today,' Joe said, after taking a swig of beer. 'I was telling Finn about it on the way in. One of the councillors, Bert Small, came to see me. He's one of the two who brought up the whole dog beach issue last year. It seems Finn's article bore fruit.'

'Yeah?' Surely the man hadn't come to Joe to confess?

'He came to dob in his mate, the other guy, the other councillor, Alan Coatts. I always suspected he was the ringleader. He admitted to Small he had set the bait but hadn't intended any animal to die. It had shaken him… enough for him to share with his mate.'

'Who had the sense to speak to Joe,' Finn said.

'Wow!'

'Yeah,' Joe said. 'It seems that while Small was willing to go along with banning loose dogs on the beach, he drew the line at poisoning them. We're lucky there was only one death.'

'So, what happens now?' Luke asked. Was it enough this Coatts guy had confessed to his mate who, in turn, had told Joe?

'It's in police hands now. I contacted the local station, and they promised to follow it up. I guess it may not be their top priority, but given it made the front page of *The Echo*…' he glanced at Finn, '… we should see some action. The challenge will be getting enough evidence to charge him. I doubt his mate's word will be enough.'

But it was something. 'I think that calls for another beer. My shout,' Luke said.

'To a successful arrest,' Finn said, the three men raising their glasses.

'And the freedom to reopen the dog beach,' Joe added.

The sense of exhilaration Luke had been feeling faded. Of course the beach would have to remain closed until this Coatts guy was arrested and charged. It wasn't over yet, but it was a start and, hopefully, once he was questioned, the guy would have the sense to confess.

Forty-six

Rachel would be glad to get home. She'd spent three days in Adelaide and on each of them had spent time at the nursing home with Becky. But, apart from that first day, her sister had given no sign of recognising her or interest in what she had to say. Rachel had found herself babbling on about things that had happened when they were growing up, even of the times she had joined Becky and Luke on their dates, in the hope of igniting some spark, some sign she understood. But there was nothing. She might as well have been talking to the wall. She didn't know how Andy did it, day after day.

Now she was on her way home and she couldn't wait to see Molly again, and Verity and her other granddaughters, even Luke. She hadn't contacted him while she was away, too confused about her own feelings to know what to say. She was well aware she may have seemed indifferent to him that morning before she left.

Becky's words had confused her further. She was right. Luke was hot, too hot for her. Rachel wasn't a teenager anymore She'd be sixty in less than two years. It was too late to change now. While it had been good to feel close to a man again, to feel desired, to have someone to cuddle up to in bed, Luke Findlay wasn't for her. Not only did he live in Sydney, he was planning to travel to Italy. The very word conjured up images of exotic places she could only dream about. It was somewhere she'd longed to visit, before marriage and children took over her life. Then there were her granddaughters, her B&B guests… and now Verity. There was no time in her life for any sort of permanent relationship.

She wondered how the little girl was coping with her gone. Although she'd called Jess each day and spoken to Verity before she went to bed each night, it wasn't the same as being there. In the short time the little girl had been part of her life, she'd crept into a spot in her heart, and Rachel was longing to see her again, to hear her cute English accent and watch her and Molly together.

Jess was waiting for her at the airport along with Verity and Emily.

'Grandma!' Verity raced to meet her and threw her arms around her legs. 'You came back!'

'Of course I did, sweetheart. I said I would.' She picked her up and hugged her. 'I missed you.'

'I missed you too.' Verity wound her arms around Rachel's neck as if she would never let her go.

A wave of love flowed through Rachel at the realisation of how important she'd become to Verity, and she vowed never to leave her again. This little girl had already lost too many people in her short life. Rachel wasn't going to be another. Suddenly the confusion she'd been experiencing was gone. Verity was more important than anything or anyone else. She must be the focus of her attention for as long as it took.

'Good to have you back, Mum. How was Aunt Becky?' Jess asked, as they made their way to the car, Verity still clinging to Rachel, her hands tightly clasped around her grandmother's neck. She was becoming heavy, but Rachel didn't want to let her go.

'Not great. Tell you later,' Rachel said, as she popped Verity into one of the child car seats in the back of the car, while Jess fastened Emily into the other one. She gave Verity a kiss on the forehead and patted the red curls which were so like hers had been.

'I thought we could go straight back to my place for a bite to eat,' Jess said. 'That okay by you?'

'Sure.' Rachel leant back in her seat. *It was good to be home*, she thought, as the familiar landmarks flew past.

In no time, they reached Pelican Crossing and stopped outside Jess's home. Verity clung to Rachel again when she lifted her out of the car, highlighting the wisdom of her decision. 'It's okay, my darling. I'm not going to leave you again,' she said. If she visited Adelaide again, she'd take Verity with her.

After a lunch of soup and salad, during which Rachel was able to fill Jess in about Becky, Jess asked, 'Shall I drop you off on my way to pick up the twins, or would you like to see them today?'

'On your way, please.' While Rachel loved the twins to bits, she wasn't ready for the exuberant welcome she was sure they'd give her. And she had to pick up Molly which meant she'd have to see Luke. 'Why don't you bring them round tomorrow? We can have lunch.'

'Okay. But don't you have guests arriving tomorrow?'

'Yes, but the rooms are all made up ready.'

When Jess dropped them off, Verity could barely wait till Rachel opened the door before running through the house. 'Where's Molly?' she asked when she returned to Rachel's side, her voice filled with disappointment.

'Molly's been staying with Luke and Nelson while I was gone. Remember them?'

'Yes. Can we fetch her?'

'In a little while. Why don't you show me what you've been doing at *Pelican Pals* first?' Rachel needed time to get her bearings, to work out what to say to Luke, before she was ready to face him.

*

Luke was closing up the clinic for the day when Molly let out a volley of barking. Glancing out the window of the office, he saw Rachel walking up the driveway, Verity skipping beside her. 'You knew your mistress was outside,' he said to the excited little dog with a grin. 'I'm happy to see her too.' He washed his hands and went out to greet them.

'Good to see you, Red. When did you get back?' he said, as Molly danced around Rachel and Verity and jumped up on the little girl making her squeal with delight.

'This morning. Jess picked me up and we had lunch before she dropped us back home. It's good to be home.' She smiled, but Luke thought there was something forced about it.

'How was Becky?'

Rachel grimaced and mouthed, 'Later.'

'Do you have time to stop for coffee? I have chocolate biscuits,' he said to Verity.

'Can Molly come too?'

'And Nelson,' Luke said, noting the boxer had now joined them, curious to see what was happening. 'But no chocolate biscuits for them.'

Verity giggled. 'Grandma came back,' she said, taking Rachel's hand.

Luke raised an eyebrow. Then he realised. She'd lost her mother, then her father had left. She must have worried that Rachel had gone for good too. 'I'm sure your grandma will never leave you,' he said, noting how she clung to Rachel's hand. Was this what Rachel's forced expression and her lack of communication was all about?

'Coffee would be good. If it's not too much trouble.'

'Of course not.' How could she imagine it would be? He was so pleased to see her he wanted to pick her up and twirl her around, to kiss her until she cried for mercy. But he sensed something had changed between them, and Verity was here, so he led her and the little girl across to the house, the two dogs following.

'How was Molly?'

Luke had made coffee. He and Rachel were sitting on the back veranda, and Verity, having drunk a glass of milk and eaten one of the chocolate digestive biscuits, had joined the dogs in a game with a ball.

'She was good. She missed you, but she and Nelson get on well together.' He glanced at Rachel, trying to gauge her expression. 'I missed you too.'

She didn't react to his comment. 'You asked about Becky.' She sighed. 'I hated seeing her like that. It's as if the life has gone out of her, leaving an empty shell.'

'I'm sorry to hear that. Were you able to speak with her at all?'

'I spoke. She only said a few words on my first day, when she seemed to recognise me.' Rachel's lips tightened, and Luke wondered what those words had been. But Rachel didn't enlighten him. 'Andy visits her each day. He's a good man.'

Becky was lucky. It must be hard when the love of your life suffers from a disease that takes her from you while she is still alive.

This wasn't going well. He had been looking forward to Rachel's return, but it was as if a barrier had gone up between them. Had something happened when she was in Adelaide? He searched around for something to say, to break the awkward silence which had grown between them.

Rachel spoke first. 'Any more news about the poisonings?'

'Some. The police haven't charged anyone yet... insufficient evidence. But Joe told Finn and me that one of the councillors has ratted on his mate.'

'One of those who wanted to ban dogs from the beach?'

'I believe so.'

'Oh! I hope they can get the evidence they need. Is the beach still closed?'

'Until they can be sure it's over.'

'And it may not be until they can find enough evidence to charge him. What a mess, and a disaster for the tourist industry. People come here to enjoy the beach. I know it's not the surf beach, but it's a beautiful stretch of white sand.'

'Yeah.'

Verity came running up, Molly and Nelson behind her. 'Can we go home now, Grandma? Molly wants to go home.'

Rachel smiled. 'I think *you* want to go home,' she said, 'and it's almost time for your bath.' She rose.

'Can I see you later?' Luke asked.

'Not tonight. I need to spend time with Verity, get myself organised.'

'Tomorrow?' Luke hated to hear the pleading note in his voice. What was happening to him?

'Jess is bringing the girls over, and I have a new batch of guests arriving.' Rachel hesitated, then said, 'Sunday. Why don't you come to breakfast. If you come at nine, the guest breakfast will be over.' She seemed about to say something else but didn't.

'Breakfast at nine on Sunday. I'll look forward to it.' Luke wanted to give her a hug, but recognised she might not welcome it. He watched despondently as she and Verity headed off, Molly running along beside them. 'What was all that about?' he asked Nelson, shaking his head in disbelief.

Forty-seven

It had been hard to be dispassionate with Luke when all she wanted to do was to throw herself into his arms, but Rachel had made her decision, and no matter how difficult it was going to be, she knew it was the right one… for her… and for Verity.

The little girl had been so excited to show her the drawing she'd made at *Pelican Pals* while Rachel was in Adelaide and to write her name for her. And the way her little body had cuddled into hers when Rachel read to her from *Green Eggs and Ham* – the same Dr Seuss book Alexander had loved so much – before bedtime, only reinforced her decision.

But now, as she sipped a glass of wine in the quiet house, the only sound Molly's gentle snoring, Rachel wished things could be different. She picked up her iPad and sent an email to Alexander, filling him in with news of Verity and telling him about her visit to Adelaide. He'd always been close to Becky, who had a soft spot for her only nephew. As soon as she finished, she picked up the phone to call Steph, to invite her to join them for lunch tomorrow. She suddenly felt an urge to have her family around her. Maybe it was seeing Becky, realising how quickly things could change, maybe it was a reaction to the decision she made about Luke, a need to justify it to herself.

Steph and Chloe were delighted to accept, with Steph saying, 'We had our six-week ultrasound yesterday and I can't wait to show it to you.'

Rachel's heart bloomed at the reminder of the new life about to enter the world, another addition to her family, and she gave thanks for her blessings. She didn't need a man to fill her life. *She already had all she needed*, she thought, dismissing the memory of the lonely nights she'd spent before Luke came on the scene, replacing them with the recollection of wakening to Verity's sweet little body curling up to hers, and the sound of the little girl calling her *Grandma* in her endearing English accent, so different from that of her other granddaughters.

'And I have you, too, Molly,' she said to the sleeping dog, who had been her faithful companion since Kirk died. 'What would I do without you?'

*

Next day, Rachel had no time to reflect on what might have been. As soon as Jess and the girls arrived, the twins demanded they go to the beach, so there was the customary kerfuffle finding buckets and spades, applying sunscreen and packing towels, water and snacks. Then they were off, an excited Molly dancing among them, climbing down the steps to the beach.

This morning, the beach was busier than usual. Since the dog beach was still closed, several of the local dog owners had begun to bring their pets here. Rachel didn't mind. She loved dogs and was happy to see them run free, but it did change the secluded nature of the beach.

When she and Jess set up the beach cabana shelter tent which she'd purchased at Christmas, and set out the beach mat under it, the twins, Verity and Molly headed for the water.

'Stay at the edge till Grandma and I join you,' Jess called after them, as they raced off to join two other dog owners and their animals.

'They'll be fine,' Rachel said, shading her eyes and recognising old Agnes with her spaniel, and Finn with his grandson and Bluey. 'I know those people. They'll make sure they don't come to any harm.'

By the time she and Jess joined the girls with Emily, Agnes and her dog had moved on, but it appeared the girls had made friends with Finn's grandson and his dog.

'This is Sandy and his dog's called Bluey like the one on television,' Verity said. 'But this Bluey doesn't look like the other one.'

Rachel and Jess laughed as the blue roan spaniel cavorted in the waves with his owner.

'Sandy goes to our school,' Gemma said.

'He's in grade two,' Indie added in awe.

Verity sidled up to Rachel. 'Sandy doesn't have a daddy,' she whispered. 'I told him I don't have a mummy, and he said I can share his.'

'Oh, sweetheart, that's kind of him.' Rachel's eyes moistened. She looked up to see Finn. 'Did you hear what your grandson told Verity?'

'I did. It almost made me weep.'

'Me, too.'

With Finn agreeing to watch the children… and the dogs, Rachel and Jess were able to have a proper swim, the familiar peace the ocean always generated stilling Rachel's worries and bringing her a much-needed sense of calm. By the time they returned to shore, she was feeling much better than she had when she awoke, and the sight of Steph and Chloe waiting for them gave her an additional lift.

Lunch was the usual chaos. They ate in the garden with Molly managing to get in everyone's way and the girls dropping titbits to her when they thought the adults weren't looking. When both children and dog went off to investigate the garden, and the grownups were enjoying coffee, Steph grinned and said, 'We have something to show you,' and pulled out her phone.

For a moment, Rachel wasn't sure what she was looking at, then her eyes focussed on the blob in the centre of the screen.

'See,' Steph said pointing. 'That's the umbilical cord and these tiny buds are the beginnings of our baby's arms and legs.' She squeezed Chloe's hand.

'Oh, Steph!' For the second time that morning, Rachel's eyes moistened. She remembered her own excitement when she first saw ultrasound images of Jess, then of Steph, then Alexander. The thrill never got any less. Now it was Steph and Chloe's turn to wonder at the miracle of a new life.

'If it's a girl we plan to call her Rachita,' Steph said, 'a diminutive form of Rachel. It's actually an Indian name meaning *created*, which is really appropriate too.'

Rachel was so moved, she was speechless, but Jess said, 'I like it. What made you choose it?'

Steph looked at Chloe and grinned. 'Actually, it's the name of a character in one of our favourite television programmes. DI Rachita Ray is an English detective. We liked the name so looked it up and love the meaning and the idea that it's a link with you, Mum.'

'I guess we just have to hope you have a girl then,' Rachel smiled.

Forty-eight

Rachel's guests, an elderly couple from Melbourne, and a young family with a boy a little younger than Verity, had already left for the day, intending to spend it on the beach. Fortunately, Verity had left too. The previous day, the twins had talked so much about their activities with Nippers, where they went every Sunday morning, that Verity had wanted to see for herself. Jess had picked her up on their way to the surf beach where the sessions were held. She was happy to go, confident in the knowledge Rachel was safely at home with Molly and would be there when she returned.

Luke had shot her a strange look when he arrived with Nelson, giving her a kiss on the cheek as usual. Now, Nelson and Molly were outside, and Luke was sitting at the kitchen table drinking coffee.

Rachel's stomach was churning as she cooked a fresh batch of scrambled eggs and bacon and dropped slices of sour dough bread into the toaster. She'd been awake half the night trying to work out what to say to Luke, how to word it in a way that wouldn't hurt him. She didn't expect he had feelings for her, no more feelings than the normal desire of a man for a woman he found attractive and who was available. Had she been too available, flattered by his interest, lonely after living alone for so long? She was the one who'd be hurt by her decision, but better now than in a few weeks' time when he went back to his life in Sydney.

When Rachel had served breakfast and taken a seat, Luke stared at her. 'What's up, Red? You seemed very on edge on Friday and this morning you're strung out with tension. Have I done something to upset you?'

Rachel flinched. She hadn't realised she was so obvious. She had hoped to delay this conversation until they had finished breakfast, but seeing his expression, she knew it couldn't wait.

Breakfast grew cold as Rachel stumbled with words in her attempt to explain her decision ending with, 'So I think it best if we remain friends. You'll be gone soon and…' Her voice broke.

'You can't mean it, Red, not after…' Luke stared at her as if she'd gone mad.

'I do, Luke. I'm sorry.' Rachel couldn't say any more as images of the times they'd spent together, moments she'd cherish for ever, flitted through her mind. Maybe she *was* mad. She knew all her friends would tell her so. Her heart dropped. They'd all find out. They knew she'd been seeing Luke, that she and he… Would they believe she'd been the one to end it? But she couldn't think of that now. 'It's for the best,' she repeated, picking up her cup with a hand that was shaking so much the liquid threatened to spill over.

Luke's lips tightened, his eyes narrowed. Rachel had never seen him like this.

'Well, I guess that's that,' he said. He went to the door, called Nelson, then man and dog left, the door slamming behind them.

What had she done? Rachel looked at the untouched plates of eggs and bacon. She pushed hers away, dropped her head onto her arms, and began to weep.

Rachel had no idea how long she sat there. She was brought back to the present by a wet tongue on her ankle and Molly's gentle 'Woof'.

'Sorry, Molly. Did you think I'd forgotten about you?' She picked the little dog up and hugged her, but Molly, scenting the food on the table, tried to wriggle free.

'You'd like some of that, wouldn't you?' she asked. She knew she wouldn't eat it. Would she ever eat scrambled eggs and bacon again without remembering this morning? Rising she scraped the plates into a delighted Molly's bowl and went to wash her face. Verity would be back soon, and Rachel didn't want her granddaughter to see her like this.

*

Luke strode across the bluff, Nelson running to keep up with him. He was filled with suppressed anger, unable to fully comprehend what had just happened. He had arrived at Rachel's for breakfast, anticipating a pleasant meal, maybe the chance for a cuddle if Verity was playing with the dogs. He'd missed the closeness which had developed between him and Rachel when she was gone and was looking forward to a resumption of their relationship. Instead… He shook his head. He'd never understand women.

Back home, he mooched around the house, unable to settle. At the sound of his phone ringing, his hopes rose. Maybe it was Rachel calling to apologise, to say she'd been wrong. It wasn't Rachel's voice, but Joe's.

'Glad I caught you. Good news. We have a result. The police brought Coatts in for questioning – the councillor we suspect of setting the baits,' he added, when Luke didn't respond. 'He broke down and confessed, so they've charged him.'

'Right. Thanks for letting me know.'

'Are you all right? I thought you'd be more pleased.'

'Sorry.' Luke tried to rouse himself, to bring himself to sound more enthusiastic. 'I just had some bad news.'

'Oh, I'm sorry. Want to talk about it?'

'Not really. But I could do with some company.'

'That I can do. *The Grand*? I'm free now if you are.'

'See you there in twenty minutes. We can celebrate our win,' Luke said, trying to inject some enthusiasm into his voice, but failing.

Luke sluiced his face with cold water to hide the ravages of the tears he would never admit to shedding. What had taken place at Rachel's that morning had shocked him. Not what she said, though that had been bad enough. What had shocked him most was the realisation of the strength of his feelings for her. What had started as a pleasant way to pass the time in Pelican Crossing, with an attractive woman who he knew had hero-worshipped him as a teenager, had turned into something more. They hadn't known each other long, but in that short time, he'd fallen in love with Rachel.

Forty-nine

Rachel didn't know how she'd made it through the last two weeks, only seeing Luke in the distance, and avoiding times when she knew he and Nelson would be on the beach. She could see them from her window, his tall figure, the large dog running by his side. He seemed to do a lot of running these days, running or surfing. Both activities which would keep his mind occupied.

Could he be missing her as much as she was missing him? Rachel thought of the sleepless nights, the times when she dozed off only to wake again in the early hours, the times when she picked up her phone to call him, only to drop it again. Now Verity was sleeping the whole night in her own bed, Rachel's felt empty again. Only two more weeks and he'd be gone back to Sydney, and she wouldn't have to face seeing him on the beach and wonder what he was thinking.

But today was Verity's birthday, and last night Alexander had made good his promise to arrive before her big day and had surprised the excited little girl. It had taken two stories from Alexander, and Rachel agreeing to allow Molly to stay with her, for Verity to go to sleep.

'She seems back to normal now,' Alexander had said when he joined Rachel in the living room where she'd poured them both a glass of port. 'It was a hard decision, Mum, but the only one I could think of at the time. I've missed her.'

Rachel hadn't replied, remembering the tears, the sleepless nights, the times Verity had crawled into bed with her. But he was right. He was in no position to bring up a child on his own and, no matter how much Rachel loved her son, she knew how thoughtless he could be at times. A young child needed security, and Rachel could provide that. There was always Jess, but with three of her own…

'It's my birthday!' A little whirlwind flew into Rachel's bedroom and flung herself onto the bed, followed by Molly who jumped up too.

'Happy birthday, my darling,' Rachel said, hugging the wriggling little body.

'Daddy's still asleep,' Verity said in disgust. 'Can we have breakfast?'

'Let me get up, shower and dress. Your daddy had a long flight yesterday. He must be tired. Can you dress yourself?'

'Can I wear my party dress, the one I got for Christmas and wore to the twins' party?'

'Of course. It's your birthday. You can wear whatever you want to.'

'Yay!' Verity slid down from the bed and, went off to get dressed, Molly following, like her shadow.

Alone again, Rachel smiled to herself. It was Verity's birthday. They were having a party. She'd put on her happy face, and no one would guess her heart was breaking. She hadn't realised how much it would hurt when she told Luke of her decision, assuming it would be a bit like pulling off a band aid – hurt for a moment, then the hurt would gradually lessen till it was gone completely. But that hadn't happened, at least not yet.

She'd tried to make light of it when she met her group of friends for lunch, saying it had been one of those things, never meant to last, and had brushed off their sympathetic comments. But it had hurt. Without meaning to, determined to keep her heart intact, she'd fallen hopelessly in love with Luke Findlay.

There were no guests to worry about today, so Rachel made banana pancakes for Verity and Alexander as a treat, then set to making the special birthday cake Verity had asked for, while Alexander took Verity – inappropriately dressed in her party dress – to the beach with Molly who rarely left her side.

The party started with the arrival of the twins who were as excited as if it was their own birthday. Verity was showered with gifts, but the one she liked best was from her new friend, Sandy, who had brought his dog, Bluey, with him. It was a pair of shorts, a tee-shirt and a water bottle, all based on the Bluey cartoon character. 'He chose them himself,' Adele, Sandy's mother, whispered to Rachel when Verity opened the parcel, her eyes shining with excitement.

As the party progressed, Rachel was pleased to see Alexander take an active role in organising the games and appearing to be enjoying himself. She also noticed how he and Adele often seemed to be standing together, either watching the children play or chatting. She wondered if this might be the start of something but was too afraid to hope. Finn's daughter had lost her husband in a drowning accident over a year earlier, and Rachel knew Finn would love to see her move on and provide Sandy with a father. She remembered Verity telling her how Sandy had said she could share his mother and thought how wonderful if it could really happen, and he could share her father too. She mentally crossed her fingers. *Maybe it wasn't too farfetched*, she thought as she watched Alexander laugh at something Adele had said to him.

'Wow,' Rachel said to Alexander, when the last guests had left. 'It was fun, but I'm glad it's over. I may be getting too old for kiddie's parties.'

'You'll never be too old, Mum,' Alexander said fondly, giving her a hug. 'I thought you were wonderful.'

'Thanks.' Rachel glowed. Alexander wasn't normally so fulsome with his praise. 'But those twins… they'll be the death of me.'

'They are a bit much,' Alexander agreed. 'That Sandy kid's nice, and he's very gentle with Verity. She seems to adore him.'

'His mum's nice too,' Rachel risked saying.

To Rachel's surprise, Alexander blushed. 'We spoke. She told me about Sandy's dad. She understands.'

Rachel gazed at her son in surprise. Had she been right in thinking there was more to his relationship with Anthea than he'd told her? She thought it best not to comment.

'She's invited Verity and me to tea tomorrow. Sandy wants to show Verity some tricks he's taught Bluey,' he added by way of explanation.

'That'll be nice,' Rachel said, feeling tentatively optimistic. It was probably too soon for both of them, but perhaps in time… Especially if Alexander kept his promise to come back frequently to see Verity.

Rachel was exhausted by the time she fell into bed that night. As she relived the events of the day, she took comfort in the possibility of

Alexander and Sandy's mother finding common ground and forming a relationship. It would be good, not only for them, but for both children who already seemed to have formed a bond. And, of course, there was the possibility, if that were to happen, that Alexander might return home for good. As her eyes started to close, Rachel acknowledged how much easier it was to plan for the future of others than to make good decisions for herself. She wondered what Luke was thinking right now, if he ever thought of her, of what might have been.

Fifty

Luke was conscious his time in Pelican Crossing was drawing to an end. There were only two more weeks before he'd be finished here and heading back to Sydney.

On the one hand, he'd be glad to leave. It was agony knowing Rachel was living just a short distance away across the bluff. She might as well have been on the other side of Australia for all the good it did him. Their paths hadn't crossed since that fateful morning when she'd told him she didn't want to see him again. She hadn't put it as bluntly as that, of course, saying they could still be friends. But despite sharing a beach, she and Molly had never been there at the same time as him and Nelson. He suspected she was deliberately avoiding him, and perhaps he didn't blame her. It saved any awkwardness.

On the other hand, he wasn't looking forward to returning to Sydney, to seeing his family home being turned into a nursery. Each time he spoke with Josh on the phone, his son reported one more item they'd bought for the baby. The house must be overflowing with baby paraphernalia by now, and soon there would be the baby itself. While he had always looked forward to becoming a grandfather, it had never occurred to him he'd be sharing a house with his grandchild and its parents.

He'd miss Pelican Crossing too. While he'd been hesitant to return, he'd discovered he enjoyed the peace and tranquillity of the coastal town where he'd grown up, the place which still held so many pleasant memories. And he'd developed a renewed enthusiasm for the beach and surfing. Nelson liked it too. It would be difficult to return to walking on concrete paths on a busy thoroughfare, or in the confines of the park, instead of enjoying the freedom of a deserted beach, to breathe in car fumes instead of the scent of the ocean. His old schoolmates, led by Troy, were already planning a farewell for him. He didn't think he could stomach it.

Tired after a busy day at the clinic, Luke was considering his options, one of which was his proposed trip to Italy. He was actually checking out flights and accommodation when an email from Bob dropped into his mailbox. This was nothing new. Luke and Bob had kept in constant touch since Luke arrived in Pelican Crossing, Luke reporting on local and clinic news, and Bob providing effusive accounts of life in the States which he was enjoying. Luke wasn't exactly in the mood to read another of Bob's diatribes about how wonderful life was in the United States where everything seemed to be bigger and better than back here in Pelican Crossing.

He fixed himself a coffee before reading it. The first section contained all the usual bluster about the weather, the food, the people. Then Luke's eyes widened as he read,

I know how much you appear to be enjoying being back in Pelican Crossing so, although this may come as a surprise to you, I'm confident you'll agree. To my great delight and I must confess, surprise, I've been invited to become a visiting lecturer with the faculty here. It would mean I'd be staying for another six months, possibly longer. I'm hoping you'll see fit to continue your good work at the clinic for that period. Can you get back to me as soon as possible as the Dean needs to know if I can accept his kind offer?

Luke didn't read any further. This was the last thing he'd expected. If only he and Rachel were still close, still speaking even, he could discuss it with her. But as things stood, could he bear to stay?

*

The sun was peeping over the horizon when Luke went down the steps to the beach with Nelson next morning. After reading Bob's email, he hadn't been able to sleep. If he accepted the offer, it would mean he would run the risk of seeing Rachel every day, of being reminded of what might have been. The thought of what it could be like for her to have become a permanent part of his life sent his heart racing. But what about his plan to travel to Italy, and Josh and Abby back in Sydney? It was all too hard.

Leaving Nelson to wander down to the ocean, Luke sat on a grassy tussock, his hands round his knees, staring out to sea, his thoughts in a whirl.

'You look very pensive this morning.'

Luke looked up to see old Agnes gazing down at him. Although the dog beach had reopened, he'd noticed that some of the old guard were still bringing their dogs here. Agnes was one of them. 'I have a lot to think about.'

'Sometimes a worry shared is a worry halved.' Agnes pulled up her long skirt and sat down beside him. Her spaniel had joined Nelson in the surf.

Luke managed a chuckle. It was something his grandmother used to say too. Maybe it wouldn't hurt to speak to old Agnes. Who was she going to tell? 'I doubt you can help me,' he said.

'Why don't you try me? There's not much I haven't heard over the years.'

Luke stared at the old woman for a few moments, then he began, telling her about Rachel, about Bob's offer, and about his indecision. 'It's crazy,' he said as he finished. 'I'm not a kid. I should be able to make up my own mind. I don't know why I'm dithering like this.'

Agnes's eyes met his, and Luke saw a world of wisdom in the old, lined face. 'Rachel's a good woman. She's had a tough life. It wasn't easy for her when her husband got sick, but she rose to the challenge. Then she set up her B&B business while taking care of her grandchildren. Now, I hear her son has presented her with another grandchild to take care of – on a permanent basis. I can understand why she might be cautious about forming a relationship with someone like yourself whose life and family are interstate. And you're about to become a grandparent yourself, you say?'

'Yeah.' When she put it like that, Luke could see Rachel's point of view. 'But…'

'How do you feel about her?' The old woman didn't mince words.

'I love her.' It was the first time Luke had said it out loud.

'Have you told her?'

'No, she…'

'Don't blame Rachel. How can she know how you feel if you haven't told her? She's not a mind reader.'

But you are?

'So, you're suggesting…?' Luke's pulse raced.

'Here's your opportunity.' Agnes rose to leave. 'Don't waste it.'

Looking down the beach, Luke saw Rachel walking along the edge of the water, Molly prancing at her heels.

Fifty-one

Rachel's heart lurched at the sight of Luke sitting on the wild grass at the edge of the beach with old Agnes. As she watched, the woman rose and called to her dog who was frolicking in the waves with Luke's boxer. Rachel bit her lip. She hadn't expected him to be on the beach at this time in the morning.

When she'd left the house, both Alexander and Verity had been sound asleep and Rachel had decided to take the opportunity for an early morning walk to blow away the cobwebs, as her mother would say. She had a lot to think about, mainly whether or not to continue the Bed and Breakfast business which had been her lifeline since Kirk died. But now she had Verity to care for, to provide company for her in the evenings when memories threatened to overwhelm her, she didn't have the same need for strangers to fill the void left by Kirk's death.

Soon she might have Alexander's company too. Last night, after Verity was asleep, they'd had a long chat during which he'd revealed how much he was missing Verity, his weariness with the social round in the busy city and his decision to look for a position in Australia, closer to Pelican Crossing, one which would enable him to work from home part of the time. 'If you think you can cope with me, Mum,' he'd said with his familiar grin.

While it was the last thing Rachel had expected, she'd been delighted and, her heart brimming with happiness at the prospect of having all three of her children living close by, assured him she'd be overjoyed if it were to happen, and that coping was the wrong word. Alex had hugged her then.

When she saw Luke get to his feet and start to walk towards her, Rachel's first instinct was to flee, but Molly had run ahead and was gambolling in the shallow water with Nelson. *She* couldn't move. It was if she had been turned to stone. Suddenly Luke was there, right next to her, looking as handsome as ever in a pair of cut-off jeans and a white tee-shirt that clung to his body like a second skin. On closer inspection, his eyes appeared bloodshot and the lines around them seemed to have deepened. *Had he been having trouble sleeping too?*

'Red.' He nodded.

Rachel's heart lurched again at the sound of the familiar nickname. She'd missed hearing it on his lips. 'Luke.' This was as awkward as she'd anticipated. It was why she'd been at pains to avoid him and had succeeded… until now. But he had every right to be here. She didn't own the beach.

'I'm sorry.'

'I'm sorry.'

They both spoke at once, but what did he have to be sorry about? Unless it was being here on the beach at this time of the morning. 'It's a lovely morning,' she said brightly, trying to suppress the butterflies in her stomach. *How could he still have this effect on her?*

'We need to talk,' he said.

'I don't think so.' *What could he possibly have to say that would interest her?* Though she was curious.

'I'm sorry,' he said again, 'sorry I've been such a fool. Meeting you again took me back to a time when life was so much simpler, when it seemed as if anything was possible.' He pulled on his beard.

Rachel was conscious of the crash of the waves on the shore, and the high-pitched yapping of their two dogs having fun. She tried to focus on what Luke was saying, hoping he would finish soon and leave. Being so close to him reminded her of times she'd been trying to forget resurrected emotions she'd thought she had quashed.

'Sorry,' he said for a third time. 'I'm not putting this well.' He pushed a hand through his hair. 'What I'm trying to say is that it's been hell. I've missed you so much. I can understand your thinking. You didn't want to become involved with someone who was about to leave. But what if I didn't… leave? What if I stayed, stayed here in Pelican Crossing? I've fallen in love with you, Red. I want to spend the rest of my life with you. Can I dare hope you might come to feel the same about me?'

Rachel stared at him, unable to believe her ears. *Had Luke actually said he was in love with her?* She'd dreamt about this moment so often, she couldn't believe it was actually happening. She blinked rapidly, feeling dizzy. Was she going to faint? 'You… I…' she stammered.

'Are you okay?'

Suddenly, Luke's arms were around her. *Had he really said he was going to stay in Pelican Crossing, that he loved her… or had she imagined it?* 'Did you say…'

'I love you. I love you, Red. Maybe I've always loved you, ever since you were that pesky fourteen-year-old hanging around Becky and me, but especially now you have become this desirable woman, a woman who makes my legs weak, who…'

'I love you too,' Rachel said. 'I tried not to fall in love with you, almost persuaded myself I hadn't. I…' But before she could say any more, Luke picked her up, her feet left the ground, and she was being whirled around as easily as if she was as light as Verity. 'Stop it, you big fool, Let me down!' she yelled, her voice causing the two dogs to race over barking wildly, no doubt thinking someone was in danger.

Luke and Rachel both burst out laughing. He lowered her so her feet touched the sand again but kept hold of her and kissed her, first on her forehead, then her eyelids, her cheeks, ending on her lips where his lips stayed for so long, Rachel almost lost her breath. 'Not here,' she said weakly.

'Then where? Do you want to go home?'

Rachel shook her head. 'No. Alexander and Verity are there.'

'Looks like it's Bob's place, then.' Luke tilted his head in the direction of the steps leading to Bob's house and the clinic. It was lucky it was Sunday. The clinic would be closed.

When they reached the house, Luke left the dogs outside, before pulling Rachel into his arms again. She melted into his embrace. This was where she belonged. She felt like a breathless girl of eighteen, her pulse throbbing in her ears and her legs weak with desire as his lips covered hers hungrily.

'I've been dreaming of this,' Luke murmured between kisses, his breath hot against her ear, his lips sending shockwaves through her entire body.

How could she have denied herself this, Rachel thought, feeling her knees weaken as his mouth descended on hers again and again.

They only pulled apart when they heard the dogs whining and scratching at the door. 'They're hungry,' Rachel said, remembering she hadn't fed Molly before they went to the beach.

Luke let them in and, after making sure they had food and water asked, 'You?'

Rachel shook her head. She wasn't hungry for food. She just wanted more of Luke.

'I think we have something to celebrate,' Luke said, 'How about champagne, then...' He glanced towards the bedroom.

Rachel blushed, a delicious shudder heating her body.

'Champagne at this time of a morning, and on an empty stomach?' Rachel giggled, feeling heady, as if she'd already drunk two glasses of champagne.

'Why not? Luke said. 'It feels as if all my Christmases have come at once.'

Rachel savoured the moment, watching the man... her *lover*, open the champagne and pour two glasses.

'To us, and our future together in Pelican Crossing,' Luke said, raising his glass.

'To us,' Rachel repeated raising her glass to join his. It might not be Christmas, but this was the best surprise ever.

The End

If you've enjoyed Rachel and Luke's story, I'd love if you could leave a review on Amazon and/or Goodreads. A few words will suffice, no need for a lengthy review. It will mean a lot to me and help other readers find my books.

I'm thrilled so many of my readers are enjoying this series set in Pelican Crossing and are making friends with my characters.

The fifth book in the series, *Safe Harbour in Pelican Crossing* is Erica's story. Those of you who have read the earlier books in the series will remember her from A New Dawn in Pelican Crossing. She is Joe's sister.

After the death of her abusive husband, *Erica Masters* returns to Perth, eager for a fresh start and the birth of her granddaughter. But when she learns her husband has changed his Will in favour of their son, leaving her with nothing, she flees to seek refuge in Pelican Crossing, the place she once called home.

Having sold his fishing boat after a bitter divorce which left him to bring up his two teenage sons, *Jamie Whittaker* has found success with his fishing charter business. Thrilled by the arrival of his first grandchild, he is stunned when his teenage flame, Erica, reappears in town.

As the pair reconnect, old feelings resurface, but Erica remains guarded after her painful past. Jamie, determined to win Erica's heart once again, manages to break through her defences until a family tragedy turns their lives upside down.

With everything unravelling around them, can these two troubled souls build a future together?

If you enjoy emotional reads, you'll love this gripping tale of love and second chances.

You can order here https://mybook.to/SafeHarbourinPC

From the Author

Dear Reader,

First, I'd like to thank you for choosing to read *A Christmas Surrpise in Pelican Crossing*. I hope you've enjoyed visiting Pelican Crossing as much as I've enjoyed creating it.

Like all my other books, although it is part of a series, it can be read as a standalone.

If you'd like to stay up to date with my new releases and special offers you can sign up to my reader's group.

You can sign up here

https://maggiechristensenauthor.com/subscribe/

I'll never share your email address, and you can unsubscribe at any time. You can also contact me via Facebook, Twitter or by email. I love hearing from my readers and will always reply.

Thanks again.

Acknowledgements

As always, this book could not have been written without the help and advice of a number of people.

Firstly, my husband Jim for listening to my plotlines without complaint, for his patience and insights as I discuss my characters and storyline with him, for his patience and help with difficult passages and advice on my male dialogue, and for being there when I need him.

John Hudspith, editor extraordinaire for his ideas, suggestions, encouragement and attention to detail, and for helping me make this book better.

Jane Dixon-Smith for her patience and for working her magic on my beautiful cover and interior.

My thanks also to early readers of this book –Maggie and Louise for their helpful comments and advice, to my son, Todd, for his knowledge of visiting a craft brewery and to fellow writer and vet, Bernadette Rowley, for ensuring I had accurate information about veterinary practice. Any mistakes are my own.

And to all of my readers, reviewers and bloggers. Your support and comments make it all worthwhile.

About the Author

After a career in education, Maggie Christensen began writing contemporary women's fiction portraying mature women facing life-changing situations, and historical fiction set in her native Scotland. Her travels inspire her writing, be it her trips to visit family in Scotland, in Oregon, USA or her home on Queensland's beautiful Sunshine Coast. Maggie writes of mature heroines coming to terms with changes in their lives and the heroes worthy of them. Maggie has been called *the queen of mature age fiction* and her writing has been described by one reviewer as *like a nice warm cup of tea. It is warm, nourishing, comforting and embracing.*

From the small town in Scotland where she grew up, Maggie was lured to Australia by the call to 'Come and teach in the sun'. Once there, she worked as a primary school teacher, university lecturer and in educational management. Now living with her husband of over thirty years on Queensland's Sunshine Coast, she loves walking on the deserted beach in the early mornings and having coffee by the river on weekends. Her days are spent surrounded by books, either reading or writing them – her idea of heaven!

Maggie can be found on Facebook, Twitter, Goodreads, Instagram, Bookbub or on her website.

https://www.facebook.com/maggiechristensenauthor
https://twitter.com/MaggieChriste33
https://www.goodreads.com/author/show/8120020.Maggie_Christensen
https://www.instagram.com/maggiechriste33/
https://www.bookbub.com/profile/maggie-christensen
https://maggiechristensenauthor.com/